A MURDER OF CROWS

MIA MOON

A Wild Ink Publishing Original

Wild-ink-publishing.com

Paperback ISBN: 978-1-958531-97-6

Ebook ISBN: 978-1-958531-98-3

❀ Formatted with Vellum

*For my daughter Kassandra. My ray of light. You will always be
my greatest inspiration...*

PROLOGUE

*E*mber ran out the back patio screen door into the bright fall sunlight. She was so excited to be outside that she didn't even care about the screen door slamming shut, even though she knew her mother would have plenty to say to her about it later. All she wanted was to be outside in the crisp October air. She loved autumn, she loved the smell of the dry leaves, wood burning fireplaces in the distance, and the cool breeze in her long black hair which was wild, down to her waist, and flowed freely behind her like tendrils of black smoke. Ember loved having her hair free and not constricted with tight braids or ponytails. She especially hated brushing it. It was a constant battle with her mother who preferred her hair neatly put up. She had fought with her mother earlier about the tangled mess.

"Ember!" her mother screamed. "How many times do I have to tell you to run a brush through that rat's nest?"

Ember's bright yellow eyes rolled. She was so sick of trying to control everything she did. It was, after all, her hair. It wasn't like she was a child anymore. Her 13th birthday was just a few weeks away. Besides brushing the waves and tangles out of her hair somehow felt wrong to Ember. Like brushing out each little snarl was taking a little bit of herself away.

Witch, that was also a word that Ember's mother hated. Ember didn't mind it though, even if some people in their small town said it to them in a mean way.

"Victoria, it's fine! And besides I like my rat's nests!" Ember yelled back at her mother over her shoulder.

"I would actually prefer to live in one if it got me away from you" she whispered under her breath.

She didn't hate her mother, but she never felt connected to her. So much that she never could bring herself to call her Mother. The word sounded unnatural in her ears. But Ember had always felt like an outsider in her own family. Her father was never home, a government job that Ember really didn't understand kept him away. Sometimes Ember thought he stayed away on purpose. Like he was uneasy being around her. But most people were uncomfortable around her. It was only her grandmother who Ember felt understood her. The only one who never tried to correct her on her messy hair or the dirt on the hem of her dress. She traveled a great deal and Ember missed her terribly when she was away. But when she was home, she would take Ember on long walks in the woods, telling her all about the plants and flowers around them. She would also spend hours telling Ember stories about her family and the magic that they could conjure. Ember lay on the soft grass looking up at her grandmother's beautiful face, as she spun yarns about witches and how they could control animals. "Is that true, Grandmother?" she would ask.

Carmen would smile and stroke Ember's messy hair, "I would never lie to you my sweet girl, you have magic in you," she would whisper.

But all those thoughts fell to the back of Ember's mind as

she felt the cool grass and crunchy leaves under her bare feet. She ran past the family dog, a big fluffy Alaskan Malamute named Karina.

"Good morning wolfy girl!"

Karina looked up from the piece of bark she was enjoying and gave a little howl in return.

Ember sometimes liked to pretend that Karina was a ferocious, wild, dire wolf, one that had magical powers and had grown to twice her size and could be ridden like a horse into battle. But she was an older dog whose idea of excitement was a good snack and a warm bed. Even at her age, the dog was protective of Ember, her sharp pale blue eyes always watching. Never missing a single detail. She tracked Ember as she ran past her down to the creek at the end of the yard. Even from her plush spot on the grass, Karina could sense Ember wasn't in danger. So, with a big yawn she returned to chewing on her bark.

Ember stopped at the edge of the yard with a gasp and looked down at the clear cold creek water, the forest of trees standing right across. There used to be a red bridge connecting the yard to the dense woods beyond the creek, but a heavy rainstorm washed it away last summer. So, the only way across was the large steppingstones that scattered along the creek bed. She stepped down the small embankment that led to the water, pausing for a moment and closing her eyes. To Ember this was a portal, a door to another world. A world full of magic where anything was possible. She opened her eyes and took her first step onto the large stone. The sunlight shone on the water and made all the different colored pebbles glitter like gemstones. She smiled to herself as she skipped over a few more stones to the moist, dark soil on the other side. She pulled herself up to the grassy ledge. The wind picked up and rustled through the trees as she took her first steps into the woods. Then, she ran. She ran as fast as she could into the cluster of trees and tall grass. She could hear the birds stirring on the branches above her. Crows. She didn't even have to look up to know the crows were there. They were always there, waiting. The flapping of their wings echoed in her ears, in her chest. Like her heartbeat and their wings were in sync. Like a drum. Beating faster and faster. Louder and louder until that was all she heard.

So, she ran deeper into the woods. She glimpsed back and saw the crows flying close behind. She laughed and ran until she collapsed into a pile of orange leaves under the big oak tree. Her hair spread out around her head like a dark halo. She breathed in deep and opened her eyes to see them all peering down at her, their onyx eyes shining.

"You all almost got me today" she said with a big smile.

The crows cawed in unison, as if to agree with her. She closed her eyes and drifted off to sleep, with the soft breeze of their wings fanning her. Here she felt safe. Here she felt at home.Among the trees and the crows…

CHAPTER 1

*E*mber taped up another box and stacked it on the growing pile that was almost hitting the low ceiling in the small living room of her parents' colonial house. Packing up the small house she grew up in was a lot more difficult than she anticipated. She walked around the room; the old wooden floorboards creaking under her weight, and wondered how a lifetime of memories could be all packed away in a room full of boxes.

So many memories, tucked away in every corner, sticking to the ivory walls like cobwebs. She couldn't stay stuck in the old house with whispers of the past. She wiped her forehead with a long sigh and marked all the furniture she was planning on donating with big red stickers. It had been a month since her mother died. Ember could still hear her voice calling to her from the room down the hall. Victoria had been sick for a long time before she passed, bedridden. Ember had quit her job at the bookstore to take care of her, spending her days tending to every need and listening to stories of her youth.

Ember would listen quietly, never really interrupting. It

always seemed that her mother had wanted to tell her something through the stories. Like some revelation was on the tip of her tongue, but she never seemed able to tell. Something that she had buried so deep inside that only now had begun to scratch and gnaw to get out. So, Ember listened. It made her mother appear older than she actually was, more tired. Until one day, she went to sleep and never woke up. Now it was time to sell the old colonial house in West Hartford.

Ember rubbed the amethyst stone in her tear-drop locket she had inherited from her grandmother, and held back the tears. Grandmother Carmen had worn it every day of her life. Ember would gaze up at the sparkling deep purple stone as Carmen read to her.

"This will pass on to you someday, my love," Carmen would say to her. "It will protect you, and make you stronger."

She had died the year before, and it had taken a major toll. Grandmother Carmen had been Ember's best friend in life. She was the only person who Ember felt really understood for who she truly was. She had learned so much from her. Ember looked forward to her grandmother's visit from faraway lands, her arms filled with gifts. Beautiful jewelry with different colored crystals, long flowing skirts made of fine silk, dresses in beautiful patterns, and strong-smelling herbs and plants she would brew in a big black pot on the iron gas stove. They would spend hours in that old brick kitchen making teas and tinctures. Ember loved sitting at the big wooden table listening to Grandmother Carmen talk about what each herb, plant, or flower could be used for, like she would do on their long walks in the woods together. Some broke a fever; some cured a cough or headaches. Grandmother had a recipe or cure for anything that ailed you.

Then there were the other uses of these ingredients, the ones she had taught Ember. The ones she made Ember swear not to tell her parents she was being taught. She would pull out the old, worn leather book with tea-colored pages full of small writing and interesting pictures and read Ember all the magical words and recipes. In the summer months, she would open her book right to the page she needed, set reading glasses on the bridge of her nose, brush loose strands of greying black hair with her hands back up into the side-swept pile on her head away from her face, and would say to Ember. "Go out to the backyard and pick all the yellow dandelions you can find and bring them here."

"The weeds?" Ember would ask. "Dad told me those are bad and needed to be killed."

"Blaha!! Weeds!! He would say something dimwitted!" Grandmother scoffed. "Go on! Bring me as many as you can find! And don't dilly dally! We have work to do," Grandmother said as she pushed Ember gently out the door.

So, Ember did what she asked. She wandered around the yard and picked up every bright yellow dandelion she could find using the skirt of her dress as a basket.

"Here, Grandmother! I got as many as I could find," Ember said with a sense of accomplishment.

"Wonderful, my darling. Put them here on the table."

Ember watched as her grandmother gathered all the dandelions and cut the flowers off with a small knife she pulled from her apron, and poured them into the pot of boiling water. She would place her hands over the steam coming up from the hot water and repeat the words from her book. She would turn her yellow eyes to look at Ember, "Now you, my sweet." Ember would jump up from her seat and place her hands over Carmen's and try to say the same words. The steam curled around them like wisps of smoke, taking different shapes, like clouds in the sky. Ember would watch the smoke in awe as it danced around her head, entangling in her long hair, and forming into a shape above her head. The shape of a large bird, its wings spread wide, is a crow.

"Look there, my child, this helps us see," Grandmother said with an intense look.

"What else can we see, Grandmother?" Ember laughed, as she could feel the tingling of the smoke around her but couldn't see the image of the ghostly crow above her head.

"See into the other place. See into the past and things that have yet to pass."

"We can do that?" Ember asked as the wispy crow began to fade away, leaving only small traces of smoke where it once was.

"Oh yes. And so much more," Carmen said as she smiled at Ember and squeezed her hand softly. "Sometimes we can even see those who dwell in the twilight, all around us."

* * *

A LOUD TRUCK rumbling down the street jolted Ember from her memory, making her somewhat angry. Memories of her grandmother were so realistic for her. It was like she went back in time. She could remember every detail, every smell. It made Ember miss her so much, she felt it in the pit of her stomach, like an emptiness that she could never fill.

Ember walked down the hallway to the large gold-framed mirror. She looked at her reflection and sighed. She had turned twenty-five this year, but she felt so much older, although no one would agree. Ember was a true natural beauty. Her long wavy hair hung down below her waist. It was black, with a slight blue-violet sheen in the sunlight, like the color of raven's wings. Her beautiful thin face and high cheekbones framed her most striking feature: her big yellow eyes, just like her grandmother's, looked like two candle flames in a window. They glowed with a mystery and intensity that made most people uncomfortable. With delicate hands, she tried to smooth out her simple pale blue dress. It hung somewhat loosely on her slender frame. Ember preferred simple skirts and dresses she made herself from the old dress patterns she found in the attic. She hated going out to stores, especially to buy clothes. All the racks and bright colors overwhelmed her. Not to mention the glares and whispers she would hear behind her back.

"There goes that Wildes girl," strangers would sneer as they gave cold and unwelcoming stares as they crossed the street to avoid passing her on the sidewalk.

Having the last name Wildes in her town had made it difficult for Ember growing up, or for anyone in her family, really. It seemed that even today, the old memories of witchcraft and dealings with the devil were alive and well. Her ancestor, Sarah Wildes, had been accused of witchcraft and executed back in Salem during the trials. Not that the women in the Wildes family ever did much to quench those rumors. All except Ember's mother, Victoria. She did everything she could to "fit in" with the tennis-playing, country club wives of Connecticut. Her mother spent so much money on dresses in the latest fashion, doing her hair and makeup like the women in the glossy magazines that Ember would see in the checkout line at the supermarket. She tried everything she could to try to impress other people, but to no avail. The town's folk would just look at Victoria with judgment behind their eyes, and whispers of disapproval under their breath. The word, that word, inevitably making its way out of their lips....

Witch

As Ember stared at her own reflection in the mirror, her wrinkled dress and messy hair, she smiled to herself. She never really cared very much about how others perceived her. She learned to live with the stares and snickers behind her back as she walked down the street. She became used to people crossing the sidewalk if they saw her coming towards them, and she liked it that way. She never really cared about being around others. She preferred solitude, preferably in nature with the company of animals. She would spend her days walking alone in the woods, the crows in the trees above her the only company she needed. She would sit in the tall grass, crumbling the bread she had made in the morning, and watching as the crows would come to gobble up as much as their bellies could hold. Ember would laugh as some would fly away with bigger pieces in their beaks to enjoy as a snack later. She would sit with the crows every day, for hours, sometimes finding small shiny things they would leave for her, as if to say thank you for the bread, nuts, and berries she would feed them. Every day she would discover a new present, coins, little pieces of metal, even jewelry. She would look up at them flapping their wings in the trees and smile. "You all have become quite the accomplished little thieves." They would all caw in approval, the sounds floating down to Ember like waves.

"Enough daydreaming," Ember said, bringing herself back to the present. No time to sit with the crows today, much to do.

She needed to finish sorting through the last of odds and ends in the house in what little time she had left. To figure out what she was going to keep and what she would donate. She had struggled over the decision to sell the old house, the house she had spent her entire life in.

Her father had left it and everything in it when he moved down to Florida. He had asked Ember to join him, but the thought of the hot, humid days in a small condo with her retired father was not something that appealed to Ember. He left a week after her mother's funeral, and for her it was a relief. Now they talked on the phone occasionally, sharing pleasantries about the weather and his newfound love for fishing. He sounded happy to Ember, and that was good enough for her.

So, instead of living in a house full of ghosts, Ember decided to sell, which to her surprise didn't take very long. It was a beautiful house, a two-story colonial with a mudroom in the front, a grand staircase with curved banister, large picture windows that filled the living room with warm sunlight in the summer and were the perfect spot to sit and watch the snow fall in the winter. But what she would miss most was the large backyard.

The yard had two large oak trees to the west that created the perfect shady spots for lounging on long summer days, and to the east was the best spot for the large garden. Ember grew all sorts of vegetables, herbs, and an array of colorful flowers that brought honeybees and butterflies. At the end of the property was a small creek that divided the yard from the woods beyond.

Ember loved playing in those woods as a child. She spent every minute she could in those woods alone. It was another world to her, a magical world full of fairy folk and wondrous creatures. A place where she had magical powers and could control the weather. And most magical of all were the animals that could speak to her, the crows that she loved so much, and she would understand their squawks and caws, and speak back. Sometimes it was like she could feel what they felt or even see through their eyes. For Ember, it was so real. So vivid in her mind. But as the years passed, the thoughts of her magical woodland became more distant, almost like a dream. At times, she wondered if it all was a dream. Some nights she still woke suddenly, as if someone or something was calling her back to those woods, and to the crows, waiting for her return.

As much as she would miss the house and everything about it, Ember felt like it was time to move on. She had this restless feeling building up in her for a while, a feeling that would keep her up at night. A feeling, like a storm is coming. Sometimes she could almost sense it, like the feeling of electricity in the air right before a thunderstorm. She was tired of waiting, tired of the feeling of restlessness, so she made the decision to say goodbye to the only place she'd ever known and start fresh in a new place. It wasn't a hard choice for Ember, deciding where she wanted to start over. There was only one place, Salem, Massachusetts.

It made perfect sense to Ember to go to the place where her ancestor Sarah Wildes had lived and sadly had been executed for witchcraft. Ember remembered her teachers talking about the Witch Trials in school. She always felt that they wanted to avoid the topic, especially in front of her, considering that everyone knew she was related to Sarah Wildes. But Ember wanted to learn more. She remembered the stories her grandmother had told her about her family's past, and she read every book she could find about Salem and about Sarah, and now she would be able to live there. That gave her a strange sense of comfort, like she was finally truly going home.

She took one last look at herself in the mirror and walked back into the living room to continue what seemed to her the impossible task of finishing packing when she heard the front door open. She didn't have to look up to see it was her friend Tristan walking in holding two cups of coffee. "Hey, Em, you in here? I come bearing gifts," Tristan called out in his usual cheerful voice as he made his way through the maze of boxes and furniture to Ember.

"Cardboard brown? So not your color," he said playfully.

"How are you holding up, Em?" he asked as he handed Ember the warm cup.

"Better than I thought, really. I think I'll be done sometime in the next 100 years," she said with a grin.

"Well, girl, you know I will be happy to take some of the antiques off your hands," he said with a sly grin, his blue eyes sparkling.

Tristan was one of Ember's only friends. He and his husband had moved up from Alabama and bought the house next door a few years back. They instantly became close. Tristan was tall with long flowing golden blonde hair down to his shoulders that he usually kept up in a tight bun. His intense pale blue eyes were piercing but warm at the same time. Ember loved his laid-back and easy-going personality, not to mention that he always had a witty comeback to every uncomfortable situation. He made Ember laugh, which was one of the things that she loved about him the most. She also secretly envied him in a way.

He always carried himself with the confidence that she wished she had. A thick skin that he had grown over the years. He understood what it was like to be misunderstood and judged for simply being who you were. So, he never questioned Ember about the rumors in town about her or her family. Never looked down on her, just loved her for who she was.

"You know I would have come and helped you pack, but I hate packing," he said jokingly with that southern drawl that Ember loved.

"I am going to miss you," Ember replied.

"Oh, you aren't getting rid of me, honey. I am going to come and visit you every chance I get. The hospital will just have to deal without me."

"You know, I'm sure Salem can use a nurse with your sense of style," Ember teased.

"Look, I know I have told you this before, but I'm so happy and proud of you. I know you love being in this big house alone. This is a huge step, but I know it's the right one. I know you will love it there, and maybe, just maybe, you will finally meet a guy and go out on a date, "he said as he sipped his coffee. "You know a date," he joked.

Ember threw her head back and laughed. "A date? I wouldn't even know how to act on a date or who would even ask me?" Ember laughed as she twirled her hair around her finger.

"Oh, come on, Em," Tristan said. "You never give any guy a chance. Promise me that you will. You don't have to marry the guy, just go out and have some fun. You deserve it."

She smiled at Tristan. "Ok, I promise. Maybe I'll just cast a love spell on the first guy that says hello to me."

"That a girl!" Tristan laughed, knowing she was kidding. They would often joke about her witch label and how everyone thought she cast spells for every reason. The thought of dating, though, made her palms sweat. She had gone on a few dates with some local boys, all ending in disaster. She thought about the one time a boy tried to kiss her. She was so startled that she jolted her head back so fast that she hit the window of his car with a loud thud. She giggled to herself, remembering the awkward look on his face as she tried to explain that he simply had surprised her. But that was the last time she saw him.

"You know, what I'm really hoping for," Ember said, her tone turning a bit more serious. "I would love to make friends, like girlfriends. Even just one girl." She shrugged her shoulders. "I don't know, it sounds nice."

"Oh, I see how it is!" Tristan said, laughing. "You want to start a coven or something, and I'm not girly enough."

They both laughed as Ember picked up a pillow from the nearby couch and threw it at him playfully.

"You will always be my best girlfriend," Ember replied.

"Aw, thanks. No, but seriously, Em, I get it, and I am so certain that you will. You will be in Salem!" he said excitedly. "I am so sure you will meet some great friends. Just as long as you remember who your bestie is."

"Always," Ember replied, and she meant it.

"Ok, so are you going to help or what?" she said as she took the last gulp of coffee.

"I suppose," Tristan said with a smile.

They spent the rest of the day chatting and filling up the rest of Ember's belongings into boxes until everything was neatly packed away.

"I couldn't have finished without you," Ember said as she was finally able to lie down on the old brown couch.

"I know," Tristan said as he sat down on the oversized chair in front of her.

"Truck comes in the morning," she stated, "then I'm finally off."

"It will be a nice drive, I'm sure. Just take your time and text me when you get there," he said, almost like a big brother. "I've got to get home; Drew is probably thinking I ran away with you." Tristan stood up and opened his arms.

"Wait, goodbyes now, you aren't seeing me off in the morning?" Ember asked.

"Not good with long goodbyes," Tristan said with a little bit of sadness in his voice.

Ember jumped up from the couch and into his arms, hugging him tight.

"Not goodbye. Just I'll see you later, ok?" she said, holding back tears.

"Ok, I'll see you later," Tristan said as he pulled away and gave Ember a kiss on the cheek.

As he started to move towards the front door, Ember suddenly remembered that she wanted to give him something. A little piece of her so she would feel like they would always be together."Wait, before you go. I have something for you."

Ember yelled over her shoulder as she ran to the desk in the foyer and opened the top drawer. "Here, I thought you might like this," she said, pulling out a shiny silver chain and locket. "I found it at an antique store, sitting in a case all the way in the back." She handed the locket to Tristan. "And see, it has your initials engraved on the front. How perfect is that?"

Tristan looked down at the beautiful old locket and smiled at her kindness. "It's absolutely perfect," he said.

With one last hug, he was gone. Ember stood in the doorway for a while, watching him walk slowly back across the yard to his house. She knew he wouldn't look back, and he didn't. It had gotten dark out, and the wind had picked up a bit. The rustling of the leaves had grown louder, and she shivered as her gaze moved up to the top of the tall oak tree. Then she saw it. At first, she wasn't sure. She had to squint to see, but as her eyes adjusted, she was sure. A crow sat slightly on one of the lower branches. It was so still that at first Ember didn't know if it was real. It didn't move or make a sound. I just watched her. Ember was startled at first by the sight of the rather large crow, but the more she looked at it, the more at ease she became. "Hey there, little thief, "she whispered. "Why are you here all alone?"

The crow just sat on his high perch and looked at Ember. A cold chill washed over her, making the hairs on the back of her neck stand up. She looked back at the crow, waiting for it to speak, like she had imagined in her dreams as a child, but it said nothing. Ember shrugged.

"That's crazy," Ember said quietly to herself. "I'm just tired. "And with that, she closed the door slowly. "Crows talking to you? Really, Ember?" She shook her head, trying to clear the fog of her childhood dreams, her long hair brushing across her back. She walked back into the living room and lay back down on the soft couch. She was too tired to go upstairs to her room. She just wanted to close her eyes and go to sleep. As she felt herself falling deeper and deeper into sleep, all she could see in her mind's eye was one thing: the crow, watching her silently, not moving, just waiting.

CHAPTER 2

Claire stepped out from her apartment on Essex Street and into the brisk autumn air. The night wrapped around her as she tried buttoning her coat against numbing fingers. It was cold for early September. Colder than usual. Claire much preferred the warm summer months; just colored leaves and chilled wind reminded her that those days were clearly over. She walked down the empty street and really appreciated how quiet it was. October was extremely crowded. The city would soon be packed with people who come to celebrate and enjoy all the spooky festivities. The whole town would be filled with groups of young girls wearing matching witches' hats, giggling as they passed all the shops with T-shirts that said 'Witch City' on the front, hanging from the shop windows. Or they would be found taking pictures with the dozens of street performers that lined Essex. Claire hated Halloween, preferring the smell of the nearby ocean over the over-bearing scent of apple cider and everything pumpkin. She was thankful to enjoy a quiet night before all the madness began.

She walked briskly; even though Salem had been a safe town in the past, she didn't like to walk alone late at night, especially with everything that had been in the news lately. Women going missing had given Claire chills up her spine, but she shrugged it off. She was on her way to meet some friends at one of the local bars down by the wharf. She rarely went out, but her friends begged her to join them for at least one drink. So, Claire agreed and headed out. Her own footsteps echoed as she crossed the old, uneven, cobblestone street and headed towards Salem Harbor. Claire took a deep breath and inhaled the salty sea air, enjoying the beautiful scenery, with a quarter moon reflecting clearly against the dark water. Suddenly, off in the distance, she heard soft crying coming from near the dock. At first, she thought it might have come from the nearby restaurants, so she kept walking slowly. Then she heard it again, but louder. She was sure this time. It was a low whimpering, maybe a cat, or worse, a woman crying. She stopped and crept quietly towards the empty dock. She followed the whimpering sound down under the dock to the water's edge.

"Hello," Claire called. "Is someone there? "Her shaking voice carried over the shallow water.

The crying grew louder as Claire moved closer under the dock to the dark water. Then she saw it, the form of a young girl.

"Hey, are you ok? Are you hurt?" Claire asked, moving closer to the girl.

Claire could barely make out the small figure in the dark shadows under the old creaking dock. She saw a girl, curled up with her legs close to her chest, wearing only a sheer long dress. No coat, or shoes. The girl's thin, emaciated limbs showed through the thin cotton fabric. Her head turned, buried against her knees, shivering in the cold, wet sand.

"Oh my god! You must be freezing!" Claire moved,

closing the gap between her and the girl until she could almost touch her shoulder. She inched a bit closer, her hand trembling as she reached out for the girl's bony shoulder. As she did, the girl's head snapped up. She realized this was no girl. Its face was twisted into a hideous open-mouthed smile. Eyes glowing silver, bright like two car headlights on a dark road. Cheeks sunken in and hollow, the skin around them like dry, sharp, grayish scales. Claire gasped at the sight of the creature. She stumbled, her ankle twisting on the wet sand, making her lose her balance and fall backwards. She tried to dig her feet in the sand to try to move away from the terrifying creature as it reached out with long gnarled claw-like hands, slicing deep gashes in her pants down to her skin, She tried to hit the scale covered arm with her hand, punching as hard as she could to make it release her, but the skin felt like armor plates; it tore the skin from her knuckles. The creature crawled over Claire's body slowly, twisting and curling its scaled-covered limbs, sniffing at her as it got closer and closer to her face. She could smell the foul breath on her cheek. Claire's eyes widened as it sat on top of her, pinning her to the cold sand. It tightly pressed down on her arm with its long animal-like claws so tightly that she was sure it was going to break. A loud snap cracked the night air as Claire's forearm shattered. A sudden rush of pain had Clarie's mouth open to scream when she felt another set of cold, wet, scaly hands come over her face from behind and cover her mouth.

Claire's mind raced. She couldn't think of anything but the pain. She tried to make sense of what was happening, but it was all happening too fast. She couldn't scream; she couldn't move. All she could do was feel the creature's weight on top of her, crushing her chest, smell its foul breath, blink to keep the saltwater dripping from its stringy hair stinging her eyes. Suddenly, two other sharp claws moved to her mouth, digging into her flesh, drawing blood from her skin. She was too petrified to move. She could see light in the windows of the houses across the street. If only someone would look out over the harbor, they would see her and the creatures that were attacking her. But she didn't see a soul. She knew that if she wanted to live, she had to fight. She frantically tried to move, to try to loosen their grip on her. She could feel long fingernails digging deeper into her skin, squeezing her neck. Her pulse beat so loud and fast, filling her ears with nothing but her heartbeat. Warm blood ran down the side of her neck and arm. As her eyes opened wide, she saw the creature's jaw disjointed and opened into a twisted smile with rows of sharp teeth. The smile became wider and wider, as it got closer to her mouth. Claire felt the breath leave her body. She could see the fog of her exhale leaving her throat and into the creature's. Life was leaving her; she knew it now. She couldn't fight it; she wouldn't fight it. All she saw was the blackness of the creature's cavernous mouth, until that darkness consumed her completely.

* * *

CLAIRE WASN'T sure how long she had been unconscious. She tried to move, but the pain overwhelmed her. Tears poured down her blood-covered face, and no sound came out when she opened her mouth. Whatever attacked her had left her for dead, alone in the cold. All she could do was lie in the cold sand and stare up at the sky. She tried to think of a time in her life when she was safe and warm. Her mind searched for any happy memory. She prayed for the pain to stop, that someone would walk by. Anyone. Then a sound came from the water. She hoped it was a boat or maybe someone walking on the dock. For a moment, she had a glimmer of hope that she might live, that help was just a stone's throw away. Claire slowly turned her head to look at the water, hoping to see her salvation, but the hope left her with the last salty tear that dripped from her eye to the sand. She could see those glowing silver eyes emerging from the still dark water. Its slimy body pulled itself up on shore, long limbs reaching like tentacles. Claire could do nothing as the ice-cold claws closed around her legs, pulling at her, dragging her into the frigid water. She tried to find the strength to speak as the creature wrapped itself around her, pulling her closer to it.

"No, no please..." she whispered. The creature hissed as the water covered them completely like a velvet blanket.

The black water engulfed her as she was pulled down deeper and deeper into the murky depths of the harbor. Claire gave in; she let go. Let go of hope, of life. She was ready. She closed her eyes and let the darkness take her.

* * *

DETECTIVE THOMAS COLE rolled over and clumsily reached for his cell phone ringing on his nightstand, knocking down the glass that he had been drinking out of the night before on the floor.

"Fuck," Thomas said as he fumbled looking for his phone. He sighed as he picked it up and saw he had five missed calls. He must have slept right through them. He groaned as he rolled over and tried to steady the dizziness in his head. He rubbed his eyes and tried to focus on the blurry screen when it rang again.

"Hey Joe, what's going on?" Thomas said, his voice sounding raspier than usual.

"Hey man, been trying to reach you all morning. We've got another body, washed up this morning in Marblehead,"

Joe said, slightly annoyed. "The team is all here, so is the captain."

"Another girl?" Thomas asked as he swung his muscular legs to the side of the bed.

"Yea, just like the others," Joe said with some sadness in his voice.

"Ok, I'm on my way." Thomas stood up from his bed and hung up the call as Joe was trying to tell him something, but he didn't care. It didn't matter; all that mattered was that there was another dead girl on his watch.

Thomas threw the phone back on the nightstand and held his head in his hands, took a deep breath, wishing that the pounding would go away. He had drunk way too much the night before, and the throbbing in his temples was proof of that. He tried to remember what happened the night before, but his mind was blank. The blackouts were getting to be far too frequent. A cup of coffee and a shower would help wash off some of the hangovers. He'd had way too many hang-overs recently. Thomas knew his drinking was out of control, but it was the only way he could numb the six years of working Homicide in Essex County. The last year had been especially difficult. Thomas, along with the Essex County homicide task force, had been working on a string of murders of young women, all in the same general age group, early to mid-twenties, all attractive and all found in or around bodies of water. It wasn't until the third body had been found that the task force was formed. The pattern was too obvious to not see that these murders were somehow related. But Thomas was at a dead end, no evidence, no witnesses, no leads. It was like these girls were magically picked up off the street and left for dead. His greatest fear was that the murders would go unsolved, or worse yet, that they would continue. But that was all detectives' greatest fear. Now on this cold morning, he worried that that fear had come true.

He stumbled into the shower and washed off the smell of bourbon the best he could. He wrapped a towel around his narrow waist and wiped the steamed-up mirror. He looked at his bloodshot eyes and rubbed the stubble on his square jawline. No time to shave, he hastily threw on the clothes he had worn the day before, grabbed a cup of lukewarm stale coffee, and rushed out the door. He was already in hot water with his Captain, and being late to a homicide scene wasn't going to improve his situation. Thomas's career hadn't always been this way. He had started out ten years prior as a wide-eyed, idealistic cop. He had grown up on the north shore, and being a cop was something he had always dreamed of. His grandfather had been a Massachusetts state trooper, so had his father. Law enforcement ran in his family. He never thought of doing anything else. His first few years on the job were exciting, and Thomas was a natural. He knew the law like the back of his hand and always followed it, no exception. Some of his fellow cops would tease him for being too rigid, and his boyish good looks didn't help. They would make remarks about his white-blond hair and his ice blue eyes. The term 'pretty boy' was used on a regular basis. He didn't mind the comments from his fellow officers; he understood that it was all part of the job. Poking fun at each other was just a way to blow off steam. Besides, he grew up with people remarking on his appearance, usually women. He was used to it, and he didn't let it get in the way of his job. Nothing would distract him or somehow make him do it half-heartedly. It was no surprise he rose through the ranks quickly, and when the opening in Homicide became available, he jumped at it. He made the choice to work in the most difficult unit. He was a detailed and thorough investigator.

He got a sense of excitement running through his bones as he walked onto a scene. Without speaking to anyone first, to see it just through his eyes. Thomas saw everything. It was as if the world slowed down, and he was able to notice things that others could not. Details that others would disregard would stand out to him. Thomas would learn every detail about the victims, who they were and their lives, getting as close to them as he could. To see their world through their eyes, to walk in their shoes. Sometimes he could have sworn that he could hear their voices, whispering in his ear, like hearing a melody on the wind, guiding him through their last moments of life. He wouldn't dare share that gift with anyone; he kept it to himself, this special bond, a secret that he shared with the people he was trying to help find peace. In the past, this talent had been instrumental for his ability to solve cases. But with these recent murders, he hadn't been able to work the way he had before. It was like something was blinding him and keeping him from connecting with the victims. A hidden force was preventing him from seeing the obvious.

Keeping him from hearing their soft whispers. This troubled him, made him short-tempered and unfocused. He felt unraveled at the edges, like an old sweater. His colleagues noticed his struggles, and snarky rumors that he was being taken off the case and sent to the department shrink had spread through the hallways of the task force offices. Thomas could take the smart-ass remarks, jokes, and rumors about his drinking. But being taken off the cases was a real fear of his. He had come too far and worked too hard on this case. He couldn't let these women and their families down; he had to keep working, but thoughts of doubt and worry about him losing his edge crept in like fog in his brain. It built up inside him like a wall, making his frustration grow, and the resentment for his job, the job that he loved, turn sour. What good was he if he couldn't help these victims? So, he drank. He drank to feel something other than this deep feeling of uselessness, to try to not see the faces of the victims in his sleep, if he could sleep.

Thomas tried to rub the alcohol haze from his eyes as he drove through the morning traffic towards Marblehead. It wasn't a far drive from his loft in downtown Salem. The way he was feeling made him grateful for that. Blue and red lights lit the narrow streets of the small neighborhood as he approached the scene and drove slowly through the rows of parked ambulances and patrol cars. He felt like he had done this way too often lately, driving up to the yellow crime scene tape, walking through the crowd of onlookers, their judgmental eyes burning in the back of his head. He could see Joe standing at the end of the road where it dropped off to the rocky shore, an impatient look on his face as he spoke to one of the crime scene technicians. With a deep sigh, Thomas shut off the engine of his unmarked SUV, swung open the door, and stepped out into the gloomy morning. Even with the clouds, the sun bothered his sensitive pale blue eyes, forcing him to squint. He searched the pockets of his coat for sunglasses as he walked over to Joe. "Of course," he whispered to himself as he remembered he left them back at his loft.

"Jesus, man, you look like shit," Joe said as Thomas approached.

"Nice to see you too, Joe," Thomas replied, as he shook the morning dampness from his hair. "What do we have?" Thomas asked as he made his way down the rocky, sandy embankment down to the water's edge, Joe following closely behind him.

"Girl looks to be in her early twenties. No purse, phone, or ID. Lady walking her dog found her. She called it in."

"Any obvious cause of death?" Thomas asked, but he already knew the answer.

"No, not yet. The Forensics are on the way. She does have some injuries. Broken arm, and some lacerations. Looks like she put up a fight. But that's about it from what I can tell," Joe replied, a bit of sadness dripping from his voice as he read the details off his small notepad.

"Broken arm? Attacks seem to be getting more violent. I'm sure the ME will find no water in the lungs like our past victims," Thomas said as he approached the girl who was lying out over the rocks, her body half in the water. She was face up, her shoulder-length blonde hair wet and slicked back, eyes open, looking up into nothingness, a pale blue film over her pupils. Her arm was twisted into an unnatural angle, deep cuts around her mouth, neck, and legs. She was still fully dressed in her coat and shoes. That was a lucky break for the detectives. Sometimes clothes got pulled off in the rough water, and they lost vital pieces of evidence. Joe handed Thomas a pair of latex gloves, which he snapped onto his hands. He looked down at her wrist and saw she had a small symbol tattooed in black ink. He lifted her hand and checked under her nails. There was a black/ green substance stuck underneath them. As he put her hand back down gently, he could see her knuckles were raw and bloody.

"She has something under her nails; looks like she put up a good fight. Make sure forensics gets a sample; we might get lucky and find DNA," Thomas said, not taking his eyes off the girl's pale, lifeless face. "Make sure the ME runs her prints IAFIS as soon as possible.

Joe shook his head as he wrote in his notebook. "You got it, Tommy."

Thomas closed his eyes and tried to listen, to see if he could hear the soft sounds of the girl's voice in his head.

Anything to give him a sense of what she had been through in her final moments. But there was nothing.

Thomas looked around the scene. The crowd of nosey onlookers that had started to congregate was growing. Thomas would never understand people's morbid fascination with death. Why would anyone want those gruesome images imprinted in their brains? Thomas wished that he could wipe his memory clean of those pictures. But they were there, trapped forever.

He motioned over to Joe and said, "Hey, have those uniforms clear some of these people out of here. Unless anyone witnessed something, get rid of them."

Joe looked up at the people gathering behind the crime scene tape and sighed. "No problem, Tommy," he said as he put his notebook back in his pocket and looked back up to the crowd of people. "What about the Feds? They have been sniffing around?"

"Run interface for me; the last thing I need is some fucking federal paper pusher contaminating my crime scene."

Joe shook his head and walked back up the rocky slope to the group of people in blue windbreakers with big yellow letters printed on the back that had seemed to multiply while they were speaking.

Thomas turned his attention back to the young woman on the shore. He knelt closer and looked back into her doll-like stare. He tried to memorize every detail in her face, taking a mental snapshot of what he was seeing. It didn't appear to him that she had been in the water long. Maybe a few hours. He looked at the scratches on her mouth and neck-deep, long, ragged lacerations, almost animal-like. But that didn't make sense. There were no animals in the area that would be capable of causing injuries like that. The other victims had similar scratches but not this deep, not this violent. They were all found in or close to water, but he couldn't determine for certain that the cause of death was drowning. No water in the lungs, no bloating. So how were these women dying? That was the question that had been haunting Thomas for months. Along with the most important question, who? Who was killing and leaving no evidence? He saw the pattern. All young, all locals, and all dumped in water, and all dead, but with no extreme obvious injury. He couldn't find anything else they all had in common. They didn't know each other or move in the same social circles, from what he could tell. He could not find anything that tied them all together except how they met their end. Thomas rubbed his forehead and took a deep breath. Whatever he was missing was eating away at him, a little piece at a time. He needed to clear his head, to refocus. "What am I missing?" he said under his breath. Thomas's focus was interrupted as he heard Joe, along with the forensic unit, making their way down with a stretcher. Their white coats made them stand out against the crowd of people. He took one last look at the girl before standing up to meet them. "I'll find out who did this to you. To all of you, I promise." With those parting words, he began to make his way to his SUV, nodding his head at the forensics team as they passed him. Dark grey clouds had just rolled in, blocking the morning sunlight, giving Thomas's eyes some relief. Just as he reached his car door, it started to rain.

"Great," he thought to himself. All he wanted to do was go home, be alone with his own thoughts and his bourbon. 'Just one drink,' he thought to himself. Enough to steady my nerves and maybe get rid of this headache. A little hair of the dog always did the trick. But he decided against it. He had to stay sober, to keep working. He owed it to this girl. He owed it to all of them. He pushed the ignition button and started the truck as the rain fell heavier, the droplets distorting the windshield. Thomas hit the windshield wipers and sat there for a moment, listening to the rhythmic back-and-forth sound of the wipers against the glass. He finally put the SUV in gear and headed to his office. It was going to be a long day.

CHAPTER 3

$\mathcal{E}$mber rolled down the window of her old Ford Bronco and felt the chilly ocean air on her face. The sky was overcast, silver grey clouds moving across the sun. A slight drizzle fell, but she didn't mind. She loved the feeling of rain on her face. She inhaled the salty, briny smell of the ocean as she drove down Lynn Shore Drive. She looked over the beautiful scenery and smiled. She always loved the ocean. The mysterious deep sea fascinated her, and now being so close to the rolling white-capped waves gave her a new sense of excitement. As she drove down the seaside street, she admired the grand Queen Anne Victorian mansions built high over the sea cliffs. Each one more majestic than the next. She wondered how they must look on the inside, how it must feel to live in such a big, beautiful home, waking up to see such a breathtaking view. How lucky it must be. She smiled to herself, because she felt like the lucky one. Even though she wasn't going to live in a huge mansion, she was on her own, starting a new life. She felt like anything was possible. A sense of freedom washed over as she drove down the picturesque highway and turned off when she saw the sign for downtown Salem. She had never been to Salem but already had a feeling of familiarity, of excitement. The air smelled like home, the rain, the salty air, the falling leaves. It made her feel safe, something that she was not expecting. She turned the Bronco down to North Washington Square Drive, the main street that ran by the center of town, Salem Commons. The tall oak trees that lined the Commons were already changing from green to beautiful shades of orange and red, signifying that fall had definitely arrived, Ember's favorite time of the year. She parked her car at an open stop right in front of a quaint-looking three-story house with green shutters. She stepped out of the truck onto the sidewalk and looked at her new home. She could see that it was once a large house, now split up into several small apartments. She grabbed a few bags out of her back seat and headed up to a large wooden door. She searched her pocket for the key, unlocked the front door, and stepped into the foyer. A small table with magazines and some mail sat against the wall across from apartment 1A. With a deep breath, Ember unlocked the door to her new home.

She stepped inside the small apartment. Thin beams of golden light came in from the half-open curtains. It made the dust in the room sparkle as it floated lightly through the air. The warm glow of the hardwood floors gave the space a cozy, welcoming feeling. She dropped her bags in the center of the room and took it all in. This was hers. Boxes and furniture were scattered from here to there, movers only arriving the day before. She walked over to the old fireplace on the other side of the room. She bent down and looked for the chain that opened the damper plate. She pulled it down and felt the air moving down the flue past her hand, bringing down old soot and ash. She dusted her hands as she stood up and walked to the large picture window, pulling back the green velvet curtains and letting the room fill with rainy daylight. Ember stood there for a bit, watching people walk along the paths of the Commons. A group of children playing, throwing a ball to a small dog on the grassy fields. It all looked so perfect, so peaceful. She finally broke away from the window and walked the short distance to the kitchen. It was small, but warm. Perfect to sit with a cup of tea on a cold winter's day. A small stained-glass window above the gas stove cast rays of blue and green light over the ivory walls. Ember couldn't think of a better place for her potted herbs. She hummed to herself as she walked across the living area to the bedroom. Two wood frame box windows lined one wall of the room, casting shadows on the low ceiling. It was just big enough to fit her bed, a small nightstand, and her vanity that she inherited from her grandmother. Ember couldn't part with the old table and tarnished silver mirror. It was one of her most cherished pieces of furniture. Through a small door was the bathroom. A big, beautiful claw-foot tub sat right in the center of a black and white checkered floor, and the tall pedestal sink with brass knobs under a gold-framed mirror completed the room. It was a change from the large house she had grown up in, but Ember welcomed the change and was excited to begin making the space a home. So, she wasted no time tearing into the cardboard boxes and unpacking more of her beloved items. She hung bundles of dried herbs she had made in the kitchen above the window over the fireplace on the mantle. A large broomstick she had made one chilly autumn night was perfect above the kitchen entrance. She hung old pictures of her family on the walls, including one of her grandmothers. The black and white picture was faded, but it did little to diminish the beauty. She was young in the image, properly in her early twenties. She was sitting on the hood of a classic car with a large curvy chrome bumper, her hair up in the style of the time. Bright lipstick painted on her lips. She looked so happy, so carefree. Ember looked at it for a long time. She could almost smell her perfume, lily of the valley. She could always feel around her, always so close.

Snapping back to reality, Ember remembered one of the most important things she brought with her. She ran back outside to her truck, swung open the tailgate, and pulled out her grandmother's large black pot. After she was able to balance it in both arms and kicked the tailgate closed, she approached the door of the house, realizing how hard it was going to be to open it while her arms were full. Just at that very moment, the door to the house was opened by a beautiful brunette. She stood in the open doorway and smiled.

"Hi! Looks like you need a hand. I'm Chloe. I live right above you."

Ember looked at the girl with curious eyes. Chloe was about her age, and very petite. Her long and wavy chestnut hair was the same color as her eyes. She had it tied back in a side ponytail with a big yellow bow. She was dressed in very bright and happy colors, and it seemed to match her bubbly and happy energy.

"Oh, hi, yeah, that would be great," Ember said shyly.

She was never very good with people, especially new people. Ember was always so awkward and worried they would judge her for her messy hair and unfashionable way of dressing. But she had promised herself and her friend Tristan she would try to be more open to making friends, especially girlfriends.

"I'm Ember. It's nice to meet you. I'm just moving in today."

"Ember, that's a pretty name," Chloe replied as she held the door open.

They both walked into the tiny first-floor apartment, and

Ember put the large, heavy pot down on the floor by the kitchen.

"Oh wow, you have a lot of stuff," Chloe said as she looked around. "I love all these herbs and old pictures!"

"These are just the things I decided to keep. You should have seen what I sold," Ember said with a smile and a nervous laugh. She looked down at her dirty fingernails and hoped that Chloe wouldn't notice.

Chloe sat down on Ember's couch as if she'd been there her whole life. Ember didn't mind; she kind of liked her new friend's confidence and bubbly personality.

"I've always loved this building. I've lived here for five years. Everyone is super nice, and you're close to everything," she said as she adjusted the yellow bow in her hair.

"Have you always lived in Salem?" Ember asked.

"Boston," Chloe replied. "I still work there; I bartend at this fancy restaurant in the city. Money is good, but the rent is too expensive," Chloe explained. "So, I decided to live out of the city and take the train to work."

"Where are you from?" Chloe asked.

"Connecticut," Ember replied.

"And what brings you to Salem?"

Ember thought for a bit. She didn't want to explain to someone she had just met why she had come. It wasn't just escaping the rumors about her family, her mother dying, or her father moving hundreds of miles away. She had felt drawn here by something she couldn't explain.

Chloe could sense the hesitation in Ember and said, "It's Salem. No matter how crazy you think your answer is, trust me, it's not."

Ember looked into her warm brown eyes and smiled. "I feel like this was the only place for me to come to. Like I have always belonged here," Ember said as she gazed off. Realizing she had sounded strange, she quickly grinned, "And I heard you all threw the biggest Halloween party in the country."

"Good enough for me!" Chloe laughed.

Her response surprised Ember, in a good way. She was so easy to talk to, no judgment in her eyes. No strange untrusting glances.

"OK, so I work tonight, but maybe we can get together and have a glass of wine or something, you know, when you get settled."

"That would be great," Ember replied. She truly meant it. It was a nice feeling having plans.

"OK! It's a date. Let me know if you need anything; like I said, I'm right upstairs 2B."

"Oh, one last thing. It's usually safe around here, but lately there have been some girls going missing and missing and murdered."

"If you want to go out at night, just be careful, OK?"

"Murders? That's terrible," Ember said as she twisted a strand of black hair nervously around her finger. "I hadn't heard, but thanks for the heads up."

"Sure, us girls need to look out for each other, right?" Chloe said with a warm smile as she walked towards the door. Her face turned slightly back to Ember. "Remember to lock up."

"Yeah, will do. Thanks," Ember watched as Chloe closed the door behind her.

"Murders," Ember thought to herself and shivered. That was the last thing she expected to hear on the first day in a new place. She tried to put the thought in the back of her mind as she walked into the kitchen and began to organize her jars of herbs and potted plants. She didn't want to think about that now. She was hopeful and excited about exploring the city. She hummed to herself the rest of the day as she unpacked and placed everything in just the right spot. The last thing she carefully lifted out of a box was her grand-mother's book of spells. It was a worn leather-bound book with tea-colored pages filled with Carmen's delicate cursive handwriting. She held it close to her before placing it on the mantel over the fireplace. There, she thought to herself, now everything has a place. She was just about to go sit and rest on the couch when she remembered she had completely forgotten to text Tristan. She picked up her purse from the kitchen table and rummaged through it until she found her phone. She saw the missed calls and texts from Tristan asking if she had made it OK.

She quickly sent him a text saying she was fine and that she was sorry that she forgot to text him. Ember was sure Tristan would understand. She put her phone down and walked into her new bedroom and lay on the bed. She watched the late afternoon light shining through the lace curtains, making a pattern on the bedspread. It had stopped raining just long enough for the setting sun to cast the last few rays before it was gone, and the nighttime sky took its place. She could feel herself getting sleepy, her eyelids getting heavy. She allowed her body to relax and melt into the soft, warm bed. Her breath becoming heavier, she tried to fight the sleep soon to be upon her. Finally giving in, she closed her eyes and slowly drifted off to a dreamless sleep.

* * *

OUT OF THE stillness of her sleep, Ember was jolted awake. Suddenly, she was outside. It took a moment for her to get her bearings. Ember looked at her surroundings and realized she was in front of her apartment, looking inside through the large window.

"How did I get outside?" She thought to herself as she looked down at her own body, trying to make sense of the strange sensations coursing over her skin. Pulses of electricity radiated through her body. Instead of her long, graceful limbs, Ember saw pitch black feathers…wings. She had wings.

"This is a dream. I'm dreaming," she thought. The shocks moved throughout her fasters, creating an aura around her, lifting her off the ground. A gust of wind swirled around her so strongly that it penetrated her skin, making them one. She was made of wind and air, so light but so powerful. The feathers on her body lifted and moved in unison with her new body slowly, stretching out as far as they could go.

Suddenly, her body rose off the ground, as her wings flapped faster and faster. It was a strange and clumsy sensation at first, but quickly she glided up and over the rooftops and the tall trees, beyond the Commons towards the city. She could see the smallest of details; people walking down the street, what they wore, what they carried in their hands. She could hear their voices perfectly as they talked and laughed. Even as they whispered to each other. The rats running back and forth from the restaurant's dumpsters in the dark back alleys didn't even escape her line of sight. She began moving faster. Her movements were more purposeful in the new streamlined body, over to Salem Harbor. She glided over the dark water, the moonlight's soft blue light casting a shadow on the water underneath her. A perfectly outlined shape of a crow in flight. She swooped down lower until the tips of her wings touched the cold waves, so fast that it had all started to become a blur. Her eyes focused on the bright light ahead, coming from a tall white tower, its ethereal glow moving over the harbor, lighting up the sea as it turned slowly in circles. She flew closer to the top of the old lighthouse, circling around the massive mirror that reflected light over the dark New England waters. Closer and closer she moved towards the light, until it was so blinding, her entire field of vision was consumed by white.

Ember's eyes jolted open, and she was back in her bed, covered in sweat. Slowly trying to regain the feeling of being back in her own body, she wiggled her fingers and looked down to make sure they were all there. She breathed out, her chest falling as the air left her lungs. Her heart was beating fast; she tried to calm down as she looked around her sun-drenched room. It was morning. She slept the whole night. The dream, it had seemed so real, as if she really was flying over the city. But somehow, she knew it was more than that. It wasn't just her flying; it was as if she were seeing the world through eyes that were not her own. The sense of not being in her body was strange, but exciting, like nothing she had ever experienced. She sat up and swung her feet over the bed to the cold floor, giving her a sense of grounding. It was just a strange dream, she said to herself. She shook her long black hair as she walked into the kitchen, filled her tea kettle with water, and put it on the burner. As the water came to a boil, she pulled out her grandmother's old leather-bound book of all her recipes and incantations. Over the years, Ember had added her own spells, dreams, and thoughts, trying to match Carmen's skillful handwriting. She thumbed through the tea-colored pages full of pressed flowers and herbs and tried to remember the strange dream so she could write it down before it completely disappeared from her mind. She thought about how it had felt to fly above the water, the feeling of being so free, to be so aware of every sense. Then, she thought of the shadow she saw reflected in the water, a crow. Same as the one sitting in the tree outside her old house. Just sitting quietly, waiting, like a long-lost friend. She was so lost in thought she hadn't realized she had drawn a picture of the crow in the book. She stared at it for a long time before the whistle of the kettle brought her out of the trance. She poured the hot water over the tea bag in her favorite cup and sat silently with her thoughts, which were now filled with an image of a crow.

Ember made the decision to explore her new home. She walked into the bathroom and let the tub fill with water. After soaking in the warm water and washing her long raven hair, she wrapped herself in a fluffy towel and walked over to her closet. A long flowy black dress with large bell sleeves caught her eye. It was cold, so she grabbed her favorite wool wrap and her favorite lace-up boots. Ember then reached for her grandmother's amethyst locket. She stepped out into the hazy morning and made her way to the Commons. Fog hung low around the newly fallen leaves that crunched under her feet as she walked. Ember admired a large, regal-looking building and wondered about all the ghost stories she had read about the Hawthorne Hotel. She'd always loved reading stories and legends about Salem. She made a mental note to stop into the hotel and have a cup of tea, or even a cider at the tavern. But not today, today she kept on walking to Essex Street, the heart of town. Past the many shops, the cobblestone streets, she made her way over to Charter Street and to The Old Burying Point. Making her way through the old iron gates that surrounded the small cemetery, Ember wandered through all the faded and crooked headstones. A cold wind picked up from behind her, blowing her dark hair around her face as she slowly made her way along the twisted path, glancing at the old, faded, crumbling head-stones. Suddenly, something made her stop in her tracks. A sensation of electricity coursing through her body like a thunderbolt. Her eyes glazed down to the broken headstone in front of her. She moved in closer and focused on the name etched in the stone, Judge John Hathorne. Ember recognized the name immediately as one of the judges who presided over the witchcraft trials back in 1692. She couldn't help the wave of sadness that came over her. To think of all the pain caused by this man and men like him. How even Sarah Wildes fell to his judgment. Thoughts of Sarah suddenly overtook her as she made her way out of the cemetery just as the morning fog lifted. She followed the path that led to the witchcraft memorial that bordered the Burying Point old stone wall. She walked along the stones that lined the memorial, stopping at every stone bench that had engraved on it the names of those executed, until she found the one she was searching for. She read it aloud to herself. "Sarah Wildes July 19, 1692". She could see that someone had left flowers on Sarah's stone, and that gave her a warm feeling, to think that someone would do this small act of kindness to remember Sarah. To remember all those who lost their lives. Ember shivered at thoughts of Sarah, and what she might have been like in life. She remembered the stories about Sarah; her grandmother Carmen told her on long, cold winter nights, snuggled by the fireplace. How Sarah was considered glamorous and forward as a young girl, even being arrested for wearing a silk scarf.

"She went to jail for wearing a scarf?" she would ask Carmen, her yellow eyes wide with curiosity.

"Yes, she did. But they couldn't keep her in jail, my love. They are never able to contain us for long," she would tell Ember, her eyes glowing in the firelight.

Over the years, as she learned more about Sarah, Ember grew to admire her for having the courage to fight to be herself, in a world that condemned individuality. She gave the stone one last look and walked further down the memorial towards the harbor. As she turned a corner, a small shop caught her eye. From the outside, it seemed to be an average-looking magical shop. There were several in Salem. A plain black door that read 'Pentagram Witchcraft and Magic Shoppe' with a five-pointed star in the center. Ember had never been to a witchcraft shop. She had always grown or foraged the ingredients needed for her recipes and herb blends. She spent the long summer days at the large wooden kitchen table of the Connecticut house, making candles and incense that she would sell at the bookstore where she worked for some extra money. But an entire store of witch-craft supplies? She was intrigued and intently drawn to go inside. She pulled open the glass door and immediately was hit with the smell of frankincense in the air. She gave her eyes a moment to adjust to the low lighting before she looked around the store, trying to take it all in. A few customers wandered about the bookcases and displays of crystals and jewelry. Ember's attention focused on the tall, dark wood shelves stocked with large glass jars of herbs reaching all the way up to the ceiling. So tall that a ladder on wheels was attached to the top shelf. Next to it was a similar one stacked with old books, some so large they barely fit on the tightly packed shelves. Candles flickered, casting dancing shadows on the dark cherry wood walls, giving everything a mysteri-ous, magical glow. Just to the back was another small room, its entry covered by a large green curtain. Ember walked slowly towards the curtain; a curiosity not normal for her, but a burning began in the pit of her stomach. It pushed her closer to it. She needed to know what was behind the thick curtain. Her fingers reached out for it, and just as she was close enough to touch the velvet fabric, a small, older woman with salt and pepper hair emerged from behind the curtain.

"Oh, hello. I thought I felt someone walk in," she said to Ember as she took the reading glasses off her face to examine more closely the stranger who had wandered in off the street.

Ember, still shocked at the woman emerging so quickly from the small room, stood frozen awkwardly in place, not knowing what to say.

"Cat got your tongue, dear?" the woman said as she moved closer to Ember. "Come now, I don't bite. No need to be shy. Come, come…did you want a reading?"

"Um, no, I was just…" Ember said, stumbling over her words.

The small woman leaned in closer to Ember. "Mmm, look at those eyes, like fire. I see fire in you, my girl," the woman said as she peered into Ember's eyes, "fire..yes..but something else."

"We can sense each other, you know," the woman said as she placed her wire-rimmed glasses back on her nose. Ember stood in the same place, her feet stuck to the floor. She nervously chewed on her fingernail, an old habit she had yet to find a remedy for. "Sense what?" She asked nervously.

"Come now, dear. I might be old, but I'm not blind," the woman said as she passed Ember, "at least not yet."

She stopped in front of a small table in the back corner of the small back room.

The woman struck a match, lighting a black candle as she sat down. The wick came to life as it burned, reflecting on the large, clear crystal ball at the center of the table. She blew the match out with a small breath and then turned to look back at Ember. "I know another witch when I see one, so do you by the looks of it."

Ember wasn't ready to be so bluntly confronted with the truth about herself so soon, her first day in town. But she had made a promise to herself that she was going to try to be more open, more accepting of people and new experiences, but nothing could have prepared her for this. A witch. She had heard the word so many times in her life as a negative. But to hear it now, in this place, it didn't feel the same at all. She had never met another witch before, or she didn't think she had. She swallowed the lump that had formed in her throat before she spoke. "Mm, I'm Ember, Ember Wildes," she said, still chewing on her fingernail." I just moved to town, and your shop caught my eye."

The woman gave her a curious look at the mention of her name. She leaned over the small table,

"Wildes? I see. Well, it's a pleasure to make your acquaintance. Ember, that's a fitting name for you," she said, making a gesture for Ember to sit down across from her. "My name is Lydia Bennett. Welcome to my shop. You are very welcome here, my dear," she said, her voice sweet and warm.

"Thank you, "Ember replied as she took a seat at the table.

Lydia was small in stature but had a commanding presence. Her shoulder-length salt and pepper hair was put up in a messy bun held in place by a pencil. Her skin was smooth except for small lines at the corners of her eyes, making it very difficult to guess her age. Her bright green eyes danced behind her reading glasses that she kept on a gold chain around her neck. There was a warm way about her, Ember thought. Her voice was soothing and reassuring, almost mother-like. Ember liked her immediately.

"Would you like some tea? I could use a cup," Lydia said as she rose from the table to pick up a teapot sitting on the shelf behind her, along with a small wooden box engraved with a pentagram, and placed them on the table. Ember hesitated for a moment, but a cup of tea did sound good on this chilly morning. Lydia looked around the room. "Oh my, where did I put those teacups? Ah, there they are," Lydia reached over Ember to a shelf right above her head. Ember turned to look at the shelf that she didn't even realize was behind her. Lydia smiled at the look of surprise in Ember's eyes. "You will learn that not everything is what it appears. Especially in this place. It's filled with all sorts of nooks and crannies." She opened the wooden box and took out a small purple velvet pouch. She sprinkled some of the contents in both cups and poured the steaming hot water over it from the porcelain teapot. Ember watched the steam from the cup as it filled the space between them.

"This is one of my special blends, "she said proudly as she handed the delicate cup to Ember. "Here you go, doll. Drink up."

Ember took the cup gently from Lydia's small hand and placed it on her lips. She took a sip of the bitter tea and winced.

"Oh, it's not that bad, "Lydia laughed as she took a large sip from her own cup.

A tiny giggle escaped Ember's lips. "It's delicious." She wasn't lying. It was strong, but the tea did remind her of one her grandmother had made, long ago. Thoughts of Carmen filled her mind as she gulped down the rest.

"Your thoughts are of your mother, no, your grandmother, yes?"

Lydia's words caught Ember off guard. She suddenly felt hot; her palms began to sweat, making her put the cup down in front of her for fear of dropping it. Lydia placed her own cup back on the table and picked up Ember's. She studied the tea leaves at the bottom closely before speaking.

"You think you are lost, but you are far from it, my darling," she began to say as Ember threw her shawl off her shoulders, trying to get some air in the room that suddenly seemed a lot smaller than before.

"Are you searching for something? Or is something searching for you?" Lydia turned the cup around in her hands as she peered closely inside. "Something is searching for you. Calling to you. You have heard it all your life, but now it is so loud. You can no longer ignore it, can you? It has been waiting a long time. Hiding in plain sight, always at your back, watching…following…like a shadow."

Ember was sweating now; she felt like all the air had been sucked out of the room, making her head spin. She needed to leave; she began to stand up from her seat when she felt Lydia's hand on hers.

"The crow, you have seen him, yes?"

Ember's skin began to tingle, as if thousands of ants were running up and down her entire body, stopping her from leaving. She turned to look at Lydia as she sat back down.

"Yes, I have seen him recently," Ember said slowly, but I think he's always been there…. I can't remember when or where, but yes, the crows have always been there." Her head began to clear now; it had stopped spinning, and she could focus.

Lydia looked up from the teacup. "Yes, dear, they have been." She turned the cup to show Ember what she had been gazing at. To share the message hidden in the tea leaves.

Ember focused her yellow eyes on the bottom of the cup, to see what mystery the tea leaves held. She could instantly see the image at the bottom of the cup. It was a bird, wings outstretched as if about to take flight. Ember sat staring at the cup, not really believing what she was seeing. A crow, in the tea leaves.

"They have always watched over you, my child. You remember, running through the woods as a child, trying to outrun them?' Lydia asked, her voice sounding steady and sure.

Ember shook her head in agreement as she closed her eyes and remembered that day so vividly. The smell of the grass, the feeling of the wind in her hair, the army of wings at her back.

"Give me your hand, dear." Lydia took Ember's hand in hers. Heat began to grow between both their hands. Ember could feel it spread up her arm, into her chest, and behind her eyes. In an instant, the world around them fell away, like pieces of a broken mirror. It was like she was falling down a hole, down further and further until the world came back into focus. She opened her eyes and realized she was back home, at the old house, with the small creek that flowed over with sparkling water and into the woods of the back yard. She blinked, trying to understand. Had she traveled back in time somehow? Then she could hear them. Far away at first, but the sound came rushing up to meet her, like waves crashing over rocks. Their calls, their wings, were all around her. "Run Ember, run and be one with us," she heard whispered in the flapping of their black wings. So, she ran, ran as fast as her legs could carry her, long black hair trailing behind her, blending in with the crow's black feathers. Her lungs burning, her eyes watering from the cold air as she ran fast through the trees and the tall grass. The crows were all around her, encircling her, until she didn't know where she ended, and they began. She could feel the ground falling from under her bare feet as she was lifted into the air. The crow's wings embraced her, cradling her body close to theirs. Entangling their beaks and talons in her hair, until she was lost in a sea of obsidian feathers, lost in their blackness.

Then, as fast as she had gone to that memory, she was back, back in the small warm room. She could feel the chair under her. She opened her eyes, as tears fell from them onto her lap. Ember inhaled deeply as she noticed that Lydia had let go of her hand. She had never had a vision like that before, never. It was so real, not like a dream. She wasn't asleep; she was wide awake, more than any time in her life.

"What was that?" Ember gasped and looked at the kind woman in front of her.

"It was a vision, a message. You and the crows are linked, since birth, I suspect."

"You could see it too?" Ember asked as she whipped her brow with the sleeve of her dress.

"Oh yes, you shared it with me, brought me into that world. A talent very few possess."

Ember tried to gather her thoughts. "But why is this happening to me now?" she asked, trying to make sense of what had just occurred.

"That's a message only you can decipher, my darling. You have a very special gift. A special connection that I have never seen. I felt your presence when you walked through my door, like a storm blowing through these walls. I can see it in your eyes and in your hair. You are very powerful, my girl, and it's time that you embrace it. To become the witch that you were born to be. The Goddess walks with you. The crows are her messengers, her guardians, as they are your guardians. You must embrace this, for your calling is one of great importance."

Lydia's words were coming too fast for Ember to process. It was all too much; she didn't understand. How could she trust this woman whom she had just met, saying things that she wasn't sure she wanted to hear?

Her mind was overwhelmed. It all seemed so unreal. She exhaled slowly and looked back into Lydia's green eyes for the truth.

"I don't understand what just happened, and I don't understand what you are telling me. All I know is that whatever that was, it was real. So real that it scared me, and I really don't have anyone. I'm alone in this world," Ember's voice trailed off as she chewed on her nails. "Can I trust you to help me?"

Lydia took Ember's hand in hers, her touch surprising her. "My darling girl, you are not alone. You are like me, and we are many. Now I will admit, I don't know everything, but together I think we can find the answers. I will help you. Yes, of course I will. My sister and I are witches."

"Sister witches?" Saying the word out loud felt strange to Ember, but not terrible.

"Yes, my darling girl. My Coven. Oh, they must meet you,"

Lydia said with a reassuring smile. "I know they will love you."

Ember smiled at the kind woman with the emerald, green eyes. 'You can trust her, a voice said in her head.

Lydia held her gaze for a moment. "Well, can't sit here and daydream, can we? Much to do now," she said as she stood up and rushed Ember out of her seat. "Listen to me, my child. If you are going to learn, you must work. One of the most important things you will learn about the craft is balance. Nothing comes for free; always a price to pay. So, you will help me here, in the shop, and we will be very busy soon. I need all the help I can get. Be here tomorrow at 10am sharp."

"Wait, are you giving me a job? Or are you teaching me?" Ember asked. She hadn't expected to work, at least not for a while. The money from the sale of her parents' house had been enough for her to be able to live off of comfortably.

Lydia cut her off with a smile. "Job, yes, and lessons…all the same. Remember, balance."

Ember gave her a small nod of agreement as she collected her things. "I don't know how to thank you, Lydia."

"Don't thank me yet, love," Lydia replied. "It's going to be hard work, but go now, rest. I'll see you tomorrow," Lydia said as she rushed Ember out the shop door.

* * *

LYDIA WATCHED as the beautiful raven-haired girl walked gracefully out of her store. She laughed as she watched her. "She even moves like a bird," she said to herself.

She meant what she had told the girl with yellow eyes. In her more than thirty years of practicing and teaching witchcraft, she had never encountered someone like this girl. The power she had, and to be so unaware of it. Lydia sat back in her chair and looked at the tea leaves in Ember's cup. She felt drained, tired, but with a glimmer of hope growing inside her. She knew that taking this girl under her tutelage wasn't going to be a mistake. 'Maybe I am too old for this sort of thing,' she thought to herself. But she felt a strong message from the Goddess; she could not deny or ignore it. Even with that strong feeling, she couldn't help being somewhat frightened for Ember. That kind of power would not go unnoticed by some in this town. Her bloodline would be sensed no doubt, but when they saw who she truly was, they would stop at nothing to destroy her, of that she was certain.

She walked over to the statue of the Morrigan placed on the small table at the other end of the room and closed her eyes.

"My Lady, you must protect the girl." She waited for a response to her plea. After a long pause, Lydia heard the answer in her mind's eye. The voice and message were clear, as clear as church bells on a cloudless day. With that, Lydia understood what she must do. She walked over to the front desk and picked up the phone receiver, dialed, and listened to the ring on the other end.

"Lydia," the soft voice said on the other end.

"I found her, Mya. It's time."

* * *

EMBER WALKED towards the harbor and out to the lighthouse overlooking the water, still somewhat unsteady from the experience in the store, but with a new sense of awareness. She tried to put herself back in that vision, to feel the crows around her. The thought made her feel safe, and that brought a new feeling of hope. Hope she would not only be with people who accepted her, but that she would finally be able to understand those things that were always buried deep inside. She didn't have to hide anymore. As she stared at the deep, dark blue water, another feeling came to her, a very different feeling. One of dread, as if a storm were coming. She looked to the horizon and watched as the clear blue sky became dark with rolling gray clouds. A gust of wind blew in from the ocean. Fast, it whipped the hair across her face. She could hear thunder rolling in the distance. Yes, a storm was coming.

CHAPTER 4

Thomas sat in his SUV in front of the medical examiner's office, trying to will himself to go inside. He tightened his grip around the steering wheel and closed his eyes. His head was still pounding, and his hands slightly shook. He knew what he was going to have to see, and he was dreading it. Another girl on a cold slab. Another phone call to a family, another life destroyed. It seemed to be happening much too often, and these murders seemed to be escalating. Thomas was the first one who picked up on a pattern and tied the deaths together, which is how he ended up being the lead investigator on the case, despite the Federal Bureau of Investigation's strongly worded objections. Most of the other investigators were certain that these deaths were unrelated. But Thomas knew after the second girl, Molly O'Connor, washed up on the shore in Beverly. Molly was a pretty girl; short, bouncy curls framed her oval-shaped face. She was well-liked and had a lot of friends. She had just graduated from high school and was getting ready to head to college. A lobsterman had found her floating by his buoys. A wet mess of blonde hair caught his attention. He was so shaken that he could barely speak when Thomas tried to get his statement. The girl had no visible trauma, nothing to help determine the cause of death. No water in the lungs, so drowning was ruled out. Just some strange scratches around her neck and shoulders. Thomas had the terrible job of informing the family. To him, it was the worst part of what he did, to have to look into a mother's eyes and tell them that their baby is never coming home. He had dealt with many of the same notifications over the past year; however, it didn't make it any easier. Every time he did, it took a little part of his soul. But he couldn't think about that now. He had a job to do. He ran his fingers through his thick blonde hair before he stepped out of his blue SUV into the rainy morning and walked inside the one-story building. He shook the water from his hair as he took off his jacket and let himself inside the double door to the examination room. The medical examiner stood over a metal table, the large bright white light over his head shining down onto the white sheet covering the small body beneath. Thomas hated this room, hated the smell, like death and formaldehyde. Hated the way the stark light hurt his eyes, making it hard for him to focus.

"Morning, Doc. Sorry, I'm a little late. Been a busy morning," Thomas said as he approached.

"Hey there, Tom. No worries, my friend. She's not going anywhere." Doctor John De Luca was a short, stocky man, with an unkempt mustache and an unsavory disposition, saying off-pudding remarks that made some of the more inexperienced cops uncomfortable. Thomas had become accustomed to the dark humor in his profession. He understood that it was a way some used to cope with all the horrors they saw. De Luca put a pair of thick black rimmed glasses on his worn face and looked at the table with no emotion in his eyes. Only the lines on his skin told the true story of the terrible things he had seen over the years.

"Yeah, I figured I'd give you some extra time on this one. From what I saw on scene, she had more injuries than the previous victims," Thomas said with concern.

"Well, I can tell you with certainty that this victim does fit the MO of the past five, even with the extra injuries. She does have a broken right arm, but everything else matches up with the others. Same strange scratches on the mouth, neck, and lower extremities. A bit deeper and more jagged, I'd say, and no water in the lungs." DeLuca removed the small brown paper bags that had been put on the girl's hands in efforts to preserve evidence. He pulled out a magnifying glass and took a closer look. "Yeah, looks like she's got something under her nails. Something black could be just dirt, but I'll send it to the lab," Thomas said as he took a few steps closer to see what DeLuca was carefully scraping from under the girl's nails.

DeLuca nodded. "Looks like this one put up one hell of a fight," he said as he placed the bits of black substance in a plastic tube. "Good for you."

He placed the tubes on a metal table and sealed them with red 'evidence' tape. His attention turned back to the table as he lifted the sheet covering the small body.

Thomas stared at the girl. She was a ghostly pale blue color, the red "Y" incision stitched on her chest in contrast to the rest of her pale skin. Her small frame looked so fragile lying on that cold metal table. He closed his eyes and tried to envision what she looked like in life. How her voice might have sounded.

"You doing ok there, Tom?" DeLuca asked, as he gave Thomas a strange look.

"Yeah. I'm good," Thomas said, trying to snap his mind back to what was in front of him. He shook off his wandering thoughts and searched his coat pocket for his notepad.

"Haven't gotten the tox screen back yet, but I'll bet you

money it's clean," he said, like the other ones. I can't find a definite cause of death. Her heart, lungs, and stomach are clear. Other than the fracture to the arm and the scratches, no other trauma noted."

Thomas shook his head in agreement as the doctor gave his assessment. "Can you check her eyes for petechial hemorrhaging?"

DeLuca looked up at Thomas with a slight look of annoyance. "Sure thing," he said, not trying to hide the sarcasm in his voice.

Sensing the tension filling up the room, Thomas looked up from his notes. "Look, doc, I'm not trying to be a dick and tell you how to do your job, ok. I just got nothing. So, I'm making sure I check everything. If there's no water in the lungs, then she was killed before she was dumped. With no other obvious signs of death, then I'm thinking asphyxiation, maybe even strangulation."

DeLuca looked at Thomas and sighed. He took a step closer to the girl and examined her eyes. "The other victims had no signs of strangulation, Tom, but I'll double check." After a few minutes, he looked up." Nothing, Tom. It's clear."

Thomas shook his head and scribbled some notes on his pad. DeLuca walked away from the examination table and peeled his latex gloves off. 'Listen, I'll put a rush on the lab. Get you those reports as soon as possible, ok. How about witnesses?"

"No witness as usual, no evidence on scene either. All I have is a statement from one of her friends. They made a call to the local PD when she didn't show up for drinks. They tried to get hold of her with no luck. Apparently, it wasn't like her to just disappear like that," Thomas said as he put his notepad back in his pocket.

Dr. DeLuca picked up a yellow file off the desk behind him. "I ran the prints for you. I thought it would help. Clarie

Marks, twenty-six years old, lived in Salem. Her prints were in the system from an arrest a few years back. I have her next of kin info if you want it."

"Yeah, thanks," Thomas said. "I'm also going to need all the files on this and the autopsy pictures. Do you have a time of death?" Thomas asked as he suddenly got a sharp pain behind his eyes.

"Sometime over the last twenty-four hours. Doesn't look like the fish got a hold of her, so she wasn't in the water for long," DeLuca answered as he picked up a stack of files from the desk and handed them to Thomas.

"Thanks, Doc," Thomas said as he took the files, put them under his arm, and turned to walk out of the room.

"Hey Tom, what are your thoughts? Who do you think is doing this? Must be a local, right?"

Thomas paused at the door. "Honestly, Doc, I have no idea. "With that, he pushed the door open to walk out of the room. DeLuca's voice made him pause. "Hey kid, go home and get some sleep. You look like shit. Look, I'll swab as much as I can to see if I can find any DNA. If I do, I'll run it through CODIS. Maybe this time we catch a break."

Thomas snickered. Just when he thought DeLucca was a cold son of a bitch, he suddenly turned into a nice guy. "Sure, Doc. I appreciate it," Thomas said, knowing that the water would have destroyed any DNA on the body."

Thomas stopped outside the door and collected his thoughts. The sharp pain in his head felt like a hot knife behind his eyes. He rubbed his temples; he should listen to DeLuca and go home for some rest, or a drink. As he stood in the empty hallway, he looked up and saw a woman staring at him. She was sitting in the waiting area right outside the exam room. She might have been in her early forties, but the worry lines on her face made her appear older. Thomas gave her a small smile as he adjusted the collar on his navy blue peacoat. He was used to that sort of attention from women, even though he didn't understand it. His looks had always been a topic of conversation. Even his own mother told him that he was "too good-looking to be a cop." Thomas sometimes felt uneasy at the way women acted around him. He'd had his fair share of girlfriends over the years, not to mention drunken one-night stands, but eventually they got sick of him putting the job first. He quickly looked down, pulled his collar up over his ears, and made his way out of the building. The rain had cleared up, and the sun had started to peek through the grey clouds. Thomas welcomed the warmth and quiet inside his SUV. He sat and listened to the engine warm up. He desperately wanted a drink, but he knew he had a lot of work to do. He grabbed one of the files off the passenger seat and flipped through the pages until he found what he was looking for. The girl's parents' phone number. Their address was out of state, which he was grateful for. As hard as it was giving people bad news over the phone, he preferred it. Looking into their eyes and seeing their pain was sometimes too much to bear, especially today. He put the SUV in the drive and headed to his office.

As he drove down the narrow streets, he thought about the woman in the office and the way she looked at him. Thomas had wanted to meet someone, to be able to share his life with a person who understood him. He had given up on the dating scene, but on lonely nights, he would troll some local bars that were not in the best areas. He didn't know what he was looking for, but deep down he had always believed that there was someone out there for him. Over the last year, it had been a struggle to hold on to that notion, but he was desperately trying to. So, in efforts to stay out of trouble and out of the dive bars, Thomas left his office and went home to his roomy loft and sat at his desk, covered with papers and notes. He pored over them night after night, combing through every detail, forcing himself to look at the horrible images, until he couldn't look at them anymore. But still, there was a feeling deep inside him, an uneasy feeling that he couldn't shake no matter how many shots of bourbon he drank. Something was coming; he could sense it. What that was, he wasn't sure.

He parked his car in front of the large brick building that held his headquarters. With all the files under his arm, he made his way inside and up to his second-floor office. He pulled open the glass door marked "Homicide Task Force" and walked to his desk. As he was putting the files down, his office phone rang.

"Detective Cole," he said curtly.

"Cole! Where the hell have you been?"

Thomas immediately recognized the angry voice on the other end of the phone. "Captain Torres, it's always a pleasure to get a call from you."

"Cole, I'm not in the mood. I've been calling your phone all morning," Torres said, the anger building in his voice.

Thomas pulled his cell phone out of his pocket and saw the multiple missed calls from his captain and sighed. He must not have noticed his phone vibrating in his coat.

"Sorry, boss. I guess I didn't notice. I was busy trying to solve a multiple murder," Thomas replied, trying to not let his captain get to him; his day had been hard already.

"Don't give me your wise ass shit, Cole! I need your report on this current victim. We need some answers! The Major is so far up my ass I can taste what he had for lunch! Do you have something? Anything?"

Thomas leaned back in his chair and took a deep breath. He wasn't in the mood for his boss's colorful language, but then again, he never was. How was he supposed to explain to him that very same thought was what kept him up at night; if he could find a common thread between all six victims, he would have somewhere to start. He understood the importance of victimology; to get to know your victims and their lives. To connect with them. That's how you solve murders. But Thomas had just not been able to do that. He was struggling to try to see the world through the victims' eyes.

"Cole, are you listening? Or are you dozing off?'

"I'm working on it, boss; I will have some answers for you soon," Thomas said as he rubbed the two-day stubble on his chiseled jaw line.

"Soon?" Torres yelled, "More like yesterday," he said as he hung up the phone.

Thomas placed the receiver back with a thud as he noticed the blinking red light notifying him that he had voicemails. He started to reach for the button but stopped. He couldn't think here, and the last thing he needed was to listen to more people asking him questions he just couldn't answer. So, he collected all his files and headed out the door. He needed to be alone, in his own private place with his thoughts. Just him and the victims. No one could understand that, and he had zero interest in explaining why. He needed a drink, just one to kill the throbbing pain in his head. Just one.

He drove home; October wasn't even here yet, and already the streets of downtown Salem were starting to get crowded with tourists. Normally, Thomas loved October, but over the years, the number of tourists flocking to Salem had grown. He knew that this was only going to make the investigation more difficult. He also worried there was still someone out there watching, waiting for another girl to be in a vulnerable position. Maybe the large crowds would deter them from killing anyone, he tried to convince himself. But he knew that probably was not going to happen. He turned down Lafayette Street and parked his car in the large parking lot across from his loft building. He was almost at the front door when a cold wind blew so hard it almost pulled all the papers out of his hands. With a shiver down his spine, he looked in the direction the wind had come, his ice blue eyes narrowing, not knowing what to expect. The street was empty and quiet, almost too quiet. He felt a pull, something compelling him to walk in the direction this strange wind had come. He wanted to fight the urge, after the day he had. But he found himself walking, not really knowing where he was going, following the pull that guided him. He closed his eyes, and just for a moment, he heard it, the voices. It had been so long since Thomas had heard the whispers on the wind. He had always trusted the voices to guide him, so he followed the wind blindly until he found himself at the old Burying Point. Thomas drove by this cemetery almost every day, not giving it much thought. But there he was, standing at the iron gate. Another sharp burst of wind blew by, picking up all the orange and rust colored leaves that had fallen off the trees, causing them to swirl around him. When the leaves finally settled, he took a step into the cemetery. He walked along the path, looking at the old decaying headstones. 'Why am I here?' he thought to himself. That's when he saw her. A woman was standing in front of one of the ancient oak trees that grew on the property. She wore a long black shawl with a robin egg blue scarf. She was tall, slender, with long black hair that seemed to play in the breeze. She turned to look at him as he approached. He was stunned at her beauty and the color of her eyes, like embers from a dying flame. He had never seen a more beautiful woman. He stood in front of her, not being able to move, like his feet were planted on the ground like the gnarled roots of the old tree.

"Embers," he caught himself saying out loud.

The raven-haired woman lifted one eyebrow in curiosity. "I'm sorry, but do I know you?" she asked.

"Ah, no, I'm sorry to disturb you. I just... well, your eyes, they are very unique; they remind me of embers." Thomas said, feeling awkward. He was sure that the last thing a woman wanted was a strange man approaching her at night in a cemetery, babbling about her eyes. 'Jesus, I must sound like a creep,' he thought.

The woman came closer. She walked so quietly, as if her feet weren't touching the ground, and smiled at him. "Well, that's my name, Ember Wildes," she said as she stretched her hand out to him.

"Your name is Ember?"

"Yes. What are you, a cop or a psychic? You never know in this town," she said playfully, her yellow eyes dancing like a candle flame in the wind.

"I'm a cop, actually. Maybe you're the psychic," Thomas replied as he reached for her hand to shake it,

"Thomas Cole."

The moment his skin touched hers, he felt a shock of electricity. He could feel it starting in his hand and moving through his entire body. He had never felt anything like it. He stared into her eyes, not being able to break his gaze. Just then, the wind whipped through the trees again, stirring up the crows nestled in their warm nests in the branches. They took flight in the wind, gliding like black ghosts over their heads, breaking Thomas's trance. She let go of his hand and looked up at the crows as they fluttered overhead, swooping down as if to taunt them both to play. Thomas had never seen anything like that. This hauntingly beautiful woman stood in this old cemetery, her black hair flying fiercely around her, and crows circling over both of them. She smiled at the black birds flying all around her, as if she was welcoming an old friend, their wings softly brushing up against her hair and kissing her cheek.

"I've never seen that before. Are they trained?" Thomas

asked, again feeling nervous and awkward, a feeling he hadn't felt around a woman in a long time.

"They could never be trained or tamed. They follow their hearts; they are free," Ember said, her yellow eyes meeting his blue ones, like fire and ice.

"Well, it's getting late. I should get home. It was a pleasure to meet you, Officer Thomas Cole."

"Actually, it's Detective Cole, "Thomas said, regretting the words the minute they left his mouth. 'God, I sound like a prick,' he said to himself.

"I see." Ember said as she walked towards him, a fiery look in her glowing eyes, "Well, have a great night, detective."

"Wait, don't go. Sorry, I didn't mean to offend you. Can I see you again or maybe call you?" For a split second, Thomas was afraid he sounded desperate, but he shook that thought out of his head fast. He was captivated by this woman; he wanted her, and he wasn't going to let her slip away and walk out of his life, never see her again. Not a chance.

She turned and looked at him over her shoulder. "Don't worry, Detective, it's a small town. We will meet again." The scent of rose, vanilla, and warm sandalwood hit all his senses as the breeze blew her hair by him. He watched as she walked slowly out of the cemetery, her long skirt trailing behind her. At the iron gates, she stopped and looked over her shoulder at him, her eyes ablaze. Then in a heartbeat, she was gone, leaving Thomas standing there, in the middle of an empty cemetery, his thoughts racing, his pulse quickening. 'Did that just happen?' he asked himself. But the feeling of passion that was left lingering inside him was confirmation enough. As he began to walk away, he saw something out of the corner of his eye, a moving shadow. He stopped slowly and looked in the direction of the shadowy figure. He tried to focus on the low light. It was a woman, standing out in the small empty field next to the cemetery. She looked pale and thin, her clothes and blonde hair dirty and soaking wet. Something about the woman was unnatural; it made his skin crawl. He looked away but could still see her out of his peripheral vision. He closed his eyes and breathed for just a second. When he opened them again, she was closer, much closer. The unmistakable smell of death filled his nostrils. 'I'm not looking. I'm not looking,' he said under his breath, as the pale figure stood there, staring at him, motionless. "Fuck this," Thomas said as he looked straight ahead and walked out of the old cemetery. Never looking behind him.

CHAPTER 5

Ember sat alone on the cold brown grass at the top of Gallows Hill Park. It was a perfect Autumn day, brisk and sunny. She gazed over the tops of trees at the blue sky and over to the large water tower at the top of the hill with the witch on a broomstick painted on it. She closed her eyes and silently thought of the chance meeting she had with the handsome man in the cemetery the night before. She thought about his flaxen colored hair and his icy blue eyes and smiled. Tristan had told her to try to go on a date, to be more social. But Ember hadn't been interested in such things. Now the thought of this tall stranger with kind eyes gave her butterflies. He seemed so familiar to her; the smooth sound of his voice, his entire presence, made her feel safe in a way she had never felt with anyone. She wondered how that could be with someone she had just met. But what she had learned over the last few weeks was that she needed to trust her instincts, and whoever he was, she would see him again. Or so she hoped. Just as she opened her eyes, a large black crow with a chipped beak flew down and landed right next to her.

"Hello, Shadow," Ember said to the bird.

The bird squawked loudly. To anyone other than Ember, it would have just been a crow, making the usual sound crows make. But to her, she was beginning to understand his calls and clicks perfectly. She knew it was his way of giving her a friendly greeting. Ember had been reading and researching everything she could about crows. Trying to understand everything about their behavior. She had spent hours at the public library reading books and magazine articles about her childhood friends. She found one article in a particularly interesting nature magazine. The author of the paper explained that it was possible to befriend crows, as they could remember human faces and even use tools, like twigs and sticks, to solve problems. It went on to give instructions on how to leave food out for them every day and to be patient, and eventually they would come to you or leave shiny gifts as a thank you, a behavior that Ember was very familiar with. She remembered the coins, small pieces of metal or sometimes even jewelry that the crows would leave on the doorstep or windowsill of her old house. So, she began leaving nuts out on the steps of her front door for the local crows in efforts to make new feathered friends. She could see them in the trees above her home, staring down at her with their small black eyes. At first, they seemed cautious. But one by one they began flying down, scooping up the nuts with their beaks and flying right back up to their safe place in the dry leafless trees of late October. But as the day passed, they became more comfortable with Ember, eventually leaving their small trinkets as a show of their appreciation.

Sometimes it was difficult, considering that the streets of Salem had become busy with Halloween tourists. But Ember never missed a day with her little thieves, making sure she left food out for them. At night when she went to sleep, she could feel their presence outside her window. She knew that they were there silently watching over her. When she slept, she dreamt of them, flying together against a stormy grey sky. One began to appear more and more in her dreams, night after night. A large crow, larger than any other she had seen, with a broken beak. He first made his way into her dreams like a shadow, not fully formed, just a dark mist that would spread its wings upwards and then disappear like smoke. She would wake up and could almost see his imprint on the wall, just in those few seconds between dreaming and the waking world. But he would disappear, so she would go outside to see if she could find him in the trees or slanted rooftops. He felt so real that she was certain he would be right there, just waiting for her, but he never was. Until one night, she woke from a dreamless deep sleep to hear a pecking at her window. She quickly threw on her emerald green velvet robe and ran to the large window in her living room. There he was, sitting on the windowsill. Ember rushed out the door to the front of the apartment, hoping that he wouldn't fly away, but he didn't; he hopped over to her like a lifelong friend. She turned her head to one side as she bent down, connected her eyes with his, her long braid touching the ground.

"So, you are the shadow I've been seeing," she said to the crow.

He gave her a reassuring squawk, clicking his broken beak as he ruffled his feathers and gazed his small black eyes back at her.

"Then that's what I'll call you, Shadow," Ember said to her new companion.

He had been at her side every day since that night, sometimes leaving her an array of little gifts at her doorstep. He would even come inside her apartment and perch on her bed post, sometimes snuggling himself on one of her pillows, claiming it as his own. When he wasn't at her side, he was never too far behind. Ember would see him circling above her as she walked through the streets, or hopping from tree to tree behind her, like the Shadow he was.

She had been working at pentagram for the last few weeks as well. Even though the store was very busy with curious visitors, asking for tarot readings or browsing witchcraft supplies, Ember didn't mind; it made the days go by fast. After the store closed, she and Lydia would stay long into the night. Ember was learning so much from Lydia's tutelage, every night learning more and more. Ember was a dedicated student, and her mind was like a sponge, soaking up everything she could.

Lydia had noticed the large crow circling about the front window of the store, pecking at the glass, eating bits of popcorn, or other food that the tourists had dropped while walking down the streets enjoying the Halloween festivities. Until one day she came upon him sitting outside the store on the sidewalk. He didn't fly away as she approached him, just tilted his head from side to side as he clicked his broken beak at her.

"Aren't you a distinguished-looking gentleman?" she said as Shadow looked up at her. "You must be the shadow I keep hearing about," she said to the bird. "Come on, come inside. Enough of you loitering out here." With that, the crow flew right through the open doorway and settled on the desk in front of the store. Lydia laughed at how he made himself right at home in the store. She leaned in close to him. "Listen to me, little pet. You can stay, but you must keep your eyes on our girl. She is very important, but I think you know that." Shadow sharply turned his head and gave her a low grumbling sound as he puffed his chest out.

* * *

Ember sat on Gallows Hill so lost in thought she hadn't noticed the time. Shadow pecked gently at her hand to get her attention. She looked down at the antique gold watch and gasped.

"Oh, shit, Shadow! I'm going to be late for work!" She quickly got up from the comfortable grass, dusted off her deep red dress, and slung her bag over her shoulder. She looked down at Shadow, still sitting in the dry grass. "I'll race you, little thief," she said with a grin. In a split second, Shadow spread his wings wide and took flight over Ember's head, flapping in the direction of the store. Ember clutched the strap of her bag and ran after him down the hill. Shadow glided right over her head as she ran through the maze of Halloween tourists, glancing up at him to see where he was in the sky. She finally reached the front door of the store to see Shadow waiting for her. Ember laughed," I'll let you win this one, Shadow," she said as she tried to catch her breath.

She held the door open for him, not paying attention to the surprised looks from the people waiting in line to enter the store. Shadow flew in and claimed his usual perch in the desk.

"Sorry!" Ember yelled over the crowd of people in the store," I know I'm late! It was Shadow's fault," she said as she gave him a wink.

"I'm sure that's not true," Lydia said with a teasing tone in her voice." he's the responsible one."

Lydia had become so fond of Ember over the last few weeks she had been working with her. Even though her forgetfulness and tardiness did sometimes worry her. Ember's carefree ways reminded Lydia of her own youth. She could excuse the tardiness from time to time. She understood that it was her nature. Lydia watched carefully as Ember placed her belongings behind the register and smoothed her messy hair. Something seemed a bit different about her. Lydia stepped closer, placing her glasses on the bridge of her nose. She studied her young student and noticed a deeper flush to her complexion, a color that had nothing to do with her sprint to work. "Well, well. What's going on with you? Something is different. Could it be that you have met someone?" Lydia asked as she looked at Ember over her wire-rimmed glasses.

Ember looked at her and smiled. "It's possible. I don't know. It's too soon to tell." Ember said as she chewed on one of her fingernails, a habit that Lydia had noticed she did when she was nervous.

"I see," Lydia said as she got closer to Ember. She knew that it was impossible to keep secrets from her, but Lydia didn't press the subject. "I see, a girl must have her secrets, I suppose. Anyways, we are going to be busy today, so no time to have your head in the clouds," she said as she rushed past Ember.

Lydia was right about them being busy as of late. Not just working in the Shop, but with the work they did after the doors closed, and it was just the two of them. For weeks, Lydia had been teaching Ember how to center herself and control her power of sight. Ember was a brilliant pupil, a natural witch; harnessing power came easy to her. It was controlling that power that worried Lydia. She had discussed her concern with the Coven during their meetings over the last few weeks. Together, they had been formulating a plan to grow her abilities but also keep her cloaked and safe. They agreed Ember wasn't ready to face the forces that would try to use her for their gain. Every one of the witches in the Coven understood how important Ember was, none more than Lydia. Still, she had this impending feeling that time was running out for all of them. With Samhain, the festival where the veil between worlds was at its thinnest, it would be the perfect time for Ember to join the circle.

"Oh, I almost forgot about our lessons tonight. I think it would be the perfect time to bring you to the circle."

Ember looked at Lydia with surprise in her eyes. She had mentioned her Coven many times during their late-night magic sessions, but had never invited her to one of their secret gatherings.

"Why don't you come with me tonight, my dear?" Lydia said as she pulled off her glasses. "The Coven is dying to meet you, and it is the last full moon before Samhain."

Ember knew how important this time of year was. Samhain was one of the most sacred holidays for witches, the day when the veil was thin, and the dead could cross over into their realm.

"I've been dying to meet them, but do you think I'm ready for all that?" Ember said as she looked down at her feet. She didn't want to disappoint her mentor, but she was nervous about meeting the Coven. She didn't truly trust all her newfound abilities just yet.

"My darling girl, you are ready. I wouldn't invite you if I didn't think so," Lydia said as she walked over to Ember and squeezed her shoulder gently. Ember thought for a minute. If Lydia thought she was ready, then she had no reason to doubt her. It could be interesting, meeting people like her on the full moon no less. She bit her lip before answering, "Ok, I'll go tonight."

"Excellent! I will phone Mya and tell her you are coming. I'm sure she will be excited to finally meet you." Lydia said as she walked past Ember. "We will go right after we close up tonight. We mustn't be late.'

Ember took a deep breath and looked over at Shadow, a small sense of excitement building in her.

At first, the thought of having to socialize with strangers at a party gave her anxiety, but the more she thought about it, the more it intrigued her. She had always wanted to feel accepted to be among others who understood her, and it seemed that it was finally happening. She was finally feeling more comfortable in her own skin and learning about the craft. She watched the clock for the rest of the day. Anxiety, waiting for it to be 10pm. The store stayed open late during October, which she usually didn't mind the extra hours, but tonight she was excited for the night to be over. She helped the sea of customers one by one, answering questions and educating people about witchcraft. For the first time in her life, people listened instead of avoiding her. She also loved how Shadow took every opportunity he could to show off. He would stand as still as he could, like a statue, as customers leaned in close, thinking he was a stuffed bird. In a flash, Shadow would spread his wings and caw loudly. Ember would giggle seeing them jump out of their skin after they realized he was real.

After what seemed to be an eternity, it was finally time to close. She impatiently drummed her fingers on the wooden desk as she waited for Lydia to collect her things and shut off all the lights. She looked over at Shadow, who seemed just as impatient as Ember, walking side to side on the small perch Ember had made for him. Lydia approached and, with a wink, she gestured to the front door. Ember motioned to Shadow, giving him the command to come to her, which he did almost immediately. Since the street was still quite crowded, even at this late hour, Ember placed Shadow in her bag. He preferred her shoulder, but to avoid unwanted attention from the Halloween tourists, she placed him in her bag. A tall girl with long wild black hair and a crow on her shoulder would be a strange sight indeed, even on the streets of Salem. So, he nestled safely out of sight. He peeked his head out and gave Ember a quick clicking sound to let her know he was ready to go.

All three of them walked out together, Lydia pausing to lock the Shop's door behind her.

"Where is this gathering. Where are we going?" Ember asked as they walked side by side down Charter Street.

"It used to be an old speakeasy back in the old prohibition times. It was abandoned for many years until Mya bought it and made it the perfect place for us to gather. Perfectly out of sight, unless you know what to look for," Lydia replied, a sly smile coming across her lips. It was a perfect autumn night; the full silver moon hung in a clear dark purple sky dotted with shimmering stars. The chilly wind whipped through town, coming up from the ocean and blowing the fallen leaves around their feet as they walked. Ember inhaled deeply; she loved nights like this. They turned off the main street down a small back alley to a single red door illuminated by an overhead light of the same color. Lydia knocked on the door three times, and after a short pause, the door was opened by an intense-looking woman with dark eyes and silver hair, a black streak framing her face. She smiled at both before gesturing for them to come inside. "Come in, we have all just arrived," the woman said as she turned to let them pass. Before she closed the door, she looked up at the full moon. "It's time."

Ember and Lydia followed the woman down a winding, dark, narrow staircase to what appeared to be the basement. When they reached the bottom of the stairs, the woman held open a heavy black curtain and guided them into a small room. The floor, walls, and low wood beams on the ceiling were painted black. Long tapered candles lined the walls, dripping wax onto the scrolled candelabras. The flickering candlelight cast dancing shadows on multiple portraits of woman dressed in attire from different time periods, their haunted gazes frozen in time.

More candles were placed all around the room, on the

floor, and on a long table at the head of the small, dimly lit room. The smell of frankincense and dragon's blood hung heavy in the air. As Ember stepped further, her eyes adjusted to the flickering candlelight. As she looked down, she saw a large pentacle painted on the black floor in gold paint, five large candles at each point of the star. She could see figures standing all around her, their faces half shrouded in black hoods and cloaks that touched the floor. As Ember looked around the room at the cloaked figures, it took her a few seconds to realize they were all women, twelve not counting Lydia, whom she saw donning a black cloak as she joined the others.

"Welcome, Ember," the silver-haired woman said as she approached. "My name is Mya, and I'm so happy to finally meet you." Ember studied the woman in front of her. She was in her late forties with long silver colored hair and a black streak running down the left side of her head. She had an elegant way about her, makeup impeccably done, a blood red color shading her full lips and black coal winged liner on her eyelids. She stood in front of Ember and smiled down at her bag that held Shadow. Sensing that someone was looking at him, Shadow peeked out from the safety of Ember's bag.

"Hello there, my friend," Mya said as she admired Shadow. "I hear that you have been watching over Ember." Shadow gave a small squawk in approval. "What is his name?" she asked.

"Shadow," Ember answered, her voice trembling slightly.

"Ah, so he is the shadow on the wall we have all been seeing," Mya said to the cloaked congregation as all nodded and whispered in agreement. "He came to you in a dream, yes?"

Ember nodded her head. "I saw him in my dreams, but not like he is now. More like smoke, not fully formed. I would see him glide across my walls like a ghost, but then he would disappear. Until one day, there he was."

Mya smiled at Ember." He has always been with you, Ember."

She walked around the room. "Gather round, sisters, and let's join hands and welcome Ember to the circle."

All the women stepped in closer around Ember and joined hands. The room suddenly became warm; Ember wiped a few beads of sweat from her forehead. Sensing the tension in Ember, Mya looked at her and said, "Ember, don't be afraid. We are a coven of sisters, keepers of the old ways, of the old Gods, of the old magic we hold in our blood. The same blood that runs through your veins." After a few seconds, Mya continued, "I know this all must seem so strange to you, and I know you have many questions. Together we will find answers, for when we are together is when we are the strongest."

Ember flung her bag off, as Shadow flew out and perched himself on her shoulder. He pecked at her hair almost like he was trying to comfort her. Ember returned the gesture as she nuzzled him gently.

"Shadow is more than your protector, Ember, more than a familiar. You and he are connected to him; and as you are one, so you both will be one with others. And others like him. He is a messenger, her messenger, and he has come to you with a purpose. Soon you will be able to hear each other's thoughts, see in each other's mind, and most importantly, you will learn to see and hear through him, be in his body, see what he does, feel what he feels. You will also have the power to control the entire murder, moving them at your will," Mya said as she admired Shadow, standing tall on Ember's shoulder.

Ember was trying to take in what Mya was saying; she knew she had always had a special connection to the crows, and she knew that Shadow was special. But why would he be sent to her, and by whom? Ember's skin was hot; drops of sweat dripped down her back. She pulled at the buttons on her dress, trying to get some air. "Why, why did Shadow choose me?'

"The crows didn't choose you. Goddess did. The crows are her messengers in this world. You are of the blood, my child, and your bloodline is an ancient one. You are a daughter of the goddess as your mother was, and her mother before her. You are a descendant of a powerful line of women that are linked to the goddess and all her creatures, and we are her priestesses, "Mya said as she walked around the circle.

Ember looked around the room anxiously to find the familiar face of her friend Lydia. As their eyes met, Lydia mouthed silently, 'I'm here,' reassuring Ember that she wasn't alone in a sea of strange eyes.

"Your ancestor Sarah came to this wild country to find a new way of life, but unfortunately, all she found was dirt and death. Many did. She was no witch, but I have no doubt that she heard the goddess calling to her; for some reason, she did not or could not answer. She most certainly had the power of magic, of that, I'm sure. She crossed the sea and brought the bloodline to these shores, and it's been passed down from mother to daughter in your family for generations. Your mother should have taught you, but I sense that she lived in fear. Fear of the power she possessed, fear of her own magic, bound her from it. Your grandmother, on the other hand, not only answered the goddess when called, but she made the ultimate sacrifice for you."

Ember's eyes welled up with tears from thoughts of her grandmother; she could almost smell her perfume. Her eyes shifted back to Lydia, eyes aflame.

"You told her about my family?" Ember asked, choking

back the tears, "And what do you mean my grandmother made a sacrifice?"

Lydia stepped forward, closing the gap between them. Don't be angry, my child. I had never encountered a witch like you. I sensed your power the day you crossed through my door. I didn't want to make a mistake with you, so I consulted with Mya."

Ember wiped the tears from her face with the back of her sleeve and took a deep breath." I understand," she said to Lydia as she swallowed the lump in her throat. She trusted her friend and mentor. Lydia had always shown her nothing but love and kindness. She had no reason not to trust her.

"She was a great lady, and made the greatest sacrifice a woman can make, to lay down her life for the sake of her family, to protect the bloodline," Mya said. "She gave you a necklace, didn't she? Why aren't you wearing it?"

Ember's hands went up to feel her bare neck. "I, I must have forgotten to put it on."

"Wear it, always. It was her talisman; it holds her power. She poured it into it when she left this world. It will protect you," Mya said as she came close to Ember and took her hands in hers, her large oval labradorite ring glittering in the candlelight as she moved. "We have been waiting for you, Ember. You are the one that has been prophesied. You not only are a daughter of the goddess, but you are also Her, here, on this plane, walking with earthly feet. You and your crow," Mya said, her voice rising throughout the room.

Ember's head was spinning; she felt overwhelmed and could barely breathe in the small, dark room. She wanted to run, back up the narrow staircase, outside, so she could feel the cold air on her skin. But her feet were stuck to the floor.

"What prophecy?" Ember asked, her voice a shaking, low whisper.

"It has long been foretold of a witch that would come to

this land. A witch that isn't just a daughter of the goddess but is Her in the flesh and can walk between worlds at will. A witch with fire in her eyes, the scared flame of the goddess. You are that witch, Ember," Mya said, her voice rising above their heads.

"You have felt the call all your life, Ember. Her call. She sent her messenger to guide you, to be your eyes, to be Her eyes. She sent you Shadow through dreams and visions, and he has materialized by her will. Now it's time for you to answer that call: if you accept this power, Ember, you will be one of the most powerful witches that has ever existed, alive or dead. Now it is time, time for you to become the witch you are. To embrace your power, to be one with She who is three, and the Three who is She," Mya said almost in a chant, as the other women began whispering incantations that Ember couldn't quite understand.

The room began to spin all around Ember. Her skin began to tingle and become hot to the touch. She was burning up; she felt like she was on fire. She began to shake uncontrollably. What was happening? What were they doing to her? Had they cast a strange spell that had locked her in the circle, unable to escape.

The burning sensation continued to grow and spread through her body as their chants grew louder, filling the room with their voices. Ember fell to her knees, her legs too weak to hold her. She tried to call for Shadow, but her voice was a low whisper. She could hear his call over the voices, but her vision was too blurry to see him. Suddenly, a strong gust of wind swept through the windowless room, blowing out all the candles, shrouding them in complete darkness. Silence filled Ember's ears as she slowly opened her eyes and saw a low violet glow in front of her. It took only a moment to see the light was coming from under her nail beds. The mysterious light began to spread down her fingers to her hands. The burning was almost too much for her to bear, as the purple glow now sparked into flames that covered her hands and arms. The purple flames illuminated her face, glowing in her bright yellow eyes. She looked past her hands for Mya, the room coming more into focus through the darkness.

But she was gone; in her place stood another figure forming from the darkness. It was darker than the blackness around them, a mass floating, ribbons of darkness growing from it, moving like fabric in the wind. It grew and pulsated like it was breathing in all around it, feeding off it, growing larger. Ember watched with wide eyes as the mass began to take shape, slowly, forming into the figure of a woman. It hovered closer to Ember, reaching out with ghostly hands, engulfing her with a dark embrace until it covered her completely. Suddenly, the figure ignited by glowing magenta flames that were flowing out of Ember. The fire bathed the entire room with neon purple light. The mysterious figure hovered silently over the floor, her dark hair flowing around her, moving like it was alive, her dress curling around Ember like dark purple smoke. Ember's heart beat so fast she thought it would burst out of her chest. Tears fell from her eyes, but she couldn't move, couldn't take her eyes off the ghosty woman in front of her. She was held in a trance. The woman's face was tilted downwards, obscured by the long tendrils of dark hair. Ember could hear Shadow's call in the distance, her eyes frantically searching for him. The woman's head moved up slightly, enough for Ember to see two large luminous violet eyes. She could not look away, even as she heard Shadow's flying closer, directly through the dark figure. Slowly, Ember could see his dark feathers become one with her. She watched in terror as Shadow's body disappeared in the darkness of the figure.

Ember opened her mouth to cry out for her beloved

Shadow, but no sound left her throat. The glowing bright lilac eyes burned brighter and grew larger as they fixed more intensely on Ember, until all she could see was bright purple flames. The pain of the burning flames consumed her; it was a pain like Ember could never be able to describe. Then she was falling. Falling into the darkness, further into the flames. She felt like she was going to die, like this apparition was going to take her down to whatever world she had been conjured from. Then just as fast as it began, the pain was over. She lay on her back, trying to find the breath that had left her body. She slowly opened her eyes.

It took a moment for her eyes to adjust to the grey, cloudy sky above her. Snow fell from the stormy sky, covering her face and eyelids. Ember blinked and brushed it off with her hand. She slowly sat up and looked around her. She was somewhere else, a snow-covered world. She lay in the drifts of snow, as the winter wind blew her raven hair all around her. She could see tall, majestic pine trees off in the distance, surrounded by snow-covered mountain peaks. She could hear water hitting rocks behind her, and as she turned her head, she saw a babbling creek, its dark water cutting through the whiteness of the fallen snow. Icicles formed around the rocks, glittering like diamonds even in the gloomy winter light. Snow fell all around her, making the world she was in silent, but Ember did not feel cold. What was this place, she asked herself, as she stood up. How did she get here? Suddenly she heard slow footsteps crunching in the snow behind her. The steam from her breath against the cold became visible as her heart quickened, thinking about who or what could be making its way toward her. Suddenly, she heard a familiar howl, one she hadn't heard in so many years, but would know anywhere. With one last deep breath, Ember turned. Standing in the snow in front of her was a large dog, pale blue eyes blinking under the falling snow. The wind that blew down from the mountains moved the dog's black and silver coat about. Ember gasped. She'd recognize that fur and color patterns anywhere.

"Karina!" she yelled and ran to the Malamute, wrapping her arms around her, feeling her warm fur.

"What are you doing here, girl?" Ember asked as Karina licked the snow and tears of happiness off Ember's face. Ember didn't care how her childhood dog was here or why; she was just happy to see her again.

"She missed you," said a disembodied voice from behind them.

Karina let out a small howl as she saw what had been the ghostly purple woman floating in the small dark room walking towards her. She was no longer hovering over the ground or glowing with violet fire; now she was a beautiful woman dressed in a long black dress, with bell sleeves covered in black fur that dragged across the snow. Her dark hair, the same color as Ember's, grew long to her knees and blew behind her as she walked. It was held clasped out of her face with a beautiful onyx crown. Her eyes, the color of deep violets, still had a magical glow to them.

Ember rose off her knees but kept one of her hands on Karina's back, not knowing if the woman would hurt her. "Who are you? Where am I? How is this possible?" she asked as she watched the regal woman approaching.

The woman smiled and stopped right in front of Ember, her hands concealed by her fur-covered sleeves.

"I have many names, as many as the snowflakes that fall from the sky. I am She who is three, the three in one. I am the Morrigan."

Ember immediately fell to her knees in front of the goddess and bowed her head. "I am sorry, my lady, I didn't know."

The goddess bent down and took Ember's face in her hands. Her touch felt like sparks on Ember's skin.

"Rise, my child. I have brought you to this place," the lady said, her voice sounding like wind chimes, echoing against the snow.

"And what is this place?' Ember asked as she rose off her knees to face the dark goddess.

"This is the in-between. The world at the fringe of your world," the goddess explained. "All magic exists in this world, my magic, and now you can cross into it." The Morrigan began to walk. Karina ran up to walk beside the lady in black. "I brought her to you. I sensed you needed a comforting presence here." She said, giving Karina a pat on the head.

"Where is Shadow?" Ember suddenly remembered how he had disappeared into her eerie form.

"Oh, he's here. Don't worry," the goddess said as she turned to face Ember. "He can cross the boundaries between the worlds, as will you, Ember. I have brought you here because I need you. It is time you take your power, my power. It is your time to rise, and time is something we do not have. I have bestowed you with many gifts, child. Powerful gifts that you must learn to control, but remember, with these gifts come great responsibilities. There are those that mean us harm, that want to take our magic, that want to disrupt the delicate balance between our worlds and cover them in darkness. Only you can fight those that mean harm to us. It will be difficult, and it will put you and those you love in grave danger. You will be tested, and you will have to make a choice, my child. Fight, or let the darkness consume you," the goddess said as she looked at Ember, her gaze serious, but there was a softness in her eyes.

"A war is coming, a darkness rising from a world that I can't not cross. A darkness that is hunting us, as it has hunted us before. I thought it was long banished, but somehow it has been released onto your world, and it is desperately fighting to infect this world with its poison; this cannot happen. I cannot see what magic has released this darkness. Somehow, I've been blinded to it, and I cannot cross the barrier between our worlds. I need you to be my warrior, Ember. I will give you all the weapons I can, but you must choose. Once you do, once you are on my path, there is no turning back."

Ember looked up at the gray sky. The snow was falling harder now. Her thoughts went back to just a few weeks ago, when the world was small. Now the world seemed endless, and she felt lost in its magnitude. She looked into the Morrigan's purple eyes. "I don't know if I can. If I'm strong enough. I don't even know myself anymore."

"You are, you always have been. You are so special, my beautiful child. You won't be alone. My crows will be your eyes and ears, your sword and shield. Trust them, trust yourself. Those dark forces will sense your presence, they will come for you, they will try to trick you. Don't let them. Believe in yourself, in who you are. Only you can stop the darkness that will spread across our worlds."

Ember sighed as she heard the Goddess' words. She searched her heart for the courage she needed to accept this new fate. She knew what her path was. She finally understood. Now it was time to follow it. This wasn't just about her, but all like her. If a war was coming against her and her kind, then she needed to fight.

"There will be others who will assist you on your journey. Some from your world, some from another, some that walk between. They also have a part to play in this story, as you will have a part to play in theirs," the Goddesses explained as she walked in the snow. "It is time that you embark on this journey. Too long have you waited in the shadows. Now you will move as a shadow."

Ember looked into the lady's eyes with a newfound sense of confidence; she knew what she must do. She knelt and gave Karina one last hug. "I'll see you later, girl," she whispered in her fluffy ear. She stood up and said, "I'm ready."

"Yes, and how glorious you will be, my daughter," the Morrigan said with a slight smile. "The ever-burning fire of our magic has always lived within your eyes. Now it's time to unleash it," the goddess said as she turned and walked away from Ember, Karina at her side.

"Wait! How do I get back?" Ember yelled at her, the snow falling heavier around her, making her dark future harder to see.

"Your Shadow, of course. He will be your guide between worlds. All you must do is call him to you."

Ember smiled, looking up through the tall trees blowing in the wind. She closed her eyes and called out as loudly as she could.

"Shadow!"

Her voice echoed through the pine trees and fallen snow to the figure of the woman in the distance. In a heartbeat, the beautiful woman spread out her arm and with a flash of purple light, the black hair and dress transformed into Shadow's black feathers. He hovered for a few seconds, flapping his wings. Ember put her hand out, giving him a place to land. She stared deep into his small black eyes. "Take us back, boy," she whispered.

In a blur of snow and onyx feathers, the world turned upside down, and Ember felt herself falling, falling upwards towards the grey sky. She closed her eyes and focused on Shadow's caw to keep her centered as her body fell through time and space. She could feel the floor rushing up to meet her, and with a jolt, she was back to the material world.

A gust blew in the room as Ember appeared on the floor from nothingness. At once, all the candles ignited once more, bathing the room in warm light. As they burned brighter, Ember could be seen curled up on the floor in the center of the circle, exactly where she had been before she disappeared with the mysterious apparition.

Shadow squawked and flew up into the rafters. Ember sat up slowly, lifting her head to get her bearings back. Snow melted off her hair and body, dripping water on the floor. The other women stood in amazement. Ember looked back at them, closed her eyes, and fainted, falling into the center of the pentagram.

CHAPTER 6

Thomas lay in bed and watched the first rays of sunlight stream through the floor-to-ceiling windows of his loft. The soft light shone down on his shirtless chest and cast shadows across the swirls of ink, making them almost look like they were almost moving. Thomas rarely talked or showed anyone the tattoos that covered most of his upper body. They were something he kept to himself; his life had been drawn across his skin. He looked down at his left forearm at the tattoo of a crow. He had gotten it years prior, and he remembered the vivid dream he'd had of the bird floating in his mind. He had woken up from that dream covered in sweat, the image of the crow burned in his mind. He was so moved that he had his artist place the tattoo of the crow on his arm the very next day. It had always been one of his favorite pieces.

Now he looked down at the tattoo as if it held a new meaning. It made him think about the beautiful woman with the strange eyes from the cemetery. He hadn't been able to sleep the previous night, unable to get the beautiful raven-haired woman from overtaking his thoughts. The way the birds had flown around her fascinated him. Everything about her fascinated him. The way she moved, the wildness of her hair, and the color of her eyes. Thomas had never seen eyes like hers. There was also something strangely familiar about her that he could not shake, even though their meeting was so brief.

He sat up and stretched his neck from side to side before walking over to his desk. The big, brown leather chair squeaked under his weight as he turned to look at the concrete wall behind him. He had been using the plain cement to hold all the evidence from the murder cases in a way that made sense only to him. Pictures of the victims along with copies from the case file covered every inch of the plain grey wall. He had placed his own notes and thoughts here and there on yellow sticky notes, his thoughts scribbled on the bright yellow paper, so he wouldn't forget. He would stare at the wall for hours at a time, scanning every bit of information, trying to see if something new jumped out at him.

He had to find the link between all the victims that had eluded him. From his experience, the quickest way to catch a serial killer was to find what the victims had in common. He knew these women had not been chosen at random. They had all been carefully selected. But why? The details he could not ignore were the unusual way they had been killed and the fact that they had all been found in or around water. He had run the modus operandi or MO through the FBI's VICAP database with no matches, so he would have to find what they all had in common, other than how they died. He took a picture of a smiling girl with curly red hair off the wall. Annabel Oldman, twenty-seven, first victim found. She had been missing for a week before her body was discovered on the beach near Winter Island. She had been in town visiting a friend for a few days from her parents' home in

Ipswich. She left her friend's house but never made it back home. She was a happy girl who loved horses. No enemies, no reason for her to end up on a cold beach, dead. Even though her body had more than likely been in the water for several days, she was strangely well preserved. His attention turned to the third girl. Lila Miller had been a performer and avid swimmer. At just twenty-four, she had become a very popular dancer, and Thomas could see why. She was a stunning young woman with shoulder-length dark hair and striking features. She would swim at the "Y" in the morning, so her somehow drowning was hard to believe. She had been found in Salem Harbor after she left a gig in Boston the night before. Up to that point, the other deaths were classified as undetermined, with drowning a commonly believed cause, even when the tell-tale signs of drowning were absent from the victims. But, with the discovery of the third body, it was obvious to Thomas that the absent signs were the one thing that did tie all of the deaths together. He just had to find out what it was that tied the women together in life. Thomas felt that if he could do that, he would have somewhere to start.

He looked over at the fourth victim, Jennifer Williams, twenty-two. The graduation picture of her in her nursing uniform stared back at him. She had just started work as a nurse at Salem Hospital on the graveyard shift. She had left her small apartment in Peabody but never made it to her shift. Her boyfriend called the police when her supervisor called to find out if she was coming in to work. She was found floating in the water just off the coast of Marblehead by some teenagers who had taken their parents' boat without permission. She had been in the water for two days at most. All Thomas could find was the strange scratches around her neck and shoulders.

The fifth victim, Elise Johnson, was a tourist to Salem from London. She had come to Massachusetts with some classmates for a vacation. At first, she wasn't included with the others, partly because she had been seen leaving a local bar intoxicated and walking off by herself around Salem Willows. She was found the next day by the shore. The first arriving police thought she might have slipped on the rocks and fallen into the water, her death being accidental. But, after Thomas looked at her autopsy photos and noticed the same strange scratches and no water in her lungs, he knew she was yet another victim.

Thomas reached into one of the files on his desk and pulled out a photo of the last victim, Claire Marks, twenty-six. He had taken the photo of her on vacation in California off her social media and placed it on the wall with the others. He also taped some of the other case file notes beside it and sat back down in his chair. He rubbed his eyes and looked over at the antique decanter full of bourbon. He knew it was too early for a drink, but he needed to calm his nerves and focus. He reached for the heavy glass bottle and poured some into a matching glass. He drank it down in one gulp as he sat back and looked at the wall. He wondered to himself how all these lives, with all their experiences, could fit on one plain gray wall. He could feel his head spinning and his eyes getting heavier the more he drank. He finally passed out as the glass hit the floor with a thud.

When he woke, it was dark in the loft. He opened his eyes and sat up in his chair. How long had he been asleep? What had woken him up? He tried to rub the drunken sleep from his eyes when he noticed something or someone standing in the dark corner. The figure made him jump up from his chair and search his desk drawer frantically for his spare gun. He found the small firearm and pointed it at the figure.

"Who the hell are you?" he yelled. "What the fuck are you doing here? Stay where you are! Don't move!" Thomas held the gun in his right hand and stepped cautiously closer to the person standing in the corner of his loft. Sweat rolled down his back as he tried to steady his body, even though the temperature in the room had dropped so much he could see his breath fog as his breathing deepened. The figure did not move or respond. As he moved closer, he saw it was a woman, dressed in what appeared to be a light brown coat. She was pale, so pale, like the color of a blank piece of paper. As Thomas moved closer, he saw she was wet; water fell down her body and was making a dark puddle form under her bare feet. He lowered his gun. He could see her better now; he could make out her face and the wet blonde curls. It was Clarie Marks, standing motionless in his loft.

"Claire?" he asked, thinking he must still be sleeping. "Are you ok?" He had just been looking at her lifeless corpse a few hours ago. How could she be standing in his loft? Then he had a thought that made his blood run cold. He had seen this girl in the cemetery, standing in the empty field. It was her; it was Claire. But how, how could she be standing there?

The girl said nothing, just stared at him with dead eyes, a milky pale white film over them. She slowly lifted her arm to point at the wall behind Thomas. He followed to see what she pointed at. He looked back at the wall and saw she was guiding him to her picture. Thomas snapped his head to look at the haunted girl.

"What?" he asked, his heart pounding in his ears. "What are you trying to tell me?" Thomas asked, his voice cracking as his shaky fingers gripped the trigger.

The girl just stood and continued to point. Thomas looked back at the picture and noticed a small tattoo on her wrist. A symbol that he didn't know the meaning of. As he turned back to look at the girl, she had moved silently to stand right next to him. Thomas, stunned, fell backwards onto the hard floor as she opened her mouth and screamed.

It was a high-pitched scream, like a banshee screeching, so loud that Thomas had to drop his gun and cover his ears.

The screeching in his ears was so loud, filling his head and making it feel like it was going to explode. The sound created a painful pressure behind his eyes, like a million little knives stabbing from inside his head. Just as he was about to scream from the pain in his head, the horrible sound stopped.

Thomas slowly looked up, and the girl was gone. All that was left in her place was the puddle of water on the floor. He fell backwards and lay on the cold concrete and tried to catch his breath. After a few minutes, he slowly crawled to the mysterious dark puddle that had appeared on his floor. He touched it with his fingers and brought it up to his nose. It smelled of salt and brine. He brought it to his lips to taste. Sea water. He collapsed on the floor next to the puddle and tried to collect his thoughts, tried to process what he had just seen and felt. He asked himself if it was real or if he had dreamt the entire event. He looked back at the water and was sure it was no dream. The temperature in the room felt warm again, as he gathered enough energy to stand up.

"That was a ghost," he said out loud. He needed to hear it in his own ears to believe it, to accept that paranormal experience that he had just witnessed. But why? Why did this dead girl appear? Thomas never really believed in ghosts, but he had seen his fair share of odd things living in Salem, a place known for the spirits that roamed freely. He walked over to his desk and placed his handgun on top of a pile of papers. He thought for a moment and looked back at his wall of evidence. That's when it hit him, like a bolt of lightning. The tattoo. She wanted him to focus on the tattoo. He pulled the picture of Claire off the wall and held it in his hand. This had to mean something. This might be the one detail he had been overlooking, and it had been there hiding in plain sight.

CHAPTER 7

*E*mber slowly regained consciousness. She felt groggy and dizzy. She tried to feel her own body by slowly moving her fingers and hands, trying to alleviate the pins and needles sensation that still lingered. She was cold; the melting snow made her hair and clothes damp. She shivered, as it took her several moments to realize where she was, back in the small dark basement. Shadow's calls echoed from his perch on the wood beams, helping her feel grounded in this world. Ember tried to focus on the sounds coming from her feathered companion. It soothed her. Lydia removed the long black cloak she had been wearing and threw it over Ember to try and warm her up. She kneeled and rubbed Ember's shoulder. Mya and the other women knelt by Ember and looked upon the girl who had just disappeared in front of their eyes. As Ember's vision came back into focus and she looked around, she could see their eyes full of wonderment for what they had just witnessed. Ember sat up, with Lydia's help as she steadied her breathing.

Lydia broke the silence first. "Ember, my love, can you

hear me? Are you ok?" Tears welled in her eyes as she looked at her student with worry.

"Yes, I think so," Ember replied, her voice sounding strange in her own ears, as she tried to stand up on her feet.

"You disappeared, right in front of our eyes. The dark figure took you. Where did you go? What did you see?" Lydia asked with concern, her questions coming too fast for Ember to process.

Ember, still shaking from her experience, looked at Lydia and tried to answer, but she didn't know where to begin. How to put what she had seen into words.

Mya stepped closer and took Ember's hand in hers. Her skin felt soft and warm. "Ember, take your time, you mustn't leave the circle until you have regained your strength. You have crossed over to a plane not many of us have ever dared to travel to, but you did. It takes great skill to walk between worlds, and it will drain your energy."

Ember looked into Mya's dark eyes and felt comforted by her smooth voice and kind face as she sat back down on the floor in the safety of the circle.

"We have all felt the Goddess's presence in the circle, but She has never taken form before, until tonight," Mya said, her words dripping with excitement.

"Where did she take you?" Lydia asked slowly.

Ember took a deep breath. "It was like I was burning, as if my body was on fire. Then she, the dark form, surrounded me. I felt like I was falling, like the world was turned in different directions, and then suddenly everything stopped, and I was somewhere else." Ember looked around as all the eyes in the room were on her. "It was snowing. It was snowing there. So beautiful, a world of ice and snow, but I wasn't cold. I saw the dog I had as a child, then she appeared."

Mya and Lydia locked eyes as Ember continued.

"I saw her, the Lady; she was so beautiful, raven-haired, with a crown of black jewels on her head. She was like a dream," Ember said as she closed her own eyes and remembered the stunning regal woman that she encountered in the world of snow-covered pines.

"Was it just one woman you saw? Did she speak to you?" Mya asked carefully so as to not bring Ember out of her thoughts completely.

Ember opened her yellow eyes and fixed them on Mya. "Yes, it was one woman. Why?"

"It is said that when the triple Goddess comes to you, she can appear in many forms. As smoke, or fog. In the shape of animals, a black horse, or a Raven. Sometimes she can appear as three women, the physical manifestation of the maiden, mother, and crone. Three, but still one. It seems she appeared to you as the mother, the nurturer, the dark queen," Mya explained as she stood up and took a few steps away from Ember. "When she spoke, what did our lady tell you?'

Ember swallowed, her throat dry and sore. "She said so many things, but she did say something is coming, a darkness, and it's coming for us. That we would have to fight, that I would have to fight," Ember looked down at her hands, remembering the purple that had appeared, "that I am the one who can defeat what's coming." Ember began to stand, still somewhat shaken and unsteady on her feet. "We are all in danger. There's something out there, waiting in the night, hunting us."

Mya and Lydia looked at each other in astonishment. "We have suspected this for some time, those girls, those poor girls that have been killed. They were not just random victims. My intuition is telling me that they were all of the blood and murdered because of it. Murdered by some ancient magic," Mya said as she walked around the room.

"Our kind has been hunted before, throughout the ages, and the threat has yet again come to these shores."

Lydia stood and stepped closer to Mya." We must find out who has conjured this magic, and why?"

"That we must my sister," Mya said as she held on to Lydia's hand, "and we will, for whatever is lurking through our streets will sense Ember's magic. Now more than ever, she stepped closer to Ember," you must be careful dear, and remember, your Shadow, he will protect you."

Mya turned to address the gathering of witches. "My sisters, a war is coming. The Goddess has made her message clear. Now it is time to prepare. It is a heavy burden we ask of someone so young," she said as she turned to look at Ember with pride, "but we are ready to fight next to our new sister, side by side, and face whatever horrors hide in dark places. Go now and prepare."

With that, the gathering began to disperse, slowly collecting their belongings and going one by one up the stairs that led to the street above. Only Mya and Lydia remained in the room with Ember, still standing in the protection of the circle.

"Go now, my child, you and your Shadow must go home and rest." Mya softly touched Ember's cheek, still flushed from her travels. "Know you are not alone; we are many, as many as there are stars in the sky. You are not alone." She gently brought Ember's face close to hers and placed a light, tender kiss on her lips.

With Lydia's help, Ember walked up the narrow staircase and back out the alley. They locked arms and walked through the now-empty, quiet streets of Salem in silence until they made it to Ember's front door, Shadow silently flying overhead. As Ember reached for her door and paused, she looked over her shoulder at her friend and gave her a smile. A smile that they both understood. "Thank you," Ember said to her friend and mentor.

"No, my dear. Thank you," Lydia replied warmly. Then Ember walked inside and closed the door.

Lydia stood there for a moment, the cold wind stirring her grey hair. She could smell the fireplaces in the distance. As she looked up to see the smoke rising through the chimneys, she realized Shadow had not gone inside with Ember. Instead, he sat on the iron fence across the street. Lydia turned to walk in his direction. She looked curiously at him.

"Staying out late tonight, I see," she said to him in a low voice as Shadow squawked loudly. "Yes, I won't be able to sleep either," Lydia answered right before he spread his wings and flew into the night sky. She stood and watched him until she lost sight of him in the darkness. She knew he had work to do. They all did.

In her apartment, Ember sat soaking in her claw-foot tub, letting the hot water warm her chilled body. The steam from the hot water fogged up the mirror over the sink. She inhaled the steam deeply into her lungs and let herself relax as she lowered herself in the tub, the water coming all the way up to her chin. The hot water comforted her, wrapping her up in warmth. She went over the events of the evening in her head. It had been almost like a dream, but she knew it was very much real. She thought of her mother, and sadness came over her. All those years Ember believed her mother's constant nagging to be like everyone else, to fit in, now made perfect sense. It was almost like she had tried to hide and protect herself from some unseen danger. Unseen even to her. Keeping her out of harm's way, the best she could. Ember remembered the weeks before she died, and how it seemed she wanted to tell her something yet couldn't. Whatever secrets her mother had, she took them to the grave.

Then her thoughts moved to her grandmother, and

Ember could feel hot tears building up in her eyes. Maybe that's why she stayed away for long periods of time, on her many trips, or maybe it was something else. Maybe she was searching for something, an answer to a question that someday would need answering. Regardless, she had never tried to change Ember; she had loved and encouraged her to be the person she wanted to be, wild and untamed, running through the woods, barefoot and hair tangled. When she was home, she taught her as much as she could. Staying up late into the night by the fire, reading from her book, or mixing herbs and oils to pour into brown glass bottles that she would seal with a cork and wax. Ember had loved watching grandmother Carmen, her dark, greying hair up in loose curls that fell over her beautiful, lined face. Ember had always felt loved and safe in that kitchen. Even when her mother, Victoria, would come and make her displeasure known. Her thin lips turned down into a frown that always seemed to be on her face. Only at this moment did Ember realize how old her mother had looked. She was a beautiful, elegant woman, hair dyed red, cut short into a bob that hit her chin, always perfectly in place. She dressed in the latest fashion, and her clothes and makeup were always impeccable. But the stress of trying to live up to the impossible standards she set for herself came to show in the lines that had appeared prematurely on her face, and the secret she tried to keep from Ember her whole life must have eaten her from the inside out. Only now could Ember start putting together the pieces of the puzzle that had been her mother. Still, there were so many missing pieces. However, she now understood more about her grandmother and why she felt it so important that Ember learned as much as she could of the craft, and why she felt that she needed to pass her power on to Ember. Moving away and starting a new life in a strange place had been difficult for Ember, but now it had never been clearer: she was exactly where she needed to be.

She looked down at her pruned fingers and knew it was time to get out of the water. She carefully stepped out of the tub and wrapped herself in a fluffy white towel. As she sat in bed and combed through her wet hair, she remembered Shadow had stayed outside. It was unusual for him not to snuggle on his favorite pillow and snooze next to her. She walked over to the window and peered through the curtains to see if she could spot him, but he was nowhere to be found. A sudden feeling of worry hit her, but the Goddess's voice resonated in her thoughts. Shadow was a part of the Lady, her messenger and Ember's protector. So, if Shadow was out on this dark night, he had a good reason. Ember sighed and chewed on her thumbnail, wondering where he had flown off to.

She closed the curtains and sat on the living room floor in front of the old fireplace with her legs crossed in front of her. She shivered, her wet hair making her skin goosebump. Her small apartment felt cold and empty, so Ember reached over to the stack of wood she had collected and piled it up in the firebox. Striking a match on the mantel, she watched as the flames caught the logs and the fire grew, filling the room with warm glowing light. She sat by the fire and warmed her chilled hands and feet as she pulled a thick wool blanket from the corner and wrapped herself up tight. Thoughts of Shadow still in her head, she closed her eyes and tried to connect with him.

"Shadow, show me where you are." She could feel her body growing warmer, but not from the fire in front of her. It was the same burning feeling that had begun at the tips of her fingers and ran up her arms to ignite into the glowing ghost-like purple flames. She could feel the heat travel up to her neck and face and finally to her eyes. As she opened her burning eyes, they were no longer hers, but Shadow's. The yellow color of her irises was replaced by the crow's coal-colored pupils, covering her entire eye, leaving no white visible. At that moment, Ember could see perfectly, all around her. She could see what Shadow was seeing; she was in his small streamlined feathered body as he flew over the rooftops of Salem. She tried to familiarize herself with where she was, what streets he was gliding over. Shadow flapped his wings faster as he took a sharp turn and came to a stop on a windowsill. Through his eyes, she peered inside the window to what appeared to be a restaurant Ember had never been to. It was busy with people sitting at tables, laughing and talking over plates of food and drinks as her sharp eyesight focused on one table in particular, the one closest to the wood-burning fireplace. Three women stood out from the rest of the patrons, not only because they sat in silence, but because of how beautiful they were, their skin shimmering like gold, their eyes, a strange silver color shining brightly as they caught the light cast by the fire. The first one Ember's eyes focused on was the woman sitting in the middle, slender build, glowing skin, sharp high cheekbones, and a mess of spiral black curls rolling past her shoulders. Dark smoky eye makeup rimmed her mysterious sparkling eyes, making them stand out even more. She was a rare beauty, elegantly dressed in an off-the-shoulder, form-fitting corset blouse that accentuated her small waist. Silver necklaces hung from her long, graceful neck, and her gorgeous, slender face was framed by long jeweled earrings that lightly grazed her shoulders as she moved her head. Every movement, no matter how small, was catlike, smooth, and with purpose. She had a commanding queenlike presence. Embers's crow eyes shifted to the woman to the right. The second woman, small and petite, was almost fragile-looking. Her long and straight sunny blonde hair was tucked behind one ear, and the rest hung carefree over her shoulder.

Sun-kissed freckles sprinkled over her delicate nose gave her a youthful appearance. Her most noticeable feature was her eyes, almost too large for her pixie-like face. Like the woman next to her, her eyes, too, glowed with a glimmer of silver, but hers were different. An aqua blue shade ran through them, mixing with the unique silver color, giving her a more haunting appearance that contrasted with her sunny hair and boho style flowered dress. The fringed suede jacket was two sizes too big for her tiny frame, and beaded bangles made her look like she had stepped right out of a vintage 1970s fashion magazine. The third girl was equally as beautiful as her two companions. Her short chocolate brown hair was pinned up in swirling curls around her head, in a style reminiscent of a 1920s flapper. Rosey red rouge applied generously on the apple of her cheeks matched the ruby red color that stained her pouty lips. The slinky, beaded, strappy, red dress hugged her body perfectly and left little to the imagination of the men that walked by, their gazes lingering on her perky breasts. She also shared the same silver pearl as her companions, shaded under long fake eyelashes.

They all appeared to be so different, but strangely the same. Even though they sat quietly, speaking only to each other in small whispers now and again, every person in the restaurant noticed them, acknowledging their presence as if they were celebrities. The women greeted their admirers with gracious smiles, but lowered eyes. Still, their uninterested reactions did not deter the attention they received.

Ember urged Shadow's body to move closer to the window, to get a better look at the three women who had obviously caught his attention as well. As he peeked his small head closer to the glass, the dark curly-haired woman noticed Shadow on the other side of the window, her silver eyes meeting his. She slowly stood from her chair as she locked a cold gaze onto the bird. The other women looked confused at first until they too saw what had caught their companion's attention. The spiral-haired woman said something Ember could not make out, but she could sense Shadow's body tense. With a ruffle of his feathers, he took flight off the windowsill without looking back. When Ember could see that he was flying in the direction of her apartment, she closed her eyes. After a few moments, she opened them, returning to her own vision and her small apartment. Her eyes returned to their usual yellow color as she blinked quickly. The fire had burned out and had gone dark. She felt tired, drained. She slowly stood and went to open her front door, knowing that her friend was close. As she did, Shadow came fluttering inside, landing on the armrest of her couch. Ember collapsed next to him and patted his small head.

"Is that why you wanted to stay out tonight?" Shadow lowered his head, a sign that he wanted more pets.

"You wanted me to see those women. Why?" Ember asked as she stroked his soft feathers. "They looked interesting." Shadow let out a loud disapproving squawk. "I suppose that means you don't care for them," Ember said with a small laugh. Shadow tucked his head in the folds of his wings.

"Ok, grumpy boy, you can tell me tomorrow, "Ember said as he nestled in a feathered ball next to her and fell asleep. But Ember's mind was filled with visions of her flight, and of course, of the women with the silver eyes. Who were they? And why did Shadow go out and find them? She went over each of them in her head, trying to remember every detail. They were so beautiful, uncomfortably so. The way the beautiful dark-haired one had looked at Shadow gave her a chill down her spine. He had caught her eye and somehow made her react, more than she had to all the people in the restaurant gushing over them. But why?

Ember rubbed her tired eyes; her mind was wide awake,

but her body was exhausted. She looked over at Shadow, his beak tucked under one of his wings. She curled up beside him, the events of the day catching up with her all at once. As she felt her eyes getting heavy, her thoughts wandered to the handsome detective she had met in the cemetery. His piercing ice blue eyes, so light that they almost gave off a white glow. White, like the snow-covered treetops in the in-between world. It was the last thing she remembered before. She couldn't fight it anymore, and sleep took over. Shadow untucked his head from his wing and looked over at his sleeping mistress. He moved his body closer to her and placed his head on her lap, and there he stayed all night as she slept.

CHAPTER 8

$\mathcal{I}$t was almost noon when Ember woke up curled up on the couch. She yawned and stretched her arms over her head, noticing Shadow as he lay close to her.

"Good morning, Shadow," she said as she gave him a quick kiss on his feathered-covered head.

Shadow shook out his feathers and began pruning as Ember walked into the kitchen to make some tea. As she filled the kettle, a knock sounded at the door. She was still in a towel from the night before, but she was too lazy to throw on a robe. She opened the door slightly, enough to see who was on the other side, hiding her body behind it.

"Hey Girl!" Ember immediately recognized the light, airy voice of her upstairs neighbor, Chloe.

"Oh, Hi Chloe," Ember replied, still somewhat groggy from the night before.

"I'm sorry, did I wake you? I slept in too," she giggled. "I was just on my way out to grab a coffee at a new place. You want to come with?"

The thought of being in public at a crowded, busy coffee

shop a few days before Halloween in Salem did not sound appealing to Ember at all, especially today, as she was still trying to make sense of everything that had happened the night before. Not to mention it was her only day off this week, but as she looked at her friend's bright, cheery smile and the colorful outfit that only she could pull off, it was hard to say no. Maybe a walk in the crisp fall air would do her some good. Besides, she liked Chloe and did want to get to know her better. Some light conversation and even a few laughs would help lift the heaviness of the last couple of days.

"Yes, that sounds great. I just need a second to change," Ember said with a smile as she stepped to one side, giving Chloe room to come in.

"Yay! Super cool," Chloe said as she walked inside and adjusted her leopard print beret.

She was about to sit down on the couch and saw Shadow peering up at her with curious eyes.

"Oh my god," Chloe said as she looked back at the large black crow casually sitting in Ember's living room. "Is that a raven?" she asked as she clutched her white coat.

Shadow clicked his broken beak in disapproval. "No, he's a crow. Not a raven. Common mistake," Ember said as she stretched out her hand for Shadow to hop on. Chloe looked at both in disbelief.

"You have a crow? As a pet?"

Ember laughed as she walked over to the kitchen and set Shadow down on the table. She pulled some nuts out of the cupboard and piled them in front of him. Chloe walked up behind her and stared at Shadow as he devoured his breakfast.

"He's not my pet. He's more like a friend," Ember said warmly to her friend. She realized how strange it might have seemed to Chloe, and it might have been simpler for her to just say Shadow was a pet, but Ember could never think of him that way.

"Very trendy," Chloe said as she lost interest and went back into the living room. Ember loved how easy-going Chloe was and how she didn't need any detailed explanations. That was enough for her.

Ember turned her attention back to Shadow and whispered, "I'm going out for a bit. I'll leave the kitchen window open for you. Stay close, little thief." She cracked open the stained-glass kitchen window and walked out of the kitchen to her bedroom to get dressed. She picked out a long-sleeved black dress and a long black coat. It was one of Ember's favorites; she loved the sleeves and the small row of buttons at the wrist. She was about to grab her purse when she remembered Mya's advice the night before. She turned back and opened a small wooden box on top of her vanity. She pulled out her grandmother's amethyst locket. The sparkling stone stood out against the black of her dress and hair. She took one last look in the mirror, fluffed up her already messy hair, and headed out the door with Chloe.

It was a gloomy rainy day, but that didn't stop all the Halloween tourists from gathering up and down the streets of the city. They weaved in and out of the crowds as they made their way to downtown Salem. Ember listened to Chloe as she chatted cheerfully about her week bartending. Ember loved how Chloe talked about the people she met as if Ember knew them as well. She had a fun, light, sunny way of talking, and her laugh was so contagious. Ember loved her laugh more than anything else. They finally reached the coffee shop as rain began to drizzle from the cloudy sky. They walked through the doors marked 'Witch City Brew' and were immediately met with a long line at the hostess desk inside the bright coffee shop. Ember looked around and saw that almost all the tables were taken.

"No worries," Chloe whispered in Ember's ear, "I know the owner," and with that, she disappeared into the crowd only to appear moments later behind a waitress holding two menus. They both followed her to a table at the far end of the restaurant, but still close to the front window.

"It's nice to know some people," Chloe said with a smile as she looked over Ember's outfit. "I'm loving this look on you. Very witch chic."

"Chic? Me?" Ember laughed as she smoothed out her dress. She'd never seen herself as stylish or chic.

"Oh yes! I'm loving it, it suits you," Chloe said as she looked over the menu.

"So, how's work been? Busy, right? It's so crazy around here this time of year."

"It has been crazy, but I don't mind. I like working at the shop," Ember replied.

"Plenty of people in town are looking for their fortune to be told," Chloe said jokingly. "I don't mean anything by that, you know. I respect what you all, um, I mean, you, do."

"It's ok, I get it," Ember said, giving her a smile.

"Maybe you can read my cards," Chloe said, her voice rising with excitement at the thought.

The waitress, a young girl, her hair put up in a bun, came back just as Ember was about to answer Chloe. She pulled out a pad and pen from her apron. "Hi, I'm Gina, and I'll be taking care of you. What can I get you ladies?" she asked with a friendly smile.

"I'll have a cappuccino and a chocolate croissant," Chloe said as she handed her menu back to the waitress. "And for you?" Gina asked Ember, her eyes not looking up from her pad.

"I'll have a lavender latte and a blueberry muffin. Thank you."

The young waitress shook her head, collected the menus, and walked off.

Chloe's brown eyes looked back at Ember. "Seriously, I'll have to come in and see you at the store. I've never had my cards read before."

"I can do it now," Ember said as she reached into her bag for the tarot cards that she always carried with her.

"Shut up! Really! Yes! Do it," Chloe said as she leaned in closer to Ember.

Ember shuffled the cards in her hands under the table so as not to draw attention to herself in the crowded coffee shop. She stopped as Gina came back and placed their order on the table in front of them.

Chloe sipped her coffee, her eyes falling on the front page of the newspaper. The man at the table next to her was reading. Her eyes scanned the headline in bold text, 'No Leads in Salem Multiple Murders' "It's so terrible, what happened to those girls. Makes me not want to go out alone," Chloe said as she shivered.

Ember glanced over at the headline. Mya had mentioned the murders, but Ember really hadn't paid them much thought. "I heard someone talking about it in the store the other day," Ember told Chloe, "about the last girl they found."

"I know!" Chloe exclaimed, putting her hot cup of coffee down on the table, "She was going out to meet some friends and disappeared. They found her the next day." It's like the cops don't have any clue what's going on around here," Chloe said, a disappointed tone in her voice. "I mean that cop they have working on this, oh, what's his name, Thomas something, the super-hot blonde one, doesn't seem to know what he's doing. Maybe looks are all he has."

Ember looked at Chloe, her yellow eyes suddenly filled

with curiosity. "Thomas, I think I met him the other day, in the cemetery. We talked for a while. He seemed nice."

"Wait, you met hot cop?" Chloe said as she placed her hand over her mouth to contain the giggles. "Every single woman in this town has been trying to get a date with him forever. Tell me everything! What's he like? Did you give him your number? Please say you did."

"No, no, nothing like that, "Ember said. "We just spoke for a minute or two," Ember said as she continued shuffling the deck of cards in her hands.

"Well, you should have. I've seen him around town; he's so easy on the eyes."

"Well, it seems he might have his hands full at the moment," Ember said as she looked back at the newspaper.

"True, I hope they catch the crazy that's been doing this soon," Chloe said, her attention turning back to the cards in Ember's hands. "Ok, Girl, let's see my future."

Ember smiled and pushed her coffee cup out of the way and placed one card face down on the table. As she was about to place another down, Chloe's voice interrupted her.

"Oh hey, what are you doing for Halloween? Do you have plans?" she asked as Ember looked up from the cards, the question taking her by surprise. Chloe had the ability to just change topics so quickly that it took Ember a minute to keep up.

"I don't know, I'm sure I have to work," Ember replied, as she turned her attention back to the cards.

"Yeah, me too, but after? You must come to this party with me, "Chloe said, the excitement building in her voice. "Mega VIP! It's at this super fancy mansion, over on Chestnut Street, a huge house! The woman who lives there puts on the biggest, most exclusive parties in town, and this one is the biggest. I've never gotten an invite, like I said, super exclusive," Chloe explained. "But this year I got in!" she continued. "Please, please come with me!" Chloe pleaded as she reached out for Ember's hand.

Ember's first instinct was to politely decline, but a small breeze softly swept through the coffee shop, moving and rustling the napkins on the tables. She touched her necklace and tried to listen to her inner voice. Something stirred deep inside her, the same feeling she'd had the other night looking over the ocean at the incoming storm. A strange sense of dread, accompanied by slight curiosity. The dark lady's words echoed in her head. Ember would have to be strong to fight whatever was out stalking the night. She understood one thing for certain: Things didn't happen by chance. Maybe this invitation had come to her for a reason, one still unknown to her.

She thought for a long moment. "Yes, I will definitely go with you," Ember said as she squeezed Chloe's hand.

"Yay!" Chloe exclaimed. "Ok, so it's not just any costume party, it's a masquerade ball. We have to look perfect, and we have like zero time," Chloe said as she reached into her purse and threw some money on the table, finished her cappuccino in one big gulp, and began to get up from the table. "I know the perfect place. Let go!"

Ember watched as her friend excitedly collected her things. She had never been to a Halloween party, let alone a masquerade ball. The thought did make her anxious, but she would be with Chloe. She needed to trust her intuition; something she had been working on with Lydia during the late-night lessons, and every fiber in her being was telling her to go. Maybe, she thought she would even have a little fun, even if it was for one night.

Chloe began to walk towards the door as she looked at Ember still sitting at the table." You coming?" she asked impatiently. Ember nodded as she began to stand up. She noticed she still had the deck of tarot cards in her hands. She looked down at the one card she had placed on the table. She was just going to put it back in the deck, but something told her to turn it over. She slowly flipped the card and looked at it in her hand...

The Devil.

CHAPTER 9

Thomas sat at the desk in his dimly lit office. The only light came from the open laptop in front of him. Most of the offices had cleared out early; Halloween was a big deal in town, and most people were out on the street or had taken the day off. He was thankful for the quiet of the usually bustling office as he scrolled through pages and pages of information on the internet, finding all he could about the symbol tattooed on Claire's wrist. The hair on the back of his neck stood up at the thought of the eerie apparition of Claire that had materialized. He hadn't slept the rest of that night. Not many things spooked Thomas, but the sight of a dead girl staring straight at him made his blood run ice cold. He shook off those thoughts; he had work to do. He scrolled through hundreds of images until he found the one he was looking for. A series of three interlocking circles that made the shape of a triangle. Thomas was sure he had seen the symbol before at some point in his life, although he could not recall where or when. He finally found it on a page about Celtic witchcraft and paganism.

"Witches," he sighed under his breath. He had grown up

in and around Salem all his life, so the word wasn't that foreign to him. Salem had adopted the image of the witch as its official 'mascot'. It was even the fire and police department's logo. Witches and stories of witches were just part of life here. But as he continued to read, he realized the ancient symbol meant more than he had anticipated.

"The Triquetra," he read aloud, "represents the triple Goddess. Maiden, Mother, Crone," he continued to read to himself.

His thoughts went back to Claire; however, she had shown up in his loft. She must have had an important reason for her ghost to appear to him. As he watched the sun break the windows, a new sense of renewal came along with it. Almost like a spark was lit. He had missed the whispers that used to come to him softly. They had been silent for months, leaving him in the dark, lost. Now the vision of this girl, as unsettling as it was, had given him hope. Hope that he could solve this case and put an end to the killings. So now, he had a place to start; where it might lead him, he had no clue, but he was going to keep his mind open to all possibilities. The one thing he knew for certain was that he couldn't share what he had seen. People already thought he was hanging on by a thread. The last thing he needed spreading around the department was that he was seeing dead people. That would be the last thing Captain Torres needed to hear to take him off the case and onto the department shrink's couch. He would keep this to himself until he could find some concrete evidence.

He kept finding more about this ancient symbol. But a question remained.' Why did she want him to see it? What did it mean to her?' He closed his laptop and rubbed his tired eyes. He didn't remember the last time he had gotten a good night's sleep. But this was life on the homicide unit, and Thomas had become accustomed to the long hours. His blue eyes looked over at the piles of case files stacked up next to his desk. Because of this one new piece of evidence, he would have to start again with victimology. All he needed was that one small detail, and the case would break wide open. He needed to go over all the victims' personal files, dig into their lives, learn every mundane detail about them and who they were. He pulled Claire's file first and looked over her personal details. Basic information, where she lived, worked, etc. Then he turned to all the sworn statements made by her friends and family. He carefully combed through every line, finding all he could about who she was and what she did in her spare time. He turned his attention back to the computer and clicked through pages and pictures from her social media. A picture of Clarie with some friends inside a shop caught his eye. He focused on what was in the background, and it appeared to be some kind of magical shop. Those were all over Salem, so which one was she in? He looked closer; in the background, there was a small sign, 'Pentagram Witch-craft and Magic Shoppe.'

"That's that place off of Charter Street," his voice echoed in his empty office. He knew exactly where that shop was, passing by it many times. He leaned back in his chair and remembered the last time he had been close to the shop. That night in the cemetery, he had met the mysterious woman. The one he had not been able to stop thinking about. The one with crows in her hair and fire in her eyes.

Thomas tried to put the thoughts of the beautiful woman in the back of his mind. He had to focus. If Clarie had visited a witchcraft store, and she had that symbol tattooed, maybe she was involved in witchcraft somehow. It wasn't much, but it was a start.

Thomas had ruled out any ritualistic ties to the murders at the very beginning, but this wasn't something he could ignore. He sat back in his chair and pored over the rest of the files, studying everything with a different purpose. The answers were in the files; he just had to find them.

Hours had passed. Thomas didn't know how many. His head had been buried in pages and pages of research. But it had paid off. He found the string that tied all his victims together. All the women were linked through witchcraft or were direct descendants of people involved in the witch trials of 1692. That was the one thing connecting all of them together. This was the connection he had been looking for; it had to be it. Thomas could barely contain his excitement; he felt invigorated in a way he hadn't in years. But he knew he had to tread carefully, especially with the topic of witchcraft or the trials. Before he could say anything, he first wanted to do some more research. Not online, but face to face. Talk to some locals, ask some questions, and go to that witchcraft store, of which he was certain. He was sure he could get some answers there. He took a close-up picture of Claire's wrist tattoo with his phone, threw his jacket over his shoulder, and walked out of the office to his SUV.

Thomas drove through the busy streets of Salem, passing all the Halloween visitors in their colorful costumes. He parked his truck a bit far from the store. The main streets had been closed to traffic for all the festivities, but Thomas didn't mind the walk; he needed to organize his thoughts before he got to the store, figure out how he was going to ask questions without raising alarm. Thomas made his way through the winding streets, the smell of apple cider and donuts coming from the food trucks reminding him he hadn't eaten all day. He tried to put his empty stomach to the back of his mind as he approached the glass storefront. A line of people had formed outside 'Pentagram', waiting their turn to get into the store. This was not unusual at this time of year. Thomas found a seat on the low paver wall outside the store and watched people go in and out. He hesitated for a moment; maybe he had picked the wrong day to go inside and start asking questions. As he started to stand and walk back to his car, something stopped him, a feeling that he was right where he was supposed to be, right at that moment. He didn't want to ignore his instincts. So, he made the decision to trust his gut and go inside. He stood in line behind a group of young girls who were giggling and chatting loudly and waited for his turn. After a few minutes, he was let inside through the doors. Inside, the light was soft and warm. Incense burned in different-shaped holders all around the space. As he looked around, his eyes were drawn to the large wall of glass jars filled that went all the way to the ceiling, and a wooden ladder on small wheels at one end to reach the top shelf. He slowly browsed the glass cases filled with different types of jewelry and crystals; his eyes were drawn to a silver charm on a necklace. The same symbol that Clarie had tattooed on her, the triquetra engraved in shiny metal. As he bent over to get a closer look at the charm, he heard a soft voice from the other side of the case, "Shopping for yourself, or a friend."

Thomas recognized the gentle voice before he looked up slowly and saw the raven-haired woman with flame in her eyes standing in front of him.

"Hello. Ember, right?" Thomas said, trying to hide the excitement and surprise in his voice, fearing he sounded nervous as he ran his fingers through his hair. He had never felt uncomfortable around women before, but this woman, with her strange eyes, made his heartbeat quicken.

"Yes, Ember. You remembered. It's good to see you again, Detective," Ember replied with a smile as she played nervously with the amethyst locket around her neck with her long, delicate fingers. She wasn't expecting to see the tall, blonde, handsome man standing in her store. He looked so out of place, even in the crowd of out-of-towners. She could feel her breath quickening as her eyes fell on his slightly opened shirt collar, exposing just enough of his collarbone. "Is there something I can help you with, or are you interested in a reading?"

"No, I mean yes. Sorry, I didn't realize you worked here. Um, yes, there is something you can help me with. I have a question; can you tell me more about that symbol?" Thomas asked as he pointed to the silver charm in the case.

Ember could tell that he was nervous, and that made her smile. His awkwardness gave him a boyish quality that was in stark contrast with his masculine features and chiseled jawline.

"The triquetra? It can mean a lot of things to a lot of people; to some it can represent the Father, Son, and Holy Ghost, to others the three stages of life, or the land, sea, and sky. In Celtic lore, it can also represent the Triple Goddess in all her forms, "Ember explained as she tried not to stare at his pale blue eyes that reminded her of glacier water.

"Maiden, Mother, Crone, right?" Thomas said, trying to impress Ember with the research he had done.

"Why, yes, that is correct, Detective. I didn't know you followed the craft," Ember replied with a sense of surprise.

Thomas leaned closer to her, and he could smell her perfume, a mix of roses and sandalwood. It was intoxicating, filling the air between them, titillating all his senses. He watched her full pink lips as she spoke. He found it difficult to follow the conversation when all he could think of was the taste of her lips, how her skin would feel under his skilled touch. He had to push those feelings down and try to concentrate on what he was there to do.

"Call me Thomas," he said, as his blue eyes focused intensely on her. The way he looked at her made Ember tremble under her dress. She could feel her heart beating and her skin beginning to glisten as she let his deep voice wash over her.

Without taking his eyes off her, he reached into his jacket pocket and pulled out the picture of the tattoo. "Have you seen this tattoo before, or even one like it?"

Ember leaned in to get a better look at the picture of the tattoo that Thomas had laid on top of the case. As she studied it, she could see that it was a small triquetra on someone's wrist. "No, I've never seen that tattoo on anyone," Ember said as she bit her lip. She hesitated for a moment, but her curiosity got the best of her." Does this have anything to do with the murders of those women?"

Thomas knew better than to discuss an ongoing case with a civilian, but something about her made him want to tell her everything, not just about the case, but everything about himself. Besides, maybe she could help; she did move in those circles.

"Yes, it is, the latest victim. It seems that she had come into your store." He pulled out his phone and scrolled until he found a picture of Clarie. He turned the screen to her. "Does she look familiar? Have you ever seen her in the store?"

Ember turned her attention to the phone screen. "No, never, but I just started working here a few weeks ago," Ember said.

"I didn't think you were from here; I would have noticed," Thomas said before he could stop himself, as he put his phone away.

"Well, I'm glad you did," she said as she tossed her long hair over her shoulder.

Customers began to walk up to the display cases on either side of him. "Seems like it's kind of crazy in here right now. Maybe you want to meet me for a drink after work? I would really like to ask you some more questions, you know, about this witch stuff, I mean, witchcraft. I know a small quiet place we can talk."

He really did want to ask her questions, related to his investigation being tied to witchcraft, but he had to admit that he just wanted to be alone with her.

"I would love that," Ember said, her answer surprising her. She normally would have never agreed to go to a bar with a man she had just met, but there was something about this man. The way he looked at her, the stubble on his jawline, the way his skin smelled, a mix of firewood and bourbon. It stirred up feelings she had never had before. She found it difficult to resist him. She wanted to be alone with him, in a dimly lit bar, with his strong hands on her hips pulling her body close to him. His lips on hers, the taste of bourbon on his tongue, and the sound of his deep voice whispering her name. Right as she was about to say yes, she remembered the Halloween party and how she had promised Chloe she would go with her.

"I can't tonight. I already have plans with my friend to go to a party. But maybe some other time," Ember bit her lower lip as she looked up at him.

'Jesus, that's driving me crazy,' Thomas thought to himself as he watched her bite her flushed lips. He smiled at her. Ember hadn't noticed the dimple in his right cheek before; it only added to his already beautiful face. "Sure, I understand." Thomas pulled out his wallet and placed his business card on the counter. "Give me a call when you don't have plans."

Ember picked up the card and held it between her index and middle finger. "I will," she said, leaning over the counter, the neckline of her dress opening, revealing her ample cleavage.

Thomas's eyes instantly fell on the round breasts. "I now know where to find you if you don't," he said. Something in his voice made Ember's heart skip a beat. "Have fun at your party, wildflower," Thomas said, a smile still on his face as he turned to walk away, his eyes still fixed on Ember.

Ember looked back at him, slight confusion lingering in her eyes. "What did you call me?" Ember asked, his statement making her stand straight up.

Thomas paused and stepped closer to her. "Wildflower, that's what you remind me of. So, see you around, wildflower," he said as he leaned back over the counter, his hand brushing up against hers.

Shockwaves of electricity ran up through Ember's hands as Thomas touched her. Suddenly, her eyes were filled with a vision, a vision that came fast the minute their skin met. She could see him, Thomas, standing waist deep in dark water. Grey pale hands breaking out of the water from below, winding up his torso, holding him tight as they began to pull him down, into the murky fluid. Above his head, against an equally dark sky, she saw the crows come flying in fast, together as one unit, swooping down all around him, encircling Thomas until all she could see were black wings.

Ember blinked fast, as the vision faded from her mind's eye. She looked down and saw that Thomas's hand had moved away from hers, and they were no longer touching. She stood there for a moment before she found his gaze again. "Are you okay there, wildflower? You blanked out for a minute," Thomas asked with concern in his voice.

"I'm fine, everything is fine," Ember said, giving him a big smile so as not to raise any worry in him. She didn't want to scare him away with talks of visions, but what she had seen bothered her down to her bones. How the vision of him came so fast and felt so real. Why did she have a vision of him? Why was he in water? Who was trying to pull him down? And why were the crows there?

"Okay, have a good night. Happy Halloween," he said as he turned and weaved his way through the crowd, glancing back at her a few times before he disappeared out the front door. Ember noticed the looks he got from the women in the store as he walked out. But he didn't seem to notice; his eyes never left her.

Ember tried to concentrate on work for the rest of the evening, but she couldn't get Thomas and the powerful vision of him out of her mind. She also couldn't forget the feeling of his skin on hers when they touched. The way she felt when he looked at her, as if she were the only person in the room. Thoughts of him, caressing her skin, kissing her lips, holding her body close to his, flooded her mind again as blood flooded her cheeks. She secretly wished she hadn't made plans with Chloe and had left with the tall, intoxicating man. But she had promised her, and Chloe was so excited about the party even though Ember was dreading dressing up in a fancy dress and being around a bunch of strangers, especially now when she would rather be in a dark, cozy bar with Thomas, watching his mouth as he talked. But it was too late to cancel her plans, so she did her best to get through the long day. She breathed a sigh of relief when Lydia was finally done with the last of the tarot readings and it was time to close for the night.

"What a long day," Lydia said as she closed the register. "I can't wait to head over to meet the coven. Should be a nice Samhain ceremony. You are welcome to come, my love," Lydia said to Ember as she threw her bags over her shoulder.

"Oh, thank you, Lydia, but I was invited to a Halloween party. I didn't want my friend to go by herself, especially tonight."

"I completely understand," Lydia said as she walked closer to Ember." I thought that maybe you had made plans with that very good-looking man who seemed so taken by you."

Ember laughed. "You think he was taken by me?"

"Honey, there was so much heat between you two, I

thought the store was going to burst into flames," Lydia teased.

Ember held back a giggle as she looked down at the floor, her cheeks red.

"Oh, my darling girl, I envy you. Go dance, fall in love, have a wonderful time," Lydia said as she closed the gap between them and hugged Ember tight."Tell me, where is this party?" Lydia asked as she broke away from their hug and looked at Ember over her glasses.

"Some fancy house on Chestnut Street, my friend says they have this big party every year on Halloween, and she's always wanted to go," Ember answered casually as she grabbed the broom from the corner and began sweeping the wood floors.

Lydia took the glasses off her face, let them hang on the chain around her neck, and stared at Ember. "A big house on Chestnut Street, you say, "Lydia asked, as she watched Ember closely.

"Yeah, it sounds like a fancy party. A masquerade one. We even rented these big fancy Marie Antoinette dresses to wear."

"Oh, that does sound fancy," Lydia said, the worry rising in her voice.

Sensing the newfound concern in her mentor, Ember stopped sweeping and looked back at her. "Is everything okay, Lydia? You have a weird look on your face."

"Yes, yes, of course, dear. Everything is fine, just be careful tonight."

Ember smiled at Lydia, appreciating her motherly concern. "I know, Lydia. I'll be careful. Plus, I'm going to try to sneak Shadow in with me."

"Shadow, right..." Lydia said as she looked back at the bird, snoozing in his usual place at the desk.

"My dear, I know you can take care of yourself, and I

know Shadow is always with you, but tonight, when the veil is thin, we must stay alert, for the dead walk among us on this night. Trust your instincts and listen to your inner voice." Lydia took Ember's hand in hers. "Keep your mind open to Shadow; he will let you know if there's danger near."

Ember gave Lydia a reassuring glance and squeezed her hand just as they both were startled by a loud knock on the glass door of the store. They turned to see Chloe standing outside. Ember walked over to the door for Chloe, who carried several bags in her hands. She walked in and threw the bags on the floor with a huff. "Ugh, there are so many people out there! I thought I would never make it." She looked over at Ember and ran up to hug her.

"Hey Girl! I'm so excited about tonight, it's going to be so amazing!" Chloe said with excitement in her voice as she let go of Ember and turned her attention back to the multiple bags, "I brought everything for us to get ready," she said as she began to pull garments and shoes out and place them on the counters neatly. She was so preoccupied pulling dresses and accessories out of her bags that she didn't notice Lydia. "Oh my God, I am so sorry. I didn't see you," she exclaimed as she hugged Lydia. "I'm Chloe. Ember's told me all about you."

"It's a pleasure, my love," Lydia said warmly as she returned the hug. "Well, I should get going. You two have a wonderful night." Lydia said as she picked up her purse and made her way out the door.

"Remember what I told you, child," Lydia said with a wink and a smile as she left the store.

Chloe turned to Ember as she held up a white and gold rococo-style dress complete with corset and wire hoop skirt. "I think this is going to look fab on you! It will really bring out the gold in your eyes."

Ember took the dress from her excited friend and went to

the back room to change. Realizing it was going to be harder than she expected, she called out to Chloe for help. Chloe came already half dressed.

"Okay, let's tighten you up. It's going to hurt, but that means it's going to look good, so suck it up." Ember tried to breathe as Chloe tightened the laces on her corset tighter and tighter. Then, she slipped the dress over her head and finished lacing it up. Ember allowed her friend to buzz around her, pinning her hair in large loose curls and securing it with a white flower clip. She filled her lips with light rose colored lipstick and sprayed perfume that smelled of blooming jasmine. When she was all done, Ember looked at herself in the mirror. She would never have chosen an elaborate outfit like this, but was shocked at how good she looked, just like one of the princesses in the fairytale books she loved so much as a child. She studied her reflection more closely. The steel-boned corset accentuated her delicate waist. The fullness of the skirts gave her figure even more of an hourglass appearance, and the shade of her rose lipstick brought out the beautiful hue of her cheeks. Her grandmother's necklace complemented the look perfectly. She looked over at Chloe to thank her for making her look so beautiful, but she was left speechless when she saw her friend in a red silk dress with small flowers embroidered on the bustier, hair brushed back from her face in a swoop with some curls falling down her right shoulder.

"Chloe, wow, you look stunning," Ember said as she admired her friend.

"Right!" Chloe said with that girlish humor Ember loved. She twirled in circles, as the folds of her silk skirts flowed around her. "Now, for the most important part, it being a masquerade ball and all. I did get us these masks." Chloe rummaged around in one of her bags and handed Ember an intricate gold-lace bejeweled mask attached to a small handle.

"This is amazing, thank you," Ember said as she admired the sparkly jeweled mask. She was truly touched by her friend's kindness. Chloe stood next to Ember in the mirror and threw her arm around her shoulders and pulled her close. "We are going to be the best dressed! I know it."

Ember smiled back at her friend in the mirror and hugged her in agreement. She had never been interested in fancy parties or dresses, but the ensemble that Chloe had chosen for them was exquisite, and her friend's excitement was contagious.

"Oh, look at the time. We need to go," Chloe said as she did one more quick check of her hair in the mirror.

CHAPTER 10

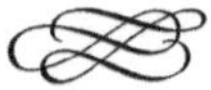

Outside in the chilly night, Ember locked the door to the store, and both girls made their way down the busy street. It wasn't a far walk to Chestnut Street, and all the people out celebrating Halloween made the dark and narrow street come alive. Salem during Halloween was a magical time. Groups of children dressed in costumes knocked on the doors of festively decorated houses. Carved pumpkins and candles flickered in the windows, giving the homes a haunted glow. Music and laughter floated through the air as they walked past the local pubs and restaurants. Ember sighed nervously as they turned onto the historic district. Looking at all the impressive homes that made up this part of town made her smile. She loved all the old houses; it was like stepping back in time. They finally arrived at the massive three-story brick Federal-style mansion. Flame-lit pumpkins and hay bales greeted them as they made their way through the iron gates that read 'Hale Manor' overhead. They both walked along the long pathway leading up to the house. Ember could see guests mingling about inside through the gossamer-covered windows, their low voices drifting softly through the house. She followed Chloe as they stepped up to the large doors. As Chloe reached for the large antique brass knocker on the door, a tall, distinguished-looking man in a royal-blue velvet coat suddenly stood in the entryway and asked in a monotone voice to see an invitation.

Chloe happily pulled the embossed paper from her small clutch and presented it to him. He scanned it with a careful eye and stepped to one side, motioning to come in. Vintage paintings lined the deep purple jacquard-papered walls. Ember looked around in awe as she followed Chloe through the open double doors that led to the grand ballroom. The ballroom was massive, with floor-to-ceiling windows on the far opposite end. Long, flowing deep emerald green velvet curtains hung from every one of the tall windows, gathering loosely on the floor like puddles of velvet. Small strings of fairy lights draped on the windows and curtains gave the room a magical forest atmosphere. The largest crystal chandelier Ember had ever seen lit the entire room with shimmering warm light that glittered off the dark cherrywood floors. Vines of dark green and orange leaves full of dark red, plum, and black flowers draped the walls and long tables full of silver bowls and trays overflowing with rich fruit, meats, and cheeses, while on the other side were tables full of cakes covered with flowers made of sparkling sugar, towers of macaroons and the finest chocolates. Butlers in black coats roamed with trays of bubbling champagne and sweet red wine, while a quartet playing classical music filled the room. Candles burning on elaborate wall sconces cast long dancing shadows on the ornate ceiling. Jack-o-lanterns of every size cast evil flickering grins from their carved glowing faces as they sat watching silently from the marble mantle that framed a fireplace with a roaring fire that warmed the expansive space from the October cold. On the wall above the fireplace hung a mirror so tall it almost reached the ceiling. Its reflection in the dim candlelight made the dancing guests appear as ghostly apparitions from long ago as they danced in their period costumes.

Ember had never been in a room so enchanting, so other-worldly, as if she had been magically transported into a gothic ghost story.

Chloe startled Ember as she came up behind her and grabbed her hand nervously. "Can you believe this place?" She whispered as she took a flute of champagne off one of the silver trays as it passed by her.

"It's like a dream," Ember responded, still in amazement at everything around her. "Do you know who lives here?"

"Her name is Sirena; wait until you meet her and her sisters. I've only met her once, but she is amazing. Super rich, super glamorous," Chloe explained as she drank the glass of champagne down. "There she is now."

Ember followed Chloe's gaze to a tall, slender woman who walked towards them. Her bronze skin glowed like gold in the warm light. Her cat-like features framed large almond-shaped eyes lined with dark makeup, which only made her eye color more piercing in the low light, a shimmering silver color like moonlight that was in contrast with her massive mane of dark spiral locks that fell freely down her back and was topped off by a gold winged crown adorned with pearls. The gold dress she wore sparkled with every slight move-ment and looked like liquid metal as it fit her body as if it had been poured. It's high collar covered her long neck, as chains of gold ran down to pearl and diamond-encrusted cuffs around her wrists. When she turned, Ember could see the dress was completely backless, showing off her exquisite muscle definition. The dress moved with her body perfectly and accentuated every curve down to the floor, its long train dragging behind her, making it seem as if she was floating on a cloud of gold. She looked like a goddess from Greek mythology, so statuesque and elegant. Ember tried not to stare at the gorgeous woman, but it was difficult not to; she captivated everyone in the room. The golden woman caught Ember's eye as she continued to move closer, walking by admirers who flocked around her, fighting for just one glance. She headed straight for Ember and Chloe, her dark rimmed eyes only focusing on them, as if no one else in the room mattered.

"Chloe, good to see you again. So happy you made it to our little soiree," she said as she gave Chloe a kiss on each cheek. Her voice was airy, like wind chimes on a summer breeze. "And who is your pretty friend? We don't believe we've been properly introduced."

"Oh, I wouldn't have missed it for the world, Sirena. This is my friend Ember. She's just moved to town not so long ago," Chloe said as she gushed over the tall woman.

"Ember, what a unique name, for such a unique looking young lady," Sirena said, as she looked more closely at Ember with shimmering eyes.

"It's very nice to meet you," Ember said, feeling a bit uncomfortable under Sirena's intense gaze, almost as if she was being studied.

"We are so happy Chloe invited you to spend the evening with us. Come, you must meet everyone." She linked her slender arm with Ember's as they walked through the crowded room. Sirena lowered the gold and pearl crown, doubling as a mask over her eyes, dark curls falling over each side of her face.

Sirena fluffed her massive head of curls back across her shoulders. "Don't mind our snakes," she whispered to Ember, her voice like bells.

"Your snakes?" Ember answered, sounding a bit confused.

Sirena laughed at Ember's question, like it was amusing

that Ember didn't understand. "Yes, our snakes," she said as she shook her head from side to side, her mess of curls moving in waves. "Our hair, doesn't it remind you of snakes?" Sirena asked as she wrapped a strand around her long, gold-painted nails, a sly grin on her face.

"Like Medusa," Ember replied, trying to hide the awkwardness in her voice with a hint of playfulness.

Sirena's expression changed from a grin to what looked like a sneer as she looked into Ember's bright golden eyes before returning a toothy grin. "Yes, exactly like Medusa. You are a smart girl," she said as she walked Ember through the crowd of people.

"You know, hair can hold great power. We can hide many secrets in our locks," she said as she stared straight ahead. People tried to greet Sirena as she walked by them, but she didn't even blink an acknowledgement. Ember held the mask Chloe had given her to her face, taking the cue from Sirena. It did give her a sense of anonymity from all the prying eyes she felt burning into her as she walked side by side with the stunning woman. Ember watched from behind her mask how enamored they all seemed. How eager they all were to have the smallest moment of her attention, even just a glance or a nod. Ember felt somewhat self-conscious walking alongside the glamorous host, but she tried not to show it. The more they walked through the enormous ballroom, the more at ease she felt. Ember suddenly had a sense of happiness that Sirena had taken such an interest in her, especially since she appeared to have no interest in anyone else.

Ember noticed how cool and smooth Sirena's skin felt against her own, almost like marble. The metal appearance of the dress only added to the cold, hard feeling. She looked at Sirena out of the corner of her eye, and her skin looked as perfect as it felt. She noticed the way the light shimmered off her cheekbones, creating a brilliant effect. They made their way out of the grand ballroom and walked down the long main hallway. Sirena slowed her pace and turned to Ember. "This old house has been in our family for generations. It was falling apart until we took it over and restored it to its former glory."

Ember listened quietly as they walked arm in arm. She admired the multiple paintings that were displayed on the walls. At first glance, Ember didn't notice what was depicted on the worn canvases, but as she looked closer, she could see eerie figures alongside strange, dark creatures painted in the oil, some with many legs and arms, reaching out from dark, stormy seas. An overwhelming sense of sadness came over Ember. 'Something bad happened here,' she thought to herself.

"Rumor has it, one of the reverends who presided over the witch trials used to have a house on this very land," Sirena continued, her voice cheerful despite the serious subject matter. "We suppose there isn't a corner in Salem that isn't haunted with tragic memories of the past," she continued to say, a grin on her face. "We have never been fond of small-town gossip or superstitions. We are sure you can relate."

"Yes, I think I can," Ember replied as the two of them had now stopped in front of a door at the end of the hall, feeling a bit confused by Sirena's question. She tried to quiet her inner monologue and really listen and feel the energy all around her, tap into that sudden sense of sadness that she had a moment before. Now it was as if a thick fog was shrouding Ember's mind. A hazy cloud surrounded her, filling her head and blinding her sight.

Sirena lifted the gold mask and slid it back on top of her head as she turned to look straight into Ember's eyes. "We know it must be difficult to be alone in a new city. A stranger in a strange land, but here you are not a stranger. Here you have friends, here are family," Sirena said as she reached out to hold Ember's hand, her skin cool as stone.

"It hasn't been bad. I have met very nice people, and Chloe is wonderful." As soon as Ember said those words, she remembered that she had left Chloe back in the ballroom. She had briefly forgotten all about her companion while she had been in Sirena's company. "I have to get back; she must be wondering where I am," Ember said as she started to turn back down the hall. Sirena's grip on Ember's hand tightened, stopping her from walking away. Her long nails wrapped around Ember's fingers. Ember was surprised how strong her grip was. "Of course, but surely not before you meet our sisters." With a smile, Sirena let go of Ember's hand and pushed open the door in front of them.

Ember slowly stepped in after Sirena, watching as the train of her gown slithered behind her. The room was a stark contrast to the rest of the house. No warm carved cherry wood, no ornate antiques or woven rugs. The walls of the room were a glossy bright red. The walls, ceilings, curtains, even the furniture and fixtures, were all the same shade of red. The only light in the room came from the huge fireplace at the opposite end, only making the blood red color of the room more intense.

Sirena walked to a small round table and poured something dark into a glass. Ember stood and watched as she drank it down and glided over to the fireplace, where two women were standing. The minute Ember saw them all together, backlit by the fire, she remembered where she had seen them before. They were the striking women that Ember had seen through Shadow's eyes. The three women with the silver eyes were sitting at a table in the restaurant. Ember's heartbeat quickened, and her skin suddenly felt warm and tingly. She tried to hide the look of familiarity as she smiled at the three women, standing motionless in front of her like dolls.

"Sisters, we have a guest. Please make our new friend Ember feel at home. Ember, meet my sisters Willow and Jasmine," Sirena said as she motioned gracefully at the blonde and brunette beside her. They both approached Ember, walking in unison, as if they were performing a choreographed dance, oddly big smiles on their faces. "Welcome, we are so excited to meet you," Willow said to Ember, her silver blue eyes glowing.

Ember smiled politely as she scanned Willow. She was small and very petite, almost elf-like. Her straight blonde hair was perfectly in place, and no makeup on her pore-less skin. She wore a light blue wispy dress with an asymmetrical bust line that was too long for her small build. Several beaded necklaces and bracelets made a rustling sound as she moved a bit closer to Ember, bumping into Jasmine's shoulder as she passed. The brunette stood silently at first. "Hello Ember," she said in a timid, but high-pitched voice as she moved very close to Ember, "it's so nice to make your acquaintance." Jasmine was taller than her sister Willow, but just as slender. Her short dark hair was styled in pin curls that framed her oval face. The beaded fringe on her black and silver dress shook as she moved, showing off her boyish figure. Her silver eyes rimmed with heavy black eyeliner.

Ember felt overwhelmed. The red room, the heat from the fireplace filling the space, making it difficult to breathe, and the odd way the women spoke and moved. A feeling of uneasiness came over Ember. She tried to clear her mind, but the fog in her head had only grown thicker. She had no reason to feel uneasy; the women had been polite and gracious. Maybe it was the same awkward, uncomfortable feeling she always had around new people, especially women who were so glamorous. She took a deep breath and tried to ground herself. 'You are okay. They are just a little odd,' Ember thought to herself. Probably a product of a privileged life filled with private tutors and finishing school. But she could not ignore the fact that Shadow had been drawn to watch them. The thought stuck like a splinter in her brain.

"Sisters, give her some room to breathe," Sirena said as she walked over to join them, waving her empty glass in the air. "You must excuse them, Ember. We don't host many intimate gatherings, and my sisters are well, a bit shy." With quick glances from Sirena's silver eyes, the other two sisters retreated to their original places by the fire. Ember immediately sensed who was in charge, and it very much was Sirena.

"I am so happy to meet all of you. Thank you for being so kind and welcoming," Ember said with a warm smile to her hosts, "but I really must find my friend. I'm sure she's wondering where I wandered off to."

The three statuesque women started at Ember blankly as she spoke, leaving an awkward silence hanging in the air.

"We promised to stay together tonight. You know, because of those women," Ember heard her voice trail off. She nervously played with the tendrils of dark hair that fell from her elegant updo.

"Oh yes, of course. Those horrid crimes, absolutely ghastly," Sirena exclaimed, her expression changing quickly to concern. "Jasmine will escort you back to the ballroom." Sirena clutched both of Ember's hands in hers. "It was so nice to meet you, Ember. We know it appears as if we have many friends, but sadly, we live a lonely existence." Ember looked back into Sirena's eyes, like mirrors, so shiny that Ember could see her own reflection in them.

"We would love it if you called on us soon," Sirena said as she let go of one of Ember's hands to gently touch her chin.

"Yes, I would like that," Ember replied, feeling Sirena's cool touch on her face.

"Come, Jasmine, take Ember to find her friend," Sirena called out to her sister without taking her eyes off Ember.

"We would love to," Jasmine responded as she slid next to Ember. As they both turned to leave, Sirena called out. "We hope you have a lovely evening, my love." Ember turned to look at Sirena to thank her, but the fiery look that shot from the pixie-like blonde standing next to her changed her mind, so she quietly walked out into the hallway, Jasmine at her side.

The warmth of the dark wood hallway was a welcome change from the bright red room. Ember exhaled softly as she glanced over at the woman beside her. They walked in silence for a while, until Jasmine broke the spell. "We know how overwhelming our sister can sometimes be," the slender brunette confessed to Ember. "We can be quite dramatic at times, but please don't let that scare you off," she continued, her voice sounding sweet. 'People in town love to gossip about our family; it can be so hurtful, but we have learned to never be ashamed of who we are."

Jasmine looked down at the floor as they approached the ballroom. She stopped and turned to face Ember." Sirena has overcome so much, so many trials and tribulations. We owe her everything." Ember studied the lovely woman in front of her. She could hear the sadness in her words as she spoke. Ember couldn't help but feel a small bit of pity for her, although she didn't understand why. A quick smile flashed across Jasmine's face, as if she realized she might have said something she shouldn't have.

"Thank you, Jasmine. It was very nice getting to know you," Ember said, and she did mean it. Jasmine did seem kind and caring. More authentic than her sisters. "I've always wondered what it would be like to have sisters. You are lucky to have each other," Ember said warmly. She had often dreamed of what it would be like to have siblings, someone to share her deepest secrets with, to have someone at your side that you could put all your trust in.

Jasmine looked at Ember wide-eyed as she spoke, her eyes momentarily looking down at the floor, then back at Ember. "Indeed." With that one word, Jasmine turned on her foot and disappeared down the hallway, the fringe of her dress shimming as she moved. Ember stood there, watching her walk away, lost in thoughts of the strange encounter she had just experienced, although it did give her a flutter of excitement. To meet these refined, oddly beautiful women did intrigue her.

"Hey! I thought you had taken off." Chloe's excited words jolted Ember out of her thoughts as she came up behind her. "Where have you been?"

Ember smiled at her friend. "I'm so sorry, Chloe. Sirena wanted me to meet her sisters."

"Really? You meet the weird sisters?" Chloe asked, her brown eyes wide.

Ember chuckled at Chloe's Shakespeare reference, even though she wasn't sure if she realized she had made the comparison. The weird sisters were a very fitting name for Jasmine and Willow.

"Yes, I met them. They seemed nice," Ember said as she looked around the hallway for the waiters carrying the trays of champagne, her throat suddenly dry.

"Really?" Chloe said, surprise in her voice. "I've only seen them a few times and, um, yeah, very weird. Listen, I've been looking all over for you. We have to go back to the party," Chloe whispered in her ear.

Ember suddenly felt drained from the evening's events. It was all so overwhelming: the party, the people, the house, Sirena and her sisters. All she wanted to do was go home, get out of the tight-fitting corset, and snuggle by the fire. "Honestly, Chloe, I think I've had enough excitement for one night," Ember said to her friend as she saw the look of disappointment that splashed across her face.

"No! You can't leave now! Girl, you will not believe who is here." She pulled Ember closer to her and whispered, "Hot cop!"

"Thomas?" Ember said, invigorated by the news. "He's here? At this party?" Ember tried to hide the sudden rush of excitement that came over her with the sound of his name.

"That's what I'm trying to tell you, "Chloe said as she pulled her friend's arm and led her back inside the ballroom through the maze of people.

They both maneuvered their way through all the other long, wide dresses as Ember imagined this was what it must have been to be a guest at Versailles, pushing through mounds of silk and organza. She glanced around the candlelit party and scanned people's faces looking for Thomas's icy blue eyes. She knew she would instantly recognize him, even in a room full of people in masks.

"Are you sure it's him you saw?" Ember yelled out to her friend over the music.

"Oh, trust me. It's him, alright," Chloe said with a huge smile as she looked back at Ember.

Ember felt his eyes on her before she saw him. She looked up to meet his gaze from across the dance floor. He was standing with a small group of people, talking and laughing loudly, but he wasn't interested in whatever they were carrying on about. He was fixed on her. He wasn't hard to miss as he was so much taller than those around him, and he wasn't covering his handsome face with a mask, although the stubble on his sharp jawline was now a little thicker. He wore white pants, black boots, a shirt, and a vest underneath a royal blue jacket with gold trim. His attire reminded Ember of a Revolutionary soldier. She could almost see him charging into battle on horseback, a sword in his hand, fierceness in his eyes. As he came closer to Ember, it wasn't battling fierceness that she saw in his eyes; it was desire. Desire for her. He walked elegantly towards her, his long legs carrying him smoothly across the floor until he was inches away from her. "Good evening, ladies. "His voice was deep and low; it gave Ember butterflies.

"Well, Detective, fancy meeting you here," Ember said, trying to keep the excitement of seeing him out of her voice, especially in the soldier's uniform.

"Yes, I heard there was a party tonight," Thomas said, his eyes making their way down Ember's body. "You look beautiful, Ember," he said, gently picking up her hand and bringing it to his lips.

Ember felt a shiver go up her spine as she felt his hot mouth on the back of her hand. She couldn't stop the rush of blood that raced through her body like a storm.

Chloe stood watching as her friend and the handsome man intensely looked at each other. She interrupted the moment, "Hi, I'm Chloe, Ember's best friend. It's so nice to finally meet you."

Thomas turned, without letting go of Ember's hand. "Chloe, yes, it's a pleasure to meet a friend of Ember's."

His eyes, usually a pale ice blue, changed to a deep aqua as he focused his attention back to Ember. "Would you like to dance?"

Before Ember could answer, Thomas pulled her waist close to him and spun her out to the dance floor. She looked back over her shoulder as Chloe mouthed, 'Have fun,' and gave her a wink.

As Thomas held Ember's body close to his, she could feel his muscular arms flex under his jacket as he pulled her in tighter. He was so tall that Ember's head rested perfectly on his chest. She inhaled deeply. His skin smelled of wood and leather. They spun around the hardwood dance floor under the crystal chandelier that cast iridescent light over them. He took her arm and placed it on his shoulders, his strong fingers slowly running down the length of her arm. The soft touch of his fingertips sent pulses of electricity through Ember's body. She felt drunk even though she hadn't quenched the thirst in her throat with a drink, but as she looked up into his eyes, a new thirst rose up in her. One that she could not contain. It bubbled up in her, about to over-flow. She was lost in his blue eyes, like an endless sea. She felt light as air, as they floated around the floor, her massive skirts swirling at their feet. She finally caught her breath enough to speak. "Are you here in an official capacity?" She asked him softly.

"You would say that?" He whispered in her ear, his breath hot on her skin, a mischievous grin on his lips.

"I just assumed, because of the uniform," Ember said, pulling slightly away from him so she could see his reaction.

Thomas laughed at Ember's tease, "I haven't worn a uniform in years, nothing like this though."

"I like this one," Ember said, her head lying back on his strong chest, feeling his heartbeat. Thomas said nothing in response, just tilted her face towards his.

"Did you follow me here?" Ember asked, her voice trailing off to a whisper as he looked deep in her eyes. The way he looked at her made Ember feel like he knew what she looked like without any clothes; it made her stomach flip.

"Would it frighten you if I said I did?" He said, his voice guttural, animalistic, like a growl.

"Yes, it would," Ember confessed to him. She was afraid of him, of how powerful he was. How his eyes wandered all over her body. The way he clenched the muscles in his jaw was as if to keep himself from devouring her completely. The intoxicating smell of his skin, the slight trace of bourbon he left behind. It felt so forbidden to her. She had no idea who this man was, or what his intentions were, and she didn't care; she wanted him, no matter what it cost her.

His lips came inches from hers. "I did follow you," he said before he pressed his lips lightly against hers. She resisted only for a moment, until completely giving herself to his kiss. She allowed his mouth to explore hers, not caring who was around them. Nothing existed at that moment, just them.

His kiss was deep and long; it made her head spin. She felt like the entire room was spinning, all around her, making her dizzy. She broke away from him and gasped for air. Her head fell backwards until all she could see was the sparkling crystal above them. It was like she was in heaven. The chandelier glittered like stars in the sky, the candles flickered around them, and the strangers in masks watched the desire building between them. Thomas let go of her hand and intertwined his in her thick, dark hair, firmly pulling her face back to his. His hands were strong; there was no fighting him. Ember didn't have the strength even if she wanted to. His lips stopped right before they touched, teasing her. She could feel his breath, hear his heart in her ears. Her legs weakened under her, and she felt as if she might fall. Sensing it, he gripped her waist harder, closer, holding her body up with one strong arm. "I don't know what spell you cast on me, wildflower, but I will never let you fall."

* * *

SIRENA STOOD in a corner of the ballroom, her two sisters standing on either side of her.

Her arms crossed in front of her body as she watched Ember and Thomas dance. The tension between them filled the room like heavy musk. Her dark eyes followed them as they moved across the ballroom. As she did, she noticed that all the eyes in the room were on them. They were so beautiful together, as they floated across the floor. She motioned to the man in the velvet blue coat. "Locke, make sure that our guests are taken care of. We are going to retire for the evening."

"Of course, madam," the distinguished-looking man said as he nodded and walked away.

"They look beautiful together, we think?" Willow whispered in Sirena's ear.

"Yes, too beautiful," Sirena replied without taking her eyes off the couple. She turned on her shapely legs and walked out of the ballroom, her sisters following close behind.

CHAPTER 11

From the paved stone wall across from the witchcraft shop, Thomas watched Ember and Chloe walk out the front door and down the street. He hesitated for a moment before falling behind them, keeping a safe distance. His intentions were to go back to his loft, to be alone with his bourbon and pictures of the victims on the wall. But the thoughts of Ember kept him from leaving, from going home. He couldn't get her out of his head, her eyes, her voice, her smell, the pout on her lips. He never let his emotions overtake him, but he couldn't deny the pull she had over him. He stayed at a distance, but close enough to not lose sight of the crowd. He couldn't help feeling a little shame, following her without her knowledge, but he was compelled to know where she was going. He watched them turn down Chestnut Street, laughing and chatting with each other. He could barely make out what they were saying, over the sound of music and trick or treaters. He stopped across from the three-story home and watched them go inside. He could see through the windows of the house and saw the large party with many guests dressed in period costumes. He didn't even pause to think about his next move. He needed to get into the party. He quickly turned and walked back down the street and toward the downtown area. He knew it would be faster if he took the side streets and back alleys towards his loft. It didn't take him long to reach the front door of his building. He ran inside his apartment door and headed straight for his closet. Thomas remembered he had an old Colonial soldier costume from a party he had gone to years prior that would be perfect. As he searched, he wondered how he was going to get inside without an invitation, but he told himself he would worry about that when he got there. All he thought about was sharing another moment with Ember, however brief. He finally found the old costume in a box at the back of his closet. He hastily removed his work shirt and jacket and slid his arms into the white cotton shirt, vest, and pants. He quickly slipped on the black leather boots and blue jacket. He took a second to look in the mirror as he ran his fingers through his hair. He hadn't shaved for a few days, and the stubble on his face was thicker, but he didn't have time for that now. The bottle of bourbon that sat on his desk looked back at him. He poured a finger of bourbon and glubbed it down, burning his throat. He reached to pour a second drink, but for the first time, in a long time, he had no taste for more. He put the empty glass down next to his phone. He saw that he had a few missed calls from work and hastily scrolled through the messages. Nothing that couldn't wait till morning, he thought to himself. Right now, he was focused on one thing.

He rushed out the door and down to the street. He walked as quickly as he could, without drawing too much attention to himself, his mind focused on getting to the party and to Ember.

No one on the street took much notice of the tall blonde detective dressed in a Revolutionary soldier uniform, not on

Halloween, no one except a lonely crow circling overhead. Had it been following Thomas since he first saw Ember and Chloe leaving the shop? Thomas couldn't recall, but it seemed he was keeping a watchful eye on his every move. Landing on a high windowsill, watching Thomas make his way through the iron gates of Hale Manor.

* * *

It was almost midnight when Thomas got back to the mansion. He stood outside waiting patiently until he saw the perfect opportunity. The doorman was distracted for a moment with some unruly kids on the front porch, trying to get more Halloween candy. It was just long enough for him to pass undetected.

He quickly stepped inside the foyer and looked around as people wandered with glasses of champagne. He suddenly became aware that he was one of the only ones who wasn't wearing a mask. That concerned him at first; the last thing he wanted was to be recognized, being that he hadn't been invited. Thomas was sure that the town's most influential people might be in attendance, so he would need to be careful.

He strolled through the groups of people casually, as if he belonged there, but making sure he kept his head down. He followed some guests as they walked down the hallway to the entryway of the grand ballroom. His eyes searched for Ember, but he didn't see her as he walked through the party trying to remember what color dress she was wearing; he was sure he would recognize her when he saw her. He quickly became aware of the interested gazes of women as he looked at them, trying to find those yellow eyes that had captivated him. But he did not see her. Just as he wondered if he had arrived too late, he looked across the dance floor and saw her friend Chloe talking close to a man by the fireplace. He searched the faces standing around Chloe for Ember, but she wasn't there. He leaned his back on the wall and carefully watched as Chloe lost interest in the man she was speaking to and walked out of the ballroom.

He stood there for a moment, seeing if Chloe would return, possibly with Ember. His intentions were clear; he was going to be with Ember tonight, to hold her close, taste her lips, and he wasn't leaving until he had.

That was when he saw her, trailing behind Chloe, as if she were being guided. Even in her bejeweled mask, her bright eyes stood out across the dance floor between them. Thomas watched her move from the hidden position against the wall. The warm glow from the chandelier illuminated her skin. He noticed how her dress accentuated her shape. His eyes traced every curve of her bust line as loose dark pieces of hair swept across her cleavage. His heartbeat quickened as he moved towards her, his eyes never leaving her.

* * *

EMBER STOOD in Thomas's embrace for what seemed like an eternity. All the sights and sounds fell away; all she could hear was her own heartbeat, in sync with his, thundering in her ears. His kiss, so deep, made her legs weak and her pulse thready. She wanted their kiss to last forever, but Thomas abruptly pulled his mouth off hers with a gasp.

"I'm sorry," Thomas breathed in her ear, "I can't control myself when I'm with you."

"I don't think I want you to," Ember said as she buried her face in his chest. She closed her eyes and listened to his breathing. She didn't understand these new emotions that were overtaking her. It all felt so forbidden, to let her guard down for anyone, especially a man. But with Thomas, it was different; he was different.

Thomas lifted her chin gently to look at her. "I can't lose control with you. No matter how much I want you, and I do want you, Ember."

Ember looked back at him as tears welled up in her eyes. "You don't know me. I'm not like everyone else. I'm afraid that when you see the real me, well… maybe you won't feel the same way."

Thomas brushed a tear away softly with his thumb and kissed the wetness on her cheek. "That will never happen." His lips lingered on her cheek for a moment, then pulled away. "Let's get out of here," he whispered, as the muscles in his jaw line clenched.

He took hold of Ember's hand and pulled her off the dance floor through the maze of people and walked out of the house into the night air. The temperature had dropped. Thomas felt Ember shiver as he put his arm around her as they walked briskly down the street, the moon hanging bright in the clear sky over them.

"Where are we going?" Ember asked him as she snuggled closer to him to keep warm, "I barely know you; I don't just run out into the night alone with complete strangers," she teased.

"I want to take you to where we first met. Besides, I don't think we are alone," Thomas said as he looked to see the large crow flying over their heads. Ember looked up to the sky. It only took a minute to spot Shadow gliding silently.

"You are taking me to the cemetery? It's late, it should be closed."

"Nothing is closed for us," Thomas said, giving her a little wink. "Besides, it's Halloween. What better night to be in an old cemetery? I don't know why, but it suddenly sounded like the perfect place." They walked the stone path covered with dry leaves until arriving at the locked iron gates. Ember turned to Thomas.

"Now what?" Ember asked as she gave Thomas a quick smile.

With that, Thomas picked her up by the waist and lifted her to the top of the four-foot rock wall that bordered the small cemetery. He jumped up next to her with ease. He stepped down from the wall in one big step and turned to bring Ember down on the ground next to him. They walked along the crumbling and tilted headstones, the wind whistling through the trees, Ember's long skirt dragging in the dirt behind her. They both stopped in front of the giant oak tree that grew out of the ancient soil. Shadow swooped down and settled on one of the low, barren branches. Ember looked up at her feathered companion and smiled. Thomas came up and stood beside her, a nervous chill coating his entire body as they both looked at the large black bird.

"Hello Shadow," Ember said as she reached her hand out towards him. Shadow jumped off the branch and fluttered over to her, taking a few hops to take his favorite spot on her shoulder. She turned to look at Thomas, his eyes wide with surprise.

"This is my Shadow," she said as she stroked his dark feathers. Thomas stepped closer and looked curiously at the bird.

"He's beautiful," he said, as he timidly reached his hand out to pet Shadow. The bird squawked loudly at first but slowly lowered his head down enough for Thomas to give him a scratch.

Ember watched as Shadow closed his eyes and enjoyed the head scratches from his new friend.

"I think he likes you, "Ember whispered with a smile. Suddenly Shadow, having enough attention, jumped off Ember's shoulder and perched on a nearby headstone. The

October wind blew a little harder, rustling the remaining leaves on the oak tree. Shadow puffed out his feathers to keep his body warm in the cold. Ember took a deep breath. She loved the smell of fall so much. The dry leaves, firewood burning in the distance, and the smell of the snowfall soon to come. She stepped closer to the old tree. "I've always wanted to come here; it was like the land has been calling me my entire life. To this place, where my ancestors lived and died."

"Your ancestors are from Salem?" Thomas asked as he watched Ember. She looked so magical, standing in the empty cemetery, looking up at the sky, her hair blowing wildly all around her.

"Yes, Sarah Wildes, she was executed during the trials," Ember explained. "From what I've read, she was a remarkable woman, fearless."

"You have that in common with her," Thomas said, as he moved towards Ember, her dark hair glowing with a blue hue from the moonlight.

Ember smiled at him. "Really? I never thought so. I've always been so afraid, afraid to live my life as I truly am. Her eyes turned downwards, a look of sadness coming over her face.

"You do, I see in your eyes," Thomas said as he studied her closely. "I have lived here all my life, so did my parents, and their parents. That is all I know. I don't really know anything about my family after that. It must be nice to know where you came from," Thomas paused for a moment before he spoke again.

"Ember, can I ask you something?"

"Yes, anything."

"Are you a witch?" Thomas asked with a hint of hesitation as he spoke the question that had been burning in his mind since he first laid eyes on her.

"Would it bother you if I were?" Ember said as she looked over her shoulder at him.

"No, it wouldn't. Not at all. I really don't understand much about it. You would think I would, growing up here."

"You aren't afraid of me?" Ember asked as she turned her body to face him, crossing her arms tightly around her.

"No, I could never be afraid of you," he said as he stepped close to her, wrapping his arms around her waist.

"You are shaking," he said softly as he pulled her into him.

She hadn't noticed her body was shaking, but it wasn't from the cold wind. Thomas held her tightly, his strong arms embracing her completely. His body was so warm, it instantly chased the chill away. He brought her chin up with his hand and looked deep into her eyes. He was so tall that Ember felt she was always looking up at him. But she didn't mind at all. His height made her feel as if he was guarding her. A shield against the outside world. Nothing else existed now, just them. He parted his lips and kissed her softly, keeping his eyes open. Thomas wanted to look at her; to see the way she gave herself to him. They lost themselves in the kiss. Ember had never felt like this before. Her whole body was on fire, the feeling overtaking her. But she didn't fight it; she let herself melt into his arms. Thomas could feel Ember's skin getting warmer through her dress. It was like her skin was on fire, and it spread throughout his own. He never wanted this moment to end; the cold wind against his warm body, the fallen autumn leaves brushing their feet, the bright moon shining down on them. The smell of her skin was like summer roses and vanilla. It was intoxicating. He finally pulled his lips off hers with a deep breath. He held her face close to him and looked in her eyes. They were glowing in the darkness like sharp flames from a roaring fire.

'Don't stop," Ember gasped as she pulled the lapel of his jacket back to her. She looked up at his bright blue eyes, now appearing a dark grey, the color of a stormy sea. The wind picked up at that moment, undoing Ember's hair from the mass of pins, allowing it to fall free and wild, swirling around them. With both hands, Thomas gently brushed the strands of black hair from her face.

"Trust me, it took everything I have to stop," Thomas said to her, his voice dropping to even a lower tone. "I've never met anyone like you, Ember. I have to confess, I've been through some dark times recently. Some days, I find it hard to get out of bed, but ever since I saw you standing here, all alone, but somehow not alone, I feel like my world has gotten a little less dark. I know it might sound crazy, but one thing I've never doubted is my instincts. I know, I was supposed to meet you here that night."

Ember gazed into his eyes as he spoke. She wanted to believe his words as they washed over her. "Things are happening so fast, it's been hard to keep my head on my shoulders," she said, her words breathy. "I want to trust you, Thomas. I do. But…I have trouble trusting, and I don't know anything about you."

Thomas sat on the cold ground next to a headstone. He took Ember's hand and motioned for her to sit beside him. She curled up next to him and put her head on his chest. She didn't know why, but it just felt right. Being that close to him. She could hear his heartbeat again, slower this time, but strong in her ears. She realized at that moment that listening to his heart made her feel calm, at ease. So, she closed her eyes.

They sat on the cold ground until the first rays of sunlight broke through the velvet sky. They talked all night, telling each other everything about their lives. Thomas listened intently as Ember told him about how she had grown up, how hard it had been with all the whispers of witchcraft and evil. She told him all about her grandmother

Carmen and how much she meant to her. She talked about her mother's passing and the move to Salem. Meeting Lydia and Chloe, and how much they meant to her. She wanted to tell him about what had happened the other night, when the Goddess revealed Her plan in the other snow-covered place, but she was afraid to. She wasn't sure what he would make of it. In turn, Ember listened to Thomas as he told her about growing up on the North Shore, how he had always wanted to be a cop, following in his father's footsteps, how much he loved his job, and the pride he took in it. Ember could hear the frustration in his voice when he spoke about the recent murder case that had troubled him for so long. She could see how much he cared about those women and how he felt almost helpless to not have gotten further in the investigation. "But I finally got a break, in a very unusual way. I found that they all have a tie to witchcraft," Thomas said as the morning sunlight shone through his blonde hair.

"Really? They were all witches. How do you know?" "You wouldn't believe me if I told you," Thomas replied, as he stood and reached to help Ember to her feet. "I'd better get you home. It's getting late," Thomas looked at the sunrise and smiled," or I should say early."

"I can't believe we talked all night," Ember said as they both made their way back over the wall and out of the cemetery. She looked over her shoulder at Shadow, making sure he was following behind them. She watched as he took off into the orange sky and flew over their heads.

"I love talking to you," Thomas said with a smile, watching Shadow.

"I loved talking to you, too," Ember said as they reached her front door. She turned to look at the fair-haired, handsome man. "Thank you for a lovely evening."

Thomas leaned in and lightly kissed her lips. "I have to go.

I have to work. Go inside, get some sleep," he said as he hugged her one last time." I'll be back later."

He watched her from the sidewalk as she walked up the steps to her apartment. She paused right before she opened the door and looked back at him. 'He is so beautiful,' Ember thought. She smiled and stepped inside, closing the door behind her.

With that, she disappeared through the doorway. Thomas stood for a moment longer, remembering the way his lips felt on hers. He finally turned and started to walk towards his loft. It wasn't a long walk, and it was a beautiful morning. He had a renewed sense of hope. That he was on the right track, not just with his life, but with his case. He had a feeling that everything was finally falling into place.

CHAPTER 12

*E*mber walked into her apartment and threw herself on the overstuffed couch, with a loud sigh. She was tired, but too excited to sleep, the events of the previous night fresh in her mind. It was all like a dream. The magical party, the beautiful ballroom, the sparkling chandelier, and her dance with Thomas, his kiss, the way his warm hands felt on her skin in the cold night air. Then her thoughts drifted to the three women that she met at the party. The Hale sisters, most of all the glamours, statuesque, wild-haired Sirena. Ember tried to remember her conversation with Sirena and her sisters. They seemed so kind, but something about them was somewhat off. Ember knew not to judge people too quickly. It had been done to her too many times. So, she promised herself to keep an open mind. Just as she thought of them, she heard a light tapping at her kitchen window. She walked to the kitchen and saw Shadow tapping the glass with his broken beak.

"Hello, my little thief," Ember said as she opened the small window so he could jump inside. "What a night, right?" she said to her friend as he hopped on her hand. "Shadow, do you believe in love at first sight?" She asked as the bird tilted his head. Ember laughed. "Don't worry, baby, you will always be the most important man in my life." She placed Shadow on the post of her bed and headed into the bathroom. She turned on the hot water and let it fill the claw tub. She turned to look at herself in the mirror. Her hair was messy and windblown; her pale cheeks still flushed from the evening in the cold.

She reached behind her and began to unlace the tight corset that Chloe had tied her into. She let the long, heavy dress fall from her body onto the bathroom floor. She reached over to a small table next to the sink and picked up a small glass bottle. She pulled the cork off and sprinkled the contents in the bathwater. She always remembered her grandmother Carmen using this herbal mix containing dandelions for many things, including helping to amplify the sight. She stepped into the tub one foot at a time and let the hot herb-infused water wash over her skin. She lay back and closed her eyes, breathing in the steam deep into her lungs. Ember let her body relax and cleared her mind. She could feel herself getting sleepy, the prior night's events catching up to her.

She opened her heavy eyelids and saw a small black dot in the clear water. She tried to focus her sleepy eyes on it as it grew larger. It was thick, almost like oil. She watched as it grew and spread out all around her. Ember felt paralyzed; she couldn't move as the dark water engulfed her. She watched with horror as water began to take shape, first into long fingers, breaking through the surface, then into a hand, rising up and reaching for her. The hand moved quickly and wrapped tightly around her throat. It squeezed tighter and tighter, shutting off her air supply. Shadow, sensing that his mistress was in danger, flew into the bathroom, frantically squawking and attempting to peck at the dark water. Ember struggled, but she was overtaken. Just when she was about to lose consciousness, the mysterious watery hand brushed up against her necklace and in an instant, it was gone, sinking back under the surface and disappearing. As it vanished, Ember regained control of her body and was able to move again. She sat up and leaned over the side of the tub to catch her breath. She looked over at Shadow, who had fallen back onto the tile floor. She looked back at the water, and it was clear, as if the mysterious thick oily substance had never existed.

She touched her necklace and remembered the Goddess' advice. Ember was glad she had listened and had worn her grandmother's necklace.

"That really happened, Shadow? It wasn't a vision?" She asked her bird who was now shaking water off his feathers. Ember stood up and grabbed a towel off the wall hook, her hands still shaking.

She stepped out of the tub and sat on the floor in front of her bed, clutching her towel. Ember chewed on her fingernail as she thought about the watery dark hand. She sensed something was strangely familiar about it, although she didn't know why. She needed to sleep; her mind would be clearer after some rest. She lay her head on the woven carpet next to her bed and instantly fell asleep.

EMBER WOKE to loud knocking on her door. Her head was still foggy as she opened and rubbed her eyes, realizing she had fallen asleep on the floor. She heard the knocking again as she stood and walked over to open the door to see Chloe, a big smile on her face.

"Well, good morning, sleepy," she said as she brushed by her. "I'm literally dying to know what happened last night.

Tell me everything! I saw you two on the dance floor. Damn, that was hot," Chloe said as she looked at Ember standing in nothing but a towel. "He's not still here, is he?" she asked with a grin, her voice a little lower.

Ember sat on the couch and gave her friend a sly look. "What would make you think he would be here?"

"Oh, come on, Ember. I saw you slink away with hot cop."

"We did have a great night," Ember said, touching her lip, remembering their kiss." he did kiss me."

"Oh, trust me, I know! Ok…I need all the details. Don't leave anything out," Chloe said as she sat cross-legged next to Ember.

"I wish I could. I have to go to work," Ember said as she stood up and walked into her room to get dressed for the day.

"You are so boring," Chloe protested. "ok, I'll let you off this time, but I'm coming back later, and I want details," she said as she jumped off the couch and gave Ember a kiss on the cheek. "Details," she yelled over her shoulder as she opened the front door.

"Hey, someone left a note taped to your door. I'll put it on the table. I'm sure it's from your sexy policeman." With that, Chloe closed the door behind her. Ember walked into the kitchen and looked at the white envelope that had been stuck to her door. It had no writing on the front, but as Ember flipped it over, she noticed a red wax seal on the back. She ran her fingers over the embossed seal. She examined it more closely and could see the image of a mermaid.

She hesitated for a moment, wondering who it could be from. She really didn't know many people in town. She cracked the seal and pulled out a small, folded piece of paper that read,

"Hello Ember,

We hope this finds you well.

It was so lovely to meet you last night. We would love the pleasure of your company this afternoon for tea.

3:00pm at Hale Manor.

With love, Sirena."

*E*mber read the note several times before it was processed in her mind. Sirena was inviting her over to her family home for tea. She felt somewhat confused about why the three sisters had taken such an interest in her, but she was intrigued. Ember found them mysterious and interesting, not to mention glamorous, something she was not.

Ember ran to her closet and shuffled through all the hangers, trying to find something suitable to wear since she wouldn't have a chance to come back home and change after work. She had never cared much for her appearance, but something about these women made her want to impress them. She finally decided on an emerald dress that she had made the year prior. It was one of her favorites with its full skirt and gathered waist. She tried to do something with her unruly mess of hair, but, as always, it had a mind of its own. She looked over at Shadow. "Well, how do I look? Is this proper for teatime?" Shadow looked at Ember lazily and ruffled his feathers with as much approval as he could muster.

She turned to look in the mirror one more time and grabbed her bag. She motioned for Shadow to get in. "Let's go, sleepy boy. Time to go to work." Shadow gave a complaining squawk and settled into Ember's bag.

Ember couldn't believe how happy she felt. For the first time in her life, Ember felt like she was exactly where she needed to be. Not only was she free to be her true self, without fear or judgment, but also, she was excited for the future and all that it could hold. She almost wished she had made this move sooner. Her thoughts moved to her father; she hadn't spoken to him since she moved to Salem. He was never very interested in Ember or what was going on in her life, but she was sure he would be happy for her. The experience with the coven still hovered over her. The Goddess 'warning was still imprinted in her mind. But Ember was happy today, and didn't want to think about it, so she pushed it to the back of her mind.

Ember got to the store just as Lydia was unlocking the front door; she looked at Ember with what could be taken as relief in her eyes.

"Good morning, Lydia," Ember said almost like she was singing.

"Good morning, dear. Don't you look pretty this morning?" Lydia responded as they got settled inside the warm store. "How was your night?" Lydia asked slowly, not looking up as she opened the store's ledger.

"It was amazing, Lydia," Ember exclaimed, as she danced around the store. Her green skirt twirling around her. Lydia watched closely as Ember danced through the store, telling her all about her night. She smiled to herself; she was truly happy for her young friend. But the happiness drained from her face when Ember spoke about meeting the three sisters.

"Oh, I see you met the Hale sisters," Lydia said as she

walked over to a bookshelf, climbed the ladder to the top shelf, and pulled out an old black book.

"Well, yes, I suppose I did," Ember said as she stepped closer to the desk where Lydia opened the book.

"Yes, Sirena, Willow, and Jasmine Hale. They come from a very old New England family, going back to before the trials. Their ancestor was the one and only Reverend John Hale."

"John Hale?" Ember asked, her interest piqued.

"Dreadful man when he was alive, and of course a main figure in the witch trials. His fascination with witches, I believe, began when he was just a child." Lydia read from the book. "When he was very young, he witnessed the execution of Margaret Jones back in 1648, and I think it affected him as an adult."

"Wait, 1648? I thought the only witch trials in this country happened here in Salem in 1692?" Ember asked, interrupting Lydia.

"Unfortunately, dear, you will learn our kind has been persecuted for centuries, not only in the old world but here in the new. Margaret was the first, but many after her went to the noose for accusations of witchcraft. Now, Hale himself interrogated and most likely witnessed horrible torture inflicted on innocent people during the trials here in Salem. He wrote a book, but it wasn't published until after his death, 'A Modest Inquiry into the Nature of Witchcraft'. He tried to explain away the atrocities to impaired judgment by demonic influences. Seems he had some regret in what he took part in, or maybe because his own wife was accused; either way, something made him change his tune." Lydia scoffed. "Didn't do much to help his reputation, or at least in the eyes of some."

Ember sat on the floor and leaned against a few big pillows, petting Shadow's small head as Lydia continued her story.

"His family had spread out all over the colony after his death; some went south while others west in search of a new life, but the memories of the trials never faded. Some of his descendants stayed here, of course, and some fell on hard times, especially after the great fire of 1914. Now, I don't know what happened after those years after the fire, but whatever they were doing brought them some success, and they built that big Federal style house on Chestnut Street. Now, the house fell into disrepair after a horrible fire, until the sisters restored it."

"Have they lived in Salem their whole lives?" Ember asked as Shadow grew impatient being in her bag and hopped over to sit on Ember's shoulder.

"So, that's where the story becomes, well, a bit clouded. No one remembers when the Hale sisters or their family came to town, or if they ever left."

"What do you mean, Lydia? No one remembers them?"

"We know they are descendants of Reverend Hale, and we know that part of their family has always been here, but no one can recall exactly when the sisters came to be. It was like one day, there they all were. They kept to themselves at first, rarely making any public appearance. Then, a few years ago, they began throwing these lavish, extravagant parties, inviting all the socialites they could, until they became part of the town's elite, if not the elite," Lydia said as she closed the book and placed it back on the shelf. "What's even stranger are the rumors about the sisters, mostly Sirena."

"Rumors, what kind of rumors?" Ember stood and made her way over to the desk where Lydia was standing.

"Well, I'm not one for small town gossip, but there are stories about people going into that house and never being seen again, particularly young girls. Strange noises are being heard at all hours of the night, not to mention how peculiar the sisters appear, almost like statues. Then, of course, what happened to Sirena," Lydia said as her voice trailed off.

"What happened to Sirena?" Ember asked curiously.

"Well, again, it's just rumors... I myself am not sure of exactly what happened, but as the story goes, when Sirena was quite young, she was being courted by a very handsome, rich man from Boston. They were set to be married. Everything was going to plan until the night before the wedding. There was a fire in the big house on Chestnut. No one knows how it started, but Sirena's entire family was killed, including her fiancé. Only Sirena and her sisters survived the flames; they say the sisters were badly burned. As Lydia spoke, Ember's face filled with horror at the thought of not only losing your entire family and the man you loved, but to also be burned. She felt terrible for Sirena and her family.

"That's so horrible," Ember said under her breath. "But wait, I saw Sirena. I didn't see any scars on her or her sisters; her skin was perfect."

"Yes, it certainly is," Lydia continued, "that's part of the mystery surrounding her and her family. After the fire, no one saw the sisters. It was like they became recluses in the old burned-out house. People would claim they saw a horribly disfigured girl standing in the windows of the old house. Others say she used the family fortune to hire the best team of surgeons in the county, but no one knows for sure. What we do know is that suddenly the mansion was repaired, and Sirena and her sisters made their appearance looking like they do now."

"Those are just rumors, right? I mean, you don't believe them. I know what it's like to have people spread untrue things about you just because you are a little different or because you've been through a lot in life." Ember looked down, her fingers twirling a piece of hair. Lydia looked closely at her young friend. "You met them. Spoke to them. What do your instincts tell you?"

Ember thought for a moment. Her time with Thomas had temporarily clouded her meeting with Sirena and her sisters. She searched her memory for every detail of their encounter. She did recall feeling very uneasy at first. Sirena's long hair and the way her voice went up and down when she spoke, almost like music. Her glowing skin was so smooth and cool to the touch.

"To be honest, I did feel uncomfortable around them," Ember confessed as Lydia moved around the desk.

"Uncomfortable how?" Lydia asked. "Try to go back to last night, put yourself back in that moment."

Ember closed her eyes and tried to remember every detail of her short time with the Hale sisters.

"They were all very beautiful and dressed flawlessly. Their skin was smooth and cool, almost like marble, and they had almost a musical quality to their voices when they spoke. They moved very gracefully, like they were floating."

"Go on, what else?" Lydia listened to every word Ember said.

"They took me to another room. Everything was red. The walls, floors, even the furniture." Ember continued, "They were almost too nice. They spoke to me as if they already knew me." Ember tried to remember more, but her thoughts quickly went to Thomas. With a sigh, she opened her eyes. "That's it, that's all I can remember."

"I see. Seems there's something clouding your sight a bit," Lydia said with a warm smile. "It's all right, my dear. New love is always exciting, but it's important not to lose your head. "

Ember smiled back at Lydia. She knew she couldn't keep secrets from her perceptive friend.

"Lydia, do you know why the Hale sisters would have a

connection to the sea, or to mermaids?" The question caught Lydia off guard. "Mermaids? Well, let me see." She took her glasses off and looked up in the distance as she searched her thoughts. "I suppose it could be because their family is from Salem, and the maritime history is so rich here. Mermaids are a part of that lore. Why do you ask?"

Ember didn't want to tell her friend about the note she had received earlier that morning. She lowered her eyes so as not to give anything away. She knew it was silly to keep the note from her, but something told Ember that Lydia wouldn't love the idea of her spending the afternoon with the Hale sisters, so she kept it to herself. She hated keeping secrets from her friend, especially since Lydia had been so kind to her. She promised herself she would tell her after she went.

The rest of the day went by fast, Halloween visitors still flocking to the store for tarot readings and souvenirs. Ember glanced up at the clock on the wall and noticed it was getting close to three, so she began to gather her things. She looked over at Shadow, napping on the top of the bookshelf, and for a split second, she had a feeling she should leave him behind, but that thought quickly disappeared.

"Lydia, I'm going to head out. I have some errands to run," Ember called out as she motioned for Shadow to climb in her bag. "I'll see you tomorrow." She made her way out the door before Lydia had a chance to ask her where she was going.

Lydia stood at the front of the store and watched as Ember hurried out, Shadow in her bag. She knew where Ember was going; she didn't need to be a witch to know the girl was hiding something from her. She was worried, but Ember had to do this on her own, for now anyway.

CHAPTER 14

SALEM, MASSACHUSETTS 1914

Sirena had never felt this excited for anything in her life. She had been so happy the last few weeks, and she couldn't believe that in just one more day she would be marrying the man of her dreams. William Warrington was handsome, educated, and came from one of the richest families in New England. As she looked at herself in the mirror, Sirena couldn't believe that he had taken such an interest in her. She tried to smooth down her dark curly hair; she hated how unruly her hair could be. She longed to have straight hair like her sister Willow. So, she did her best to make it as straight as possible. William preferred it that way, straight and long, and she wanted to please him. She was slender and tall, with a long neck and high cheekbones. Her eyes were dark brown, and she liked to rim them with black coal, even though William didn't care for makeup. Her skin was a deep bronze that tanned easily in the sun. She looked nothing like her sisters, which always made her feel uncomfortable and often the target of cruel jokes from other children in her younger years.

She had always been jealous of her two younger sisters,

not only for their looks but also for the attention given to them by their parents. Sirena was always treated differently by both her mother and her father. She had done everything she could to please her parents growing up, getting top marks in all her home school courses, reading every book in their family library, and always making sure she looked neat and put together, but she barely got any acknowledgement compared to her sisters. It wasn't until William came to the house wanting to visit with Sirena that her parents started to look at her with approving eyes.

The Hale family had fallen on hard times over the years. The aging house and grounds crumbled around them. The family kept to themselves, hiding behind the tall brick walls of the manor estate. Sirena knew the match between her and the Warrington boy would bring a new influx of funds to their family, which is why her parents were so enthusiastic about the union. But Sirena didn't mind, for once in her life, she felt special.

She finished dressing and made her way down the spiral staircase to the ground floor. She happily passed the workers hanging large garlands filled with white and pink roses on the wooden banisters and smiled as she walked into the parlor to see William standing by the front windows. Jasmine was sitting in her usual place by the window, her nose in a book. She barely looked up from her reading as Sirena entered the room.

"I'm so sorry to have kept you waiting, William," Sirena said as she hurried into the room a bit flustered.

"I would have waited forever; you are a vision, my love," William said as he gave Sirena a quick kiss on the cheek.

Sirena tried to hide how nervous she was around William. He was tall, slim-built, and had intense grey eyes. His dark hair was always neatly groomed and styled, slicked back off his clean-shaven face. It had been a very quick engagement. Her parents insisted, so Sirena hadn't gotten the chance to really get to know the handsome man standing in front of her. But she was excited nonetheless.

"Thank you," Sirena said shyly. "Everything is being taken care of for tomorrow, and all the arrangements have been made."

"I can see that. I believe we have used every rose on the east coast for this grand affair," William said, his Bostonian accent noticeable. He reached for the gold table lighter and lit the cigarette in his hand.

"Do you think it's too much?" Sirena asked with a hint of embarrassment in her voice. She wanted everything to be perfect, but didn't want to come across as extravagant. Before William could answer, Willow walked into the parlor. Sirena turned to look at her with annoyance; she knew how selfish and sharp-tongued her sister could be, and she didn't want anything to disrupt the day.

"Sirena, do we really have to wear those hideous pink dresses tomorrow?" Willow said with a whining tone, tossing her long blonde hair over her shoulder.

"If you don't wear them, you can't be a bridesmaid, Willow," Sirena replied, trying to make light of the uncomfortable situation.

"I think the dresses are pretty," Jasmine said to her older sister with a kind smile.

"You would, you have terrible taste in clothes," Willow said in a mocking tone as she hit the book out of Jasmine's hands. She laughed as it tumbled out of her hands and hit the floor with a loud thud.

Jasmine was the youngest of the three and had a quiet, passive way about her, preferring the company of books over people. She was kind and considerate, unlike their middle sister, who always had a snarky comment and made bullying Jasmine a hobby. But Sirena wasn't going to let Willow make any trouble today. She turned to pick up the book off the floor and thanked Jasmine for being sweet to her about the dress choice. She looked back over at William. He still stood at the window, but his gaze was fixed on something across the room, past her. Sirena's eyes followed his gaze to her blonde sister, who was also staring at William, a mischievous grin on her face.

Sirena stood there for what seemed like forever, as her fiancé and her sister looked at each other in a way that made her stomach drop.

The tense moment was interrupted by the wedding planner and Sirena's mother coming into the parlor and pushing the two girls out. Sirena walked closer to William as he exhaled the last of his cigarette. "Is everything all right?" She asked. "Is there something I should know?"

"Everything is wonderful. Why would you ask?" William said as he put out his cigarette butt in a nearby ashtray.

"No reason," Sirena said, trying to hide the worry in her voice.

"Wonderful, then I'll see you tomorrow." William gave her a small kiss on the cheek.

"You are leaving so soon?" Sirena asked, trying to hide her disappointment.

"I'm sure you have lots to do. Wouldn't want to keep you from it," William said over his shoulder as he stepped out of the parlor and into the hallway.

Sirena stood at the window, a lump in her throat, and watched as he walked down the street.

She convinced herself that it was just her imagination, he had chosen her, he was in love with her, and there was nothing going on between him and her sister. Willow was known for being difficult, but she would never betray Sirena like that. It was all in her head.

Sirena lay staring at the ceiling of her bedroom. She had

tossed and turned for hours, the picture of William and Willow looking at each other burned into her memory. She tried talking to her sister after dinner, but Willow had locked herself in her room with claims of a headache. She was sure it was nothing, but something about the look in their eyes worried her.

She turned and pulled the covers up over her head. Just then, she heard a noise coming from the floor above her. She sat up in bed and tried to listen to see if she could make out where it was coming from.

Muffled voices and odd movements came from what seemed to be the attic. She threw her covers off and walked out of her bedroom. She softly tiptoed down the third-floor hallway where the attic door was. Sirena pressed her ear to the thick oak door but could hear nothing. She told herself she should just go back to bed, but something compelled her to turn the glass knob.

The pitch-black staircase leading to the attic came into view as she opened the door. The soft voices came drifting down from the darkness. She slowly made her way up the creaky stairs, holding her breath so she wouldn't make a sound until she made it to the top. She peered into the dark as she took slow footsteps, her bare feet leaving prints in the dust on the old wooden floors. She walked through a labyrinth of old furniture and paintings covered in cobwebs until she found the source of the strange noise.

Sirena crouched behind an old chest and stared in shock at the scene playing out before her eyes. Willow and her fiancé were on the dusty attic floor, a small candle lighting their entangled naked bodies. William was kissing the nape of Willow's neck as she threw her head back and gasped. Sirena felt tears welling in her eyes, as rage built inside of her, consuming her. She could barely contain it as she watched her beloved William make love to her sister. She couldn't stop the flood streaming down her face onto her white nightgown.

Sirena wanted to scream; she wanted to hit them both, to hurt them, to make them feel the pain she was feeling. She couldn't breathe, like the air had been punched out of her chest. She looked around her and saw a fire poker leaning against an old chest of drawers. She reached for it and wrapped her fingers around the cold iron. She picked it up without making a noise, as she stood up and looked down at the two lovers. They were so enthralled with each other that they didn't notice the crying Sirena standing over them. She stood there trying to calm herself, and just as she realized what she was about to do, she came to her senses. She couldn't hurt anyone, especially her sister, or the man she loved. Just as she was about to put the fire poker down, she heard William whispering in her sister's ear.

"I love you so much, Willow. I would do anything for you, anything. You are the only woman I could ever love."

All Sirena saw was black; her grip tightened around the poker as she raised it over her head and brought it down hard on the back of William's head. Warm, bright-red blood splattered over the floor and on her sister's naked body.

Willow's eyes opened wide as she saw her Sirena hitting William over and over until he was no longer moving, and her white night gown was stained crimson. It took Sirena a few moments to realize what she had done. She stood, shaking, blood dripping from her face and onto a puddle that had formed on the floor. She looked at the lifeless, crumpled body of her fiancé, dark blood pouring from the gash in his head, so dark it appeared black, and she began to cry uncontrollably. Willow looked at her with disbelief and anger. She covered herself with the robe she had carelessly tossed aside.

"What did you do?" Willow screamed, tears falling from her eyes. "You killed him! You killed William!" Willow was hysterical, frantically pacing around the room. "I'm going to tell! I am going to tell everyone what you did, you bitch!" Willow screamed as Sirena stood motionless, staring at William's corpse. "You have always been jealous of me, always! William never wanted you; he loved me! He had to marry you, mother and father needed him to, for the money, but he wanted me," Willow said to her as she moved closer. "They are going to lock you away forever; I'll make sure of it. I'll make sure you rot in the deepest darkest hole there is, and we will finally be rid of you like mother always wanted."

As the words left Willow's mouth, Sirena dropped the poker, and her hands wrapped around her sister's throat. She squeezed as Willow struggled to get away.

"I loved him! I loved you both! How could you?" Sirena said through the tears, as she squeezed her sister's throat tighter with each syllable. Willow clawed at her sister's hands. Her fingernails breaking as she dragged them across Sirena's skin, leaving long red scratches.

Sirena pushed Willow back as she kept a grip on her throat, back to the candle still burning on the floor. The hem of Willow's robe caught the flame of the candle, and within seconds, the whole bottom part was fully engulfed.

Sirena released her hands from her sister as the flames spread along the floorboards to the furniture and then to the walls. Willow screamed as the flames licked up her body. She reached out to her sister for help, but Sirena just stood there, silently watching as the flames surrounded them both.

CHAPTER 15

Ember's hands shook as she stood in front of the tall, intimidating iron gates. She was nervous and wasn't quite sure what to expect. She looked down and saw Shadow still nested in her bag.

"Shadow, I'm going to need you to look around for me. Stay close, but out of sight."

Shadow spread his wings and flew to the second-floor windowsill.

'Stay sharp, I'll call you if I need you.'- Ember said in her mind, knowing Shadow would hear her. She walked through the gates up the path to the Hale mansion. Ember reached for the large brass knocker and knocked three times before an older-looking man in a suit opened the door.

"Good afternoon, Miss Wildes. You are expected. Please come in," the man said, with a faint British accent, as he stepped aside and allowed Ember in.

"Thank you so much, Mister..." Ember asked as she walked through the door into the foyer.

"Locke, ma'am." Ember gave him a small nod and followed the tall man into the parlor.

"Miss Wildes, madam." He announced and gestured for Ember to sit on one of the ornate chairs that circled a marble table.

All three of the Hale sisters stood at the same time when Ember stepped in closer to them.

"We are so happy you chose to join us," Sirena said with a smile as she walked over to Ember and gave her a kiss on each of her cheeks. Sirena's skin was cool against hers, and Ember thought about the story Lydia had told her. Sirena was dressed in a flowing black kaftan made of silk with white flowers printed on one side. It was a stark contrast to the form-fitting gold dress she had worn to the party. Long silver chain necklaces completed the look.

"Thank you for your invitation. It was a pleasant surprise," Ember said. As Sirena pulled away, she could smell her strong perfume. It was a familiar fragrance, but Ember couldn't place it. Wet soil, patchouli, and something else she couldn't identify.

Ember turned to the two sisters. "It's wonderful to see you again as well." Both of them were also dressed in floral-printed sundresses.

Jasmine walked up to her excitedly with a huge smile and threw her arms around her. "Welcome, Ember. So happy you came."

"Lovely for you to join us," Willow said as she stood and smiled at Ember from across the table.

"Locke, we will take our tea now, thank you," Sirena said to the older man standing in the doorway.

"Very good, madam," he said as he turned and walked out of the parlor.

Sirena smiled at Ember, "We know it seems like everything is so formal, but sit please, make yourself at home," she said as they all took a seat. Ember noticed they all seemed to move in unison, like every moment was a part of a well-rehearsed dance.

"It's very lovely," Ember said as she smoothed out the front of her dress, suddenly very aware of her appearance.

"Yes, we love the grandeur of the way things were in times past, so we try to keep it alive here at the manor," Sirena said as she looked around the beautiful, decorated room with a sense of pride. Just at that very moment, Locke walked in carrying a silver tray with a porcelain teapot and matching cups and saucers. Two women dressed in black and white uniforms followed behind him, their arms filled with large platters of small sandwiches and an assortment of pastries.

The staff placed everything neatly on the table in front of them and quickly left the room. Sirena reached out for the teapot and poured the hot tea into the cup in front of Ember and then her own.

"This porcelain is beautiful," Ember said, feeling a bit awkward.

"Thank you. It's a family heirloom," Sirena said as she set the pot down gently. Ember noticed how Sirena continued to speak and didn't pour tea into her sister's cups.

"We didn't get a chance to talk to you as much as we would have liked at the party. So many people, you understand."

"Yes, of course. It was such a beautiful party," Ember said as she took a sip of tea. Sirena's eyes moved to Willow as she put four sugar cubes in her cup before pouring tea over them.

"Willow, where are our manners? One sugar cube is enough; we must watch our figures," Sirena said with a disapproving tone. Her silver eyes turned back to Ember as Willow scooped out the extra sugar cubes with a small spoon and placed them on a small napkin.

"Yes, we are so sorry, sister," she said with an uncomfortable smile.

"We are so happy you think so. It's one of the biggest parties we put on throughout the year, and we must confess it is one of our favorites." Sirena continued without missing a beat. "So, tell me, Ember, where are you from? What brings you to Salem?"

Ember put her cup down and took a deep breath. "Well, I'm originally from Connecticut, but I've always wanted to come here. After my mother passed, I decided it was a good time to start fresh in a new place," Ember explained as Sirena watched her closely. "My ancestors are from here, well, on my mother's side," Ember continued, "I'm related to Sarah Wildes, so I really wanted to come to Salem and connect with my roots."

"We have that in common, a connection to the trials. Although our family's history is less than desirable," Sirena said as she stirred her tea. "We've done so much to remove that black mark from our family's name, though sadly, there are still some who think poorly of us. But we are hopeful. We should not have to pay for the sins of our ancestors, don't you agree?"

"Yes, I absolutely do agree," Ember said with a sense of confidence.

"So, how are you liking our little town?"

"I love it here. I have a job I enjoy, at Pentagram, the magic shop. I love my apartment, and I've met some very nice people." Ember's thoughts went to Thomas, and she could feel her cheeks flush.

"Yes, we did see you getting very friendly with our town's lead detective," Sirena said as she stood and walked over to the window. "Have you known Detective Cole for long?"

"No. Well... we only recently met. Is he a friend of yours?" Ember asked, glancing over at Sirena.

"No, not particularly. As a matter of fact, we are very curious about how he got into the party in the first place. Our first thought was to have him removed, of course, for trespassing, but we saw how much fun you were having, so we let him stay," Sirena said as she looked out the window. "It seemed like he was quite taken with you, almost like he was here specifically for you, but how would he know that you were going to be here?" Sirena asked as she turned her silver eyes on Ember.

"Well, I had met him a few days before, and he did stop by the shop earlier that evening," Ember explained as she put her tea down on the table.

"Really, he doesn't seem like the type who would want his fortune read on Halloween night," Sirena scoffed.

"No, he came in to ask me some questions about a case he's been working."

"Ask you questions? Oh dear, it seems like the detective is even more lost than we all thought, "Sirena said, taking her place back on the couch. "It's been dreadful, the killing of those innocent girls. The town has been terrified, and it seems Detective Cole has fumbled the investigation from the beginning. Now he's asking questions in witchcraft stores? Seems to us as if he's trying to find a scapegoat," Sirena shook her head and looked over at her sisters, who had been sitting in silence. "It would be a shame if he tried to blame these horrible deaths on a member of the witchcraft community."

"A terrible shame," Willow said as she shook her head from side to side.

"We certainly don't need that kind of hysteria in this town, not again," Sirena added, as she picked up her teacup.

"No, never again," Jasmine said in the same even tone Willow had spoken.

"No, I don't think that's what he's doing at all," Ember

interrupted. "He was just asking." Ember let her voice trail off. Her gut feeling was to not say too much about what Thomas had shared with her that night. Sirena stared at her like she was waiting for Ember to finish her sentence.

"Asking what?" Sirena asked, breaking the awkward silence.

"Oh, just if I had ever seen one of the girls in the store before. I hadn't," Ember said quickly. "That was all he wanted to know."

"Well, like we said, he has done nothing but waste time on this case; meanwhile, women are being killed. You know, there are some who say he's more closely involved than just investigating, but those are just rumors."

"What do you mean, more closely involved?" Ember asked, her pulse quickening.

"Just whisperings among some. He's been the lead investigator since the killings started. He always seems to be close when the bodies are discovered, and then, of course, there's no progress; it just makes you wonder if he has anything to do with it."

Ember shook her head. "No, that's not possible. I've spent time with him, and he's a very kind and honest man."

"Of course he is," Sirena cackled. "We are so sorry, Ember. We didn't mean to upset you." Sirena said as she reached out and put her hand over hers. "But, on the other hand, how did he know you were here, at the party last night? You don't think he followed you here, do you? It would be a terrible thing if you were involved in some sort of scandal, especially with you being so new in town."

Ember stared at the tea in her hand; she hadn't given much thought to how Thomas suddenly appeared at the party. She was so swept away by him. "I don't know. I don't think so."

"No, you are right, it was probably just a happy coincidence," Sirena said with a smile. "Would you like to take the air out in the gardens? It's a beautiful evening."

Ember was surprised at Sirena's ability to change the subject so easily. "Yes, I would love to." Ember stood and followed Sirena out the glass doors at the back of the parlor that led to a spacious, lush backyard garden. She walked down the stone steps through the maze of manicured bushes, Willow and Jasmine walking closely behind.

Sirena took Ember's arm in hers and led her down the pathway that cut through the garden. It was past dusk, the last bit of sunlight lighting up the coming night with shades of deep pink and purple. The October chill had passed, and the winter air was upon them. They walked in silence for a while, under the bare trees.

"In the spring, this garden blooms with all sorts of bright colors, but this time of year holds its own magic. Some see it as a time of death, but we believe death is its own beauty," Sirena said as she looked up at the stars just starting to appear.

They walked together to the end of the pebble path to a white gazebo in the center of the property. Gas-powered lanterns lit the darkness around them.

"It's so beautiful here," Ember said as she looked at the gazebo, its white ivy-covered archways standing out from the bare trees and dry leaves.

"We are so happy you think so, Ember, truly. We want you to feel at home here," Sirena said as she held Ember's hand in hers. "We all do." She gestured to her sisters to get closer. "Truth be told, we don't have many friends. Yes, we throw big parties, but we feel close to very few. We have been misunderstood for so long. It's nice to meet someone who won't judge us."

Ember was touched by Sirena's kindness. She couldn't believe people would spread ugly rumors about the sisters.

'They might be somewhat eccentric,' she thought to herself, 'but not anything like the stories Lydia had told me.'

Just as Ember was about to thank Sirena and her sisters for their hospitality, Shadow swooped down from his hiding place and landed on the gazebo next to them with a loud squawk.

Sirena quickly let go of Ember's hands and ran to stand between her sisters. She looked at Shadow with wide eyes and what appeared to be fear in her expression. She clung to both her sisters tightly as all began to back away from Ember.

"No, it's ok, don't be afraid. I know he's rather large for a crow, but that's Shadow," Ember said, trying to calm the sisters down. "He's perfectly friendly, I promise."

"That bird belongs to you?" Willow asked, the fear building in her voice, her silver eyes shining.

"Shadow doesn't belong to me, he's my friend," Ember explained as she extended her arm, a sign for Shadow to come to her.

The three sisters moved back even further when Shadow took his place on Ember's shoulder. "I know it seems odd, but like I said, he's very friendly."

Sirena gathered her composure and moved closer to Ember, away from her sisters. "We are sure he is very friendly. He just startled us." She looked back at her sisters, and then at Ember. "We are so sorry, we must cut our visit short. Silly thing, really. We forgot a prior engagement. Locke will see you out," Sirena said with a tight smile. "We will get together soon."

And with that, all three sisters disappeared into the garden. Ember stood next to the gazebo and felt confused at how the sisters reacted to Shadow.

"What was that all about, boy?" Ember whispered to her crow.

Shadow looked at his mistress and shook his feathers. At that moment, Locke appeared walking down the path.

"I will show you out, ma'am."

Ember followed to an open gate that led out to the street behind the house. "Please tell Sirena and her sisters, thank you from me. I didn't get a chance to," she said as she walked through the gate.

"Of course. Have a good evening, Miss." He closed the gate and walked back through the garden.

Ember stood there for a moment and tried to make sense of the sisters' reaction to Shadow. She looked up at the dark windows at the back of the house. Everything was so quiet and still. She placed Shadow in her bag and began her walk home.

Sirena watched Ember from a small window on the third floor. Her breath fogged up the cold windowpane in front of her.

Sirena heard her sisters walk up behind her.

"That was going so well," Willow said softly in Sirena's ear.

"It was, but it seems we have more than one complication," she said as she turned to face her sisters.

"We are running out of time, and we don't need any more problems," she hissed at them. "Jasmine, find out more about that detective, all you can. Find out how much he knows. Willow, find out if that mangey bird is her seer. If he is, don't hurt it, just bring it to me."

"Yes, sister," Willow and Jasmine said in unison and walked out of the room.

Sirena turned from the window and walked over to a large mirror on the wall. She touched her perfect skin. "Time is the one thing we don't have."

CHAPTER 16

Even though Thomas hadn't slept the night before, he wasn't tired. After stopping at his loft for a quick shower, a shave, and coffee, he was back at his office before anyone else had come in. He always enjoyed the quiet mornings so he could think.

Memories of the previous night came back to him in flashes: holding Ember as they danced, the smell of her skin, the softness of her lips. He had never felt so strongly for a woman in his life. Everything about her excited him, not to mention the way she made him feel like the man he knew he was. He couldn't wait until their next meeting, but for now he had to get back to his work.

He had a small lead, but it was somewhere to start. One by one, he went back over all the victims' files, combing through their backgrounds, reading statements given by their friends and families. He searched town records and databases to trace back some of the victims' ancestry.

He knew they all had one thing in common: they either practiced witchcraft or were descendants of people involved in the trials. But it wasn't the only thread he found that connected them. All of them had been guests at one of the parties held at the Hale mansion. It was certain to him now. These women had not been killed at random; they were chosen. The reason why was what he needed to find, and by whom. When he did, he knew he would find the killer. He thought about the ghostly apparition of Claire that had appeared to him and shivered.

Thomas was so consumed with his work that he didn't notice Captain Torres standing in his office.

"Cole, I don't think I've seen you in the office this early in years. I assume you have something for me," Torres said in his usual irritated tone.

Thomas looked up, surprised by his captain hovering over his desk. "I actually do, Captain."

"Alright, let me hear it," Torres said with a sigh as he sat in one of the chairs in front of Thomas's desk. Captain Ivan Torres was a smaller man in his early forties with an athletic build and tan skin. His sharp features and keen dark eyes gave him a commanding presence. When he spoke, a slight accent indicated his Brazilian heritage.

"I found a connection; all our victims were involved with witchcraft in some way, or strangely enough, descendants of families involved in the trials," Thomas explained. "Also, it seems that they all attended some of the same social events. I'm thinking that's where our suspects found them."

"What evidence do you have that ties these women to witchcraft?' Torres asked, his interest piqued.

Thomas went over every new detail he had uncovered with his Captain, only leaving out the ghostly encounter that had given him the first clue. After Thomas finished, Torres sat back in his chair.

"Tom, you are a great detective, one of the best I have. I know this case has taken a toll on you. It's been difficult for the entire unit, but I have to ask you. Are you sure about this?

It's not that I don't trust your instincts, and your evidence is compelling, but this is Salem. So, before we start talking about how witches are being targeted in this town, make sure you are on the right track," Torres said, a worried look on his face. "I don't want to cause a hysteria, so let's keep this between us."

"Sure, Cap, I'll keep it under wraps," Thomas said with a sigh of relief. He hadn't been sure how his boss was going to react to his theories.

"Also, double check the autopsy reports. Make sure we aren't overlooking anything," Torres said as he got up and started toward the door.

"Will do."

"One more thing. You said suspects. Do you think we are looking for more than one person?" Torres asked as he paused in the doorway.

"At first, no, it goes against all patterns of a serial murderer; they usually work alone. It's rare to see this type of killer work with anyone, but from the injuries on the victims, I am not so sure."

"Ok, just keep me updated. I'll try to keep the brass and the Feds away for now," Torres said as he walked out of the office.

Thomas was relieved his boss still trusted his investigative instincts, even with all his struggles over the past year. This case had haunted him since it began. Now, he felt like he was close. His attention turned back to the files on his desk. He picked up a picture of one of the victims, Lila Miller, in one of her extravagant costumes, performing at one of the parties held at the Hale mansion. He knew his next stop had to be to go back there.

He had seen the sisters before, around town, and of course had heard all the rumors. He had always chalked it up to local gossip whispered in bars. But now he was very interested in having a talk with the sisters.

He threw on his coat and headed for the door. He was tired, but he didn't want to give up the momentum. He would just make a quick informal call on the Hale sisters. See if he could pick up on anything. His Captain's words ran through his head as he started his car. He had to keep this quiet. Being suspicious of a prominent family could backfire, so he must tread lightly.

He pulled up to the large home and sat in his car watching the softly lit windows. He didn't know what to expect or if the sisters would even speak to him. He knew the eldest was Sirena; he decided it would be best to just speak with her. He walked up the stone pathway, still decorated with bales of hay and carved pumpkins, and looked to the second-story window. A shadowy figure ducked quickly behind a curtain, hiding from view.

After a few moments, he knocked on the door, the sound echoing throughout the house. After a few minutes, an older, distinguished gentleman opened the door. Thomas recognized him as the same doorman he had snuck by the previous night. Thomas worried that he might be recognized, but there was no look of familiarity on the man's face.

"So sorry to bother you. My name is Detective Cole, Essex County Sheriff's Office. I was wondering if I could have a brief moment with Sirena Hale?" Thomas said as he reached into his pocket for his wallet to show his badge and identification.

"Madam Hale is unavailable for visitors at this moment, but if you leave a business card, I will make sure she receives it," the well-dressed man said as he looked at Thomas with disdain.

"I see. Well, if you can, tell her it's very important I speak with her. I'd rather do it here, more discreet. I wouldn't want to have her come to the office." Thomas said as he pulled a card from his wallet and handed it to the doorman.

"I will see to it right away," the man said as he closed the door.

As Thomas walked back down the path to his car, he turned to look back at the windows and saw the same curtain move slightly. He was certain that the sisters were home, but he was fine waiting. He would be back, and they couldn't hide forever.

* * *

WILLOW LOOKED out the window at the handsome detective walking up to the house. She hid behind the curtain quickly when she saw him look up to the second story. She wasn't sure if he had seen her. She ran to the landing and leaned over the stairway railing to hear what was said at the front door.

Jasmine came up behind her, "Who is here?" she asked softly.

"The police," Willow whispered back. "It's that delicious-looking detective."

"Why is he here?" Jasmine asked as she nervously played with her short hair.

"Probably looking for that messy girl and her bird," Willow sneered at Jasmine.

"We better tell Sirena anyway; we would want to know," Jasmine said as she turned away from her sister.

"Fine, we will tell her," Willow said as she rolled her eyes. She turned briskly and walked up the stairs to the third floor. She knocked softly on the door before entering the dimly lit room.

"Sister, we don't mean to disturb you, but that nosy police

man was at the door," Willow said as she approached Sirena, who was standing in front of a large mirror.

Sirena ignored her sister as she admired her reflection. Her slender body was only covered by a sheer white robe that showed her silhouette perfectly even in the candlelight. Willow walked up behind her sister and put her hand on Sirena's shoulder; Sirena glanced at her in the mirror for a moment before returning to her own image.

"He's smarter than we thought he was," Sirena said to her sister without taking her eyes off herself. "We are sure the girl is helping him, even though he might not even realize it. No matter; we will just have to hurry things up a bit. Now go and take care of what we asked you both to do. We can't let him get any closer to her."

"What if he comes back?" Willow asked in a monotone voice.

"If he does, then we will deal with him. We won't let him come between us and everything we have suffered for," Sirena said, her voice rising and echoing in the spacious room.

"We trust in our sister, always," Willow said as she turned and walked out of the room, slamming the door behind her.

Sirena took a deep breath and stared back into the mirror. She reached her hand out slowly and touched the glass with the tip of her finger. Instantly, the mirror began to move, like rippling waves in a pond. Where Sirena held her finger, a black spot formed, growing larger, spreading like oil on water until it turned the entire mirror black. Sirena stepped away as she watched the mirror move like ink, swirling around, making different forms and shapes, like fish swimming on the surface of water.

"Why have thou summoned us?" A haunting voice said from the black mirror. "Have you fulfilled your end of the bargain?"

"We have not, but we have given so much already. Isn't that enough?" Sirena asked, her voice trembling.

"No!" the voice said loudly, sounding like many voices speaking at once, shaking the entire room. "We have granted you all you wished for, beauty, riches, and most importantly, the life of thy sisters. We demand payment, or you must suffer our wrath."

"We understand, but the police..." Sirena said, a tear falling from her eye.

"The laws of man do not concern us," the voice said, interrupting Sirena's plea. "Bring us she who walks with Her, and you shall never have to bring us anymore souls. Thou wilt stay beautiful forever; that was the bargain, or return to thy true form, and face judgement."

The voice shifted into an image of a horribly disfigured Sirena, her face and body covered with burns. Her left eye was gone; only a black hollow socket was left. Her long curly hair had burned off completely on one side; only small stringy patches remained. At her feet were the burned and smoldering bodies of her sisters and the rest of her family staring up at her with lifeless eyes, wailing and screeching in pain. Behind her was the bloody image of her fiancé William, his face and head badly beaten. Sirena screamed and covered her ears. "No, please, no more! We will do what you asked, but please take it away," she pleaded.

The black mirror swirled, and the horrible image disappeared, as Sirena lowered her hands from the sides of her face. The black fluid molded itself into a hand that stretched out from the confines of the mirror, reaching out for Sirena. The hand ran down her body, feeling every part of her. Sirena stood motionless as the cold hand touched her.

"Yes, we have indeed made you beautiful, a bargain though hast entered in, forged in blood. Do not forget, they belong to us," the voice whispered as the hand retreated back into the mirror, turning it back to its crystal-clear reflection. Sirena once again saw her perfect face and body, and she breathed out a sigh of relief. She hated what she had become, but anything was better than looking like a hideous monster, alone in a house filled with ghosts.

She wiped the tears away and smiled, "So be it, if a monster we shall be, we will be the most beautiful one of all," she said to herself, as her hair began moving as if alive, coiling around her face and neck, stroking her bare breasts, and her arms and down her back.

"A beautiful monster, forever."

CHAPTER 17

SALEM, MASSACHUSETTS 1914

Sirena's eyes widened as she saw the flames spread quickly from the floorboards to the walls and the curtains. Over the roar of the fire, Willow's screams of pain rose as the flames consumed her body. Willow desperately reached out to Sirena for help, but all she could do was stand and watch the horror unfold in front of her.

The attic had begun to fill with thick, black smoke that burned Sirena's eyes and throat, choking the breath out of her. She covered her mouth and nose with her nightgown and ran towards the stairs that led out of the attic. She looked back and saw her sister's crumpled body on the floor next to her dead fiancé. She hesitated for a split second, thinking she should try to go back and save her sister, but she knew in her heart that Willow was dead and there was nothing she could do.

Sirena ran down the stairs to the third floor. The ceiling was already caving in and falling, burning the dry wood planks as they began to fall all around her. One thought raced through her mind; she had to get to Jasmine's room on the second floor. The entire main stairwell was choked with black smoke, and Sirena struggled to make it down the stairs and find her sister's bedroom door. She was crawling on her hands and knees, trying to stay as low as possible away from the thick smoke. She finally made it to Jasmine's door and banged on it as hard as she could. She tried to scream, but the smoke choked her. The bedroom door finally opened, filling Jasmine's room with hot smoke, forcing her to the ground next to her sister.

"Sirena!" Jasmine screamed, "Is the entire house on fire? Where is Willow? We must get Mother and Father and get out of here!"

"There's no time. We need to leave before the house falls down around us!" Sirena screamed back as she grabbed onto her sister and began to pull her to the stairwell.

"No, I'm not leaving without them!" Jasmine said as she pulled back and started down the hallway in the opposite direction.

"Jasmine! No! Come back!" Sirena screamed as she saw her sister disappear in the smoke-filled hall. She could already see flames above her head, rolling across the ceiling like waves of fire, spreading over the doorframes and blocking her off from the direction her sister had gone. She knew there was no way she would be able to save her; she had made her choice. So, Sirena crawled back towards the stairs and tried to make her way to the first floor.

She tried to look down the long hallway to her parents' room, but it was too far. She knew she wouldn't be able to make it with the smoke and burning beams falling around her. How could she explain to her parents what she had done: killed her fiancé and let her sister burn to death? How would they ever forgive her? How would she ever forgive herself?

Hot tears marred her soot-stained face, and her lungs burned. She could feel the intense heat coming from the floors above her, and she knew it was her last chance to get out alive. So, she ran down to the first floor, as fast as she could. She could see the front door ahead of her. She was so close. She had a little bit more to go, and she would be out of the inferno. Just then, she heard wood splitting. Her eyes looked above her, and before she could move out of the way, a large beam came crashing down, knocking her to the ground and pinning her to the stairs. Sirena screamed as flames licked her face and body. She couldn't move under the weight of the beam, and there was nothing she could do but accept her fate. So, she closed her eyes and waited for death to take her.

The last thing she remembered before letting the darkness fall over her was the front door being knocked down by firemen.

* * *

Sirena woke and slowly opened her eyes. Her vision was blurry, and it took her a few seconds to realize she was lying in a hospital bed. She tried to move but was overwhelmed by excruciating pain all over her body. She tried to call for help, but her voice was just a low raspy whisper. Sirena looked around desperately for anyone to help her as a nurse in white scrubs and a paper facemask came into the room.

"It's ok, you are safe now," the nurse said as she checked all the glass bottles of fluid connected to Sirena's arm.

"What happened? Where am I?" Sirena asked as she became more aware of her new surroundings.

"You are in the hospital, dear," the nurse said with a reassuring voice.

"Hospital?" Sirena repeated, the pain becoming too unbearable, "I am burned?"

As the words left her lips, the memories came flooding

back. William and Willow making love on the attic floor, the fire poker in her hand, the feeling of blood splattering across her face. How blinded by rage she had become; she didn't even notice she had her hands around Willow's neck. Then the flames, the fire, the choking black smoke.

"My family, my sisters; where are they?"

The nurse looked down at Sirena, "I'm so sorry to be the one to tell you, sweetie, but they didn't find them."

Sirena reached up to touch her face and felt the rough, raw, open sores and a bandage on her left eye. "I want to see my face! Let me see!" Sirena screamed hysterically.

She tried to get out of bed despite the pain. The nurse pulled a string on the wall behind the bed that rang a bell. A team of nurses came running into the room. They tied Sirena's hands to the bed rails with soft restraints, as one of them pushed a syringe into the IV in her arm.

"There, this will make you feel better," Sirena heard one of the nurses say before she fell into a dreamless sleep.

CHAPTER 18

Shadow glided through the cold evening air, stretching his wings wide, letting the wind carry him over the treetops and pitched roofs of Salem. He flapped his wings to change direction and dipped to land on the fence in front of his mistress's home. His attention was on the front door of the apartment as Chloe walked out onto the street. Her bright, colorful outfit stood in stark contrast with the gloomy November day. She gave a quick glance in Shadow's direction and turned down Washington Square.

Shadow opened his wings and followed Chloe as she made her way down the cobblestone streets. He perched on a tree branch and watched her walk into a small restaurant and take a seat at a table by the window. He hopped over to the windowsill to get a closer look and saw that the table she sat at already had three other people seated, although their backs were to the window. Shadow inched closer to see who Chloe was chatting so happily with, waiting for one of the unknown guests to turn so he could make out a face and imprint it in his mind.

Just as he was about to get a look, a passerby shooed him

away from the window. Shadow squawked in disapproval and immediately took flight back to Ember's.

* * *

EMBER LOOKED at her cell and saw there were no messages or missed calls. She hadn't heard from Thomas all day, and she was feeling a bit uneasy. She bit her fingernail and thought about what Sirena had said about Thomas during tea. The comments had taken Ember by surprise. She would never have thought Thomas would be involved in any of those women's deaths. He didn't seem like the type that would hurt anyone. She never once felt an ounce of violence from him, although she did sense darkness in him.

Her thoughts drifted to the vision of Thomas in the dark water as she played with her necklace. She had allowed Sirena's words to cloud her feelings, her instincts. Something about the sound of her voice, something Ember couldn't quite place.

She glanced at her phone again and thought about her friend Tristan. She hadn't spoken to him much since she had moved away. He always had a way of making her feel better. She thought about calling him, but she decided against it. Her thoughts and feelings were a bit too scattered to hold a conversation.

Just as she put her phone down, she heard a familiar tapping at the window. She ran to the kitchen to let Shadow in.

"Where have you been?" she asked her friend as he hopped inside her warm apartment.

"It's cold out there. I was getting worried," Ember said as she rubbed Shadow's head. He didn't respond with his usual squawk but instead stared at her with his dark eyes.

"Is something wrong?" she asked as she picked him up in her hand and brought him closer to her face.

Ember looked deep into his eyes, and suddenly her sight disappeared. She was in a tunnel with darkness all around except a circle of light in the distance, like she was looking through a tube. The small circle became larger, and she realized she was seeing through Shadow's eyes. She could see perfectly everything he had seen earlier, which he was giving to her as an answer.

The trees and roofs passed under her as she flew over the city. She saw Chloe come out of her apartment and walk down the street and into the restaurant. Ember could see her friend sitting at a table, talking in her usual cheerful self to three other people with her, but she couldn't see who it was. Suddenly, she was jolted out of the vision as someone scared Shadow off the windowsill. She was back in her apartment, seeing through her own eyes again.

Ember blinked her eyes and tried to adjust her vision. Vertigo hit her hard, making her have to put Shadow on the kitchen counter to steady herself.

"You wanted me to see that. Why?" she asked Shadow as he hopped closer to her, tilting his head from side to side.

"Why Chloe? Is she alright?" As the words left her lips, a feeling of dread washed over her. She felt it deep in her gut. Chloe was in danger.

She ran back into the living room and reached for her phone. She heard the phone ring until Chloe's voicemail picked up. She called again, but Chloe still did not answer. Ember's hands shook as she held the phone. She wanted to call Thomas, but decided against it. She wasn't sure if she should tell him.

She would find Chloe herself, so she grabbed her coat and called to Shadow, "I have a terrible feeling, Shadow, and I know you feel it, too. We have to find her." She ran out the front door, Shadow flying overhead. She knew exactly what direction to go, remembering what she had seen. It was dark now, but Ember's sight was enhanced like never before, like her crow's vision had merged with her own, making her eyesight sharp and able to see in the darkness. She came to a stop at the small restaurant she had seen in her vision. She looked in the same window where Shadow had seen Chloe, but she was not there. Ember went inside and approached the young girl at the hostess desk.

"Excuse me, I'm looking for my friend. She was here earlier; she sat over there." Ember pointed to the now-empty table. "Brunette. She was sitting with three other people."

The pretty young hostess looked up and said, "Oh, yes, Hale, party of four. They left a while ago."

"Hale? She was with Sirena and her sisters?" Ember asked with surprise.

Yes, I've never met them myself. I mean, they have never come in during my shift. They are so much more glamorous in person."

"Did they leave together?" Ember asked, beginning to feel impatient at the young girl's gushing.

"Yes, they did," the hostess responded.

Ember could hear the hostess ask something as she rushed back out the door, but she didn't stop to listen. She ran into the street and looked for Shadow, who she found sitting in the tree, waiting for her. Ember looked into his eyes, and without saying a word, she said to him, 'Go to the Hale mansion, see if Chloe is there. I'm going to find Thomas,'

Shadow flapped his wings and nodded his head in agreement. 'Be careful, and be the Shadow you are, my friend.'

With that, Shadow took flight into the night sky. Ember watched him as he disappeared through the trees. She checked her cell phone. No calls or messages. She put the phone back in her bag and headed the opposite way, down the street in the direction of the Sheriff's office, hoping Thomas would be there.

* * *

THOMAS SAT BEHIND HIS DESK, the glow of his laptop the only light in the room. He typed Sirena's name into their database. He scrolled down to see what he could find under her name. He knew it was a long shot, but he had a strange feeling about the Hale sisters that he couldn't shake.

He had heard the rumors circulating in town about the sisters, but he never paid much attention. All small towns had gossip, especially about the super wealthy, although he had seen the sisters around, and they did appear a bit odd.

He searched through the database but came up with nothing. No arrests, no driver's licenses, nothing. Same with the other two sisters. He couldn't even find birth or school records. He logged off the department's site and typed 'Hale family Salem' into the search bar. In an instant, dozens of news articles popped up across his screen, some going back decades, mostly articles that mentioned tragedies that had plagued the family throughout the years. Deaths, disappearances, bankruptcies, and the fire that had almost destroyed the house completely.

Thomas scrolled down and continued to read the article, but there was no mention of how the fire started, only that all inside had been killed. He read the family's names. "That can't be right," he asked out loud as he saw the names listed. Sirena, Willow, and Jasmine Hale, along with their parents, some staff, and Sirena's fiancé. He rubbed his tired eyes and leaned back in his chair. The fire that destroyed the house and almost all of Salem was back in 1914. 'It can't be the same sisters,' he thought. Maybe a coincidence, the same name.

He did think it was strange that the sisters had no current records he could find, but with rich people, that wasn't necessarily unheard of. It wasn't a surprise they would want to keep to themselves and handle their personal affairs privately. Thomas sat up in his chair and turned his attention back to his computer. The sisters were descendants of John Hale. He had been a very influential figure in the witch trials.

He went through page after page, describing Hale's involvement in some of the examinations and interrogations of the accused, up until his own wife, Sarah, was accused by one of the afflicted girls, although she was never charged or arrested. She died soon after the trials, and Hale began writing his book, published after his death, where he suggested the court's judgement was influenced by fear of witchcraft and not by the devil, which had led to the deaths of innocent people.

So, the sisters also had a connection to the trials. He couldn't ignore that fact. This had been the one connection he had been able to find in this case. He really needed to speak to them now, no more dodging and hiding behind windows. As he got up to leave, he heard a knock on his door.

CHAPTER 19

The knock took Thomas by surprise. He wasn't expecting anyone, not at this hour. His thoughts went to Ember; he had not called or stopped by to see her like he had promised, so maybe it was her.

He smiled as he unlocked and opened the door, expecting to see her beautiful face. But instead of Ember in his doorway, a tall pale girl with short brown hair stood, dressed in a sheer tight-fitting pink dress that left very little to the imagination.

"Oh hello, can I help you?" Thomas asked, surprised by the unknown beautiful visitor.

"We are sure you can help," the woman said in a high-pitched but sensual voice. "Jasmine Hale, you came to our house asking for our sister." She breezed by Thomas and took a seat in front of his desk.

"I see. Well, it's a pleasure to meet you, Jasmine. I'm Detective Thomas Cole. Please make yourself at home," Thomas said with a hint of sarcasm as he sat back down in his chair. "I was just leaving to pay your sister another visit."

Thomas closed his laptop so she wouldn't see what he had been working on.

"Well, isn't this just perfect timing then?" Jasmine said as she shifted in the seat and crossed her long legs, the slit of the pink dress sliding open to show her thigh.

Thomas tried to focus on her face and not the smooth, silky skin of her shapely legs.

"I'm curious, Jasmine, why did you come to see me and not your sister, Sirena?" Thomas asked as his eyes moved up her lean body.

"We are terribly busy, you know, so we decided to call on you," Jasmine said as she played with one of the short curls that framed her face.

"Is that right?" Thomas asked, amused by her peculiar way of speaking. "Well, Miss Hale, I had a few questions about a case I've been working on. I'm sure you have read about it or seen it on the news. The murdered women."

"Oh, yes, of course, so dreadful, and please call me Jasmine," she responded as she focused her silver eyes on Thomas.

"Yes. So, tell me, Jasmine. Did you know any of these women?" Thomas said as he pulled out pictures of each of his victims and set them down in front of Jasmine. She leaned forward and glanced quickly at each one. "No, they don't look familiar to us."

"Not at all? Please take your time."

"No, so sorry, we've never seen any of them," Jasmine said with a smile as she leaned back in her seat.

"You never have? Well, Jasmine, the thing is, I never ask a question I don't already know the answer to. So, you want to look again? Because what's interesting is they all attended events at your home," Thomas laid down several more pictures of the victims who had been at different parties at the Hale mansion. "You mean to tell me you never saw any of them."

"Detective, we host so many parties and events at the manor. Too many to count. So many guests attend, it would be impossible to remember everyone," Jasmine said, the same coy smile on her face.

"I understand the guest list is quite exclusive, chosen by you and your sisters, I assume?"

"Yes, very exclusive. We've even heard of some sneaking in without an invitation, so you can imagine how difficult it could be to keep track of everyone," Jasmine said, pulling her skirt up just a bit more.

"I can see how that could happen from time to time," Thomas said as he shuffled some papers on his desk in an effort to not look at Jasmine's legs.

"Tell us, Detective, do you think one of our guests could be responsible for hurting these poor women? Someone who snuck in without our knowledge, perhaps? Someone who might have followed them there or maybe followed them home?" Jasmine asked, her bright silver eyes narrowing slightly.

"It's possible, as anything is possible. I am not discounting anything or anyone." Thomas replied, understanding the message Jasmine was sending.

She knew he had been to the manor on Halloween night. It was clear to him this was a veiled threat. Now there was no doubt in his mind that he was on the right track. The Hale sisters were somehow involved in these murders or covering for the people who were. Thomas just needed to find out how and why. But he needed to tread carefully; the sisters had acquired many powerful friends over the years. One word from Sirena to the right person could be a career ender. So, before he told anyone about his suspicion, he had to be sure.

"Of course, you won't," Jasmine said as she stood from the chair."We trust you will bring the perpetrators to justice."

"I would still like to speak to Sirena," Thomas said as he also rose from his seat. "I can stop by your home at your convenience, of course."

"Of course," Jasmine said as she walked around the desk. "We would love to get to know you better." Her sweet, high voice suddenly lowered in tone, almost like a whisper, but still loud enough to hear, as it floated in the air, like bells ringing in the distance. Thomas felt almost hypnotized by the sound of her voice. Suddenly, he found he could think of little else, just her voice, as it enveloped him.

"Look at you, not even trying to fight it," Jasmine laughed as she ran her finger down Thomas's jawline to his neck. "You want to love, don't you? We once wanted to love someone as well, like you perhaps. So beautiful, but that never happened, sadly. In moments like this, we dream of what love would have been like, so dream with us," she said softly as her mouth brushed his neck. "Listen to our voice, and you will tell us everything."

Thomas felt compelled to answer. Her voice flooded his mind; he was hypnotized by it. It was the most beautiful sound he had ever heard.

Jasmine pulled his face closer to her and kissed his lips softly. "There, there, beautiful boy. Now you are ours."

"Yes, anything for you," Thomas heard himself say. The words escaped his lips involuntarily. He couldn't stop them, couldn't stop the desire that had overcome him.

Just at that moment, the items on Thomas's desk began to shake, and it seemed like the entire room trembled, breaking the eerie spell Jasmine had cast over him. He pulled her hand off his face and backed away. Jasmine, startled by the sudden movement, looked around the room to find the source of the interruption.

The temperature in the room had dropped dramatically; their breath was like small puffs of fog in the air. Then in a dark corner of the office, forming from shadow, a figure began to take shape, water running toward them across the floor. Jasmine's eyes widened as she saw the figure floating closer, reaching out to her, until she could make out a face.

"Lila!" Jasmine screamed as she turned and ran for the door. But a tendril of black smoke whipped out before she could make her escape, wrapping around her, keeping her from moving.

Thomas watched the apparition surround Jasmine. He looked at the ghostly face and immediately recognized who it was. Lila Miller, the third victim. He watched as the smoke formed what was once a beautiful girl, wearing a long flowing dress, like many of the dresses she had worn in life as a performer. He watched in horror as the beautiful face turned into a sunken, shriveled death mask.

Jasmine opened her mouth, as the terrifying figure got closer, letting out a high-pitched scream so loud Thomas covered his ears in fear his eardrums would burst. With a banshee-like scream, the dark figure curled and shrank back into the shadows with a wind that tossed papers all over the office. Thomas uncovered his ears and looked in the direction Lila's ghost had disappeared, only a puddle of water remaining. He turned to Jasmine, but she was nowhere to be found. She had also disappeared, leaving his office door open.

Thomas collapsed in his chair and tried to catch his breath. He put his head in his hands and wondered what he had gotten himself into.

CHAPTER 20

The rain fell hard in big drops as Ember ran down the streets to Thomas's office. Large sheets of water blinded her as thunder rumbled loudly in the distance. She was freezing, her hair and clothes soaked completely, but she had to get to Thomas. The worry for Chloe kept her moving despite the numbness in her fingers and toes. Just as she approached the large brick building, she saw a woman run out the back door. Even in the pouring rain, she could see that it was Jasmine Hale, her sheer pink dress wet and clinging to her as she ran across the flooded street to a nearby black car.

Ember stood and watched the car drive away from the building. 'Jasmine? What was she doing here?' Ember asked herself out loud.

She could feel the doubt stirring inside the pit of her stomach, turning into jealousy. She ran to the door and went inside. She was shaking by the time she reached Thomas's office, not sure if it was from the cold or the anger building inside her. She had trusted him, believed everything he had confessed to her that night in the cemetery. 'Was it all just lies?' she wondered.

She walked towards the open door, leaving wet footprints on the concrete floor. As she entered his office, she saw Thomas at his desk, his head in his hands. She stood there silently for a moment, just watching him.

"Thomas," she said softly as she took a small step in his direction. His head shot up to look at her.

"Ember," Thomas said with surprise as she stood to greet her. "How long have you been here?"

Ember stood motionless, trying to think of something to say. Her worry about Chloe was still in her mind, but the feeling of jealousy overtook it.

"Ember, come in, you are soaking wet," Thomas said, picking up a towel from a rack on the wall and throwing it over her shoulders.

"What are you doing here, in this weather?" Thomas hadn't realized until that moment that it was raining. "Is everything ok?"

"You didn't call. Or stop by. I was going to call, but… and Chloe," Ember's voice trailed off to a whisper.

"Chloe? Your friend. What about her?" Thomas asked as he tried to rub warmth into her arms and shoulders.

"Why was Jasmine here? I saw her leaving. Was she here to see you?" Ember said in a flat voice, her eyes fixed on him.

"Jasmine, yes, she was here to see me," Thomas began to explain.

"Oh, I see. I didn't know you two were involved. I would never…"

"Involved? Ember, you aren't making any sense. Yes, she came to see me. I had some questions for her sister, but for some reason Jasmine came instead. Nothing is going on between us. Why would you think that?" Thomas started as

Ember threw the towel from her shoulders and turned away from him.

"I just don't understand why she would be here, in your office. I came here for help. I'm sorry, but I didn't know where else to go. I can't find Chloe, then Shadow saw her with them, and now I don't know where she is. So, I came to find you, and I see her here..." Ember knew she was rambling and not making any sense, but she was over-whelmed by her own feelings. She tried to swallow the tears she could feel starting to build up in her throat.

"Wait, slow down. What about Chloe? What do you mean Shadow saw her?" Thomas held Ember by her shoulders and looked in her eyes. "Ember, look at me," Thomas said force-fully. "Tell me what the hell is going on. Help me understand, because whatever is happening, it looks like I'm a part of it. Let me in, let me help you, please."

Ember looked into his blue eyes and looked for the man who had kissed her under the full moon. She wanted to trust him, to believe him, but Sirena's words came back to her, and now Chloe was missing, and Jasmine had come running out of his office. What if Sirena was right? Did Thomas have something to do with those murdered women, and was he just using them? Ember closed her eyes before speaking. "Did you follow me to the party at the Hale mansion?"

Thomas sighed, "I did... but I didn't follow you, not exactly. Look, it's not like it sounds. I wanted to be with you, to be close to you."

"So you did," Ember said, opening her bright yellow eyes.

"Yes, I did. Look, you captivated me since the moment I saw you. I meant everything I said that night, Ember. I think I'm....I think I'm falling in love with you," Thomas pleaded with her.

Ember looked down at the rainwater dripping from her face onto the floor and shook her head. "In love with me?

Really? But you follow me around, and don't tell me. Then I see another woman in your office," Ember said, anger dripping from her voice.

"Ember, no! That's not what's going on at all," Thomas said as he held her arms tightly and pushed her up against the wall. "Ember, listen to me." Ember saw the anger flaring in his ice blue eyes, turning them a dark deep blue, his voice a deep growl. The forceful way he had pinned her against the wall drove fear through her.

"I can't!" Ember screamed as she broke Thomas's grip and ran out of the office, and out of the building into the storm outside. She ran through the rain, not knowing where she was going, the anger inside her confusing her thoughts. She searched through the raindrops for Shadow, but the rain was coming down too hard for her to see anything. She called to him in her mind.

"Ember, wait!" Thomas yelled as he watched Ember run. He grabbed his jacket and took off out the door after her. He could see her running away from him through the rain, so he ran as fast as he could to catch up with her.

"Ember! Stop!" Thomas called his voice searching for her through the rain. He saw her disappear down the street and quickly ran before he lost her. It didn't take long for his muscular legs to catch up as the storm rolled in stronger and the rain fell harder, lightning breaking through the dark, menacing clouds. Thomas followed closely behind Ember into the old Burring Point cemetery, getting close enough to take hold of her hand and stop her from running away.

"Ember, please, stop! I'm not going to hurt you," Thomas said as he pushed his soaking wet hair out of his face. He held her with both arms.

"Why are you afraid of me?" Thomas asked, as Ember looked down at the ground, her tears mixing in with the raindrops. She didn't understand what had come over her.

"Ember, look at me!" Thomas's voice was loud and commanding. "Listen to me, I have always been alone. I could never get close to anyone. Never wanted to. The job was all that mattered. The fucking job! It was all I had. Until I met you."

Ember looked up into his eyes as he spoke and searched for a glimmer of truth. She wanted to believe him so desperately. To trust him, to love him. To let herself be loved. She wanted to feel like she had, under the crystal chandelier, listening to his strong heartbeat, lost in his arms.

"Look, I don't know what's been happening lately. I've seen some crazy shit. I saw some crazy shit tonight. I don't understand any of it, but I know one thing for certain, and that's how I feel about you."

Thomas let go of her arms and inched in closer to her. "I'm not going to try to make sense of my feelings for you. Like I always try to do. Because none of it makes sense, and I don't fucking care."

Thomas pushed her wet hair out of her face and cupped it with both hands. "Listen to me, there is nothing I wouldn't do for you. I would follow you to the end of the earth and back. I would lay my life down for you. Do you understand? I know you believe me." Thomas fell to his knees in the wet dirt in front of Ember as the rain hardened around them. He looked up at her, drops falling into his eyes as he blinked. 'I know you feel me." She knelt in the muddy earth with him and placed his hand on her chest. "My heart. Do you feel it?"

"Yes, I feel it," Thomas whispered as he closed his eyes. Feeling Embers' heartbeat through her wet dress. As she felt his hand on her chest, she could hear her own heart beating loudly in her ears. Ember closed her eyes and thought about the sound of his heart, how it comforted her. It was like coming home.

"My heart. It lives in you," Ember said as she pulled him close and pressed her lips on his.

No longer being able to resist the passion she felt for him, for the emotions she had mistaken for anger and jealousy were just unbridled lust. She now understood, as they kissed long and deep, their hands reaching for each other frantically. Thomas held the back of her head, his hands pulling at her wet hair, as he drew her closer, kissing her harder as he pulled her dress down over her shoulders. Ember no longer cared about anything; all she wanted was this man. She let herself get carried away by his passionate kiss. Let him pull her dress down, exposing her breasts to the cold rain. Thomas broke his lips off hers and licked the water running down her neck to her round, firm breasts. She gasped with pleasure as she felt his hot mouth on her hard nipples. She struggled to breathe as she pulled his jacket off and threw it behind him. She ran her hands down his back, feeling the muscles rippling under her touch. Thomas looked into her eyes and ripped what was left of the fabric, and tore it off her wet body. He pushed her down in the muddy earth and held himself over her. Ember closed her eyes as one of his hands reached between her legs.

"Open your eyes. I want you to look at me," he purred in her ear. Ember did as he ordered. He held her gaze as his hands found their way down to her panties. His skilled fingers pushed the soft fabric to one side. Ember exhaled as she felt his fingers deep inside her. Her breaths were muffled by his lips once more on hers, briefly, before he moved his mouth down her body, kissing the bones on her hips. She ran her hands through his thick hair as his mouth made its way further down to meet her wetness. The rain pelted them both, and thunder cracked loudly in the sky. Ember was on the verge of climaxing as Thomas pulled away. She could see his muscular, tattooed chest, water running down his chiseled abs as his strong hands held her thighs open. Her hands dug into the wet earth as she watched his sculpted body move with every deep breath.

"Do you want me, wildflower?" Thomas asked as he pushed his hair out of his face and clenched his jaw tightly.

"I want you," she gasped as he kissed the soft skin on her thigh. He held his body over hers, balancing his weight with one arm, as Ember fumbled to undo his pants and pulled them down. He held the back of her head securely in his hand and kissed her deeply as he thrust himself inside her. Thunder rolled in the sky as Thomas moaned in her ear, feeling the warmth of her body. Ember's head fell back as she could feel Thomas fill every part of her. Ember felt as if her skin was on fire. The hot tingling sensation spread all over her, consuming her, just as Thomas consumed every part of her. Both their wet bodies moved like one in the wet mud, until they both collapsed in ecstasy. He lay on top of her, and she could feel his hot breath on her neck, his heartbeat on her chest. The rain washed the sweat and mud from their skin as Thomas wrapped her up in his arms. His skin felt warm as she let herself be cradled in his embrace, their breathing syncing together as they held each other, under the fury of the storm.

CHAPTER 21

Shadow circled above the Hale mansion for a place to land and find shelter from the rainstorm. He spotted a covered windowsill high on the third floor of the house. He shook the water off his feathers as he curled up and peered in the window. Inside, he could see Sirena standing in front of a large black mirror. The image in the mirror moved and swirled, and he could hear a strange voice speaking to Sirena. He moved in closer to get a better look, knowing that whatever he saw, Ember would see. He had felt the pull of her call earlier, but it seemed to have changed from distress to excitement. Shadow could sense his mistress's emotions. He was not only her protector, but also Ember's eyes and ears. So, he watched and listened as the voice spoke to Sirena, imprinting everything he saw. The darkness swirled one last time before returning the mirror to its original state. Shadow could make out Sirena's reflection perfectly, and how her hair seemed to come alive and move like snakes around her chiseled features.

Suddenly, the door to the room flew open, and Jasmine

came running in, dripping water as she ran across the floor to her sister.

"Sister, something has happened," she said breathlessly. "We went to see the Detective as requested."

Sirena raised her hand to her sister's face, without taking her eyes off her own reflection. "Sister, please no hysterics. Remember who we are," Sirena said as she turned away from the mirror and walked over to the canopy bed in the center of the room and stretched her long, feline-like body over the red silk sheets.

"Of course, sister. We apologize," Jasmine said as she took a deep breath and tried to calm herself before continuing.

"Now, tell me, sister, what is so important that we needed to barge into our private quarters looking like a drowned rat?" Sirena said carelessly as she lay across the large bed, her hair spread out around her, still moving around her head.

"We went to see the detective as we wanted. He was suspicious of us from the moment we walked in," Jasmine began to explain as she looked down at her feet.

"Please don't tell us that we couldn't control that small town cop," Sirena said as she shot her sister a disapproving look, her silver eyes ablaze.

"We did, at first. The voice had him. He was about to tell us everything, but then something happened, something that, well, is impossible, but we saw it with our own eyes."

"Let me guess, the dirty bird girl showed up and ruined your plans with him," Sirena said as she admired her long, glossy nails.

"No. Not her, Lila," Jasmine said, her voice trembling. "She appeared, out of shadow. We believe... We believe that she was protecting him."

Sirena shot up in bed as her hair moved frantically around her, her eyes narrowing as she listened to her sister.

"What! That's impossible! We took her. There is no way

she could have escaped her prison," Sirena said as she stood up from the bed and paced the room. "This can't be. We would have felt it. Sister, are we sure that is what happened and it's not some cheap parlor trick by that witch?"

"We are sure. It was Lila. Who summoned her, we do not know, but the voice did scare her off," Jasmine said, trying to reassure her sister.

"It did? Well, that's at least something. We must find out how their souls are escaping. How are they able to cross onto this plane without our knowledge? We have no doubt that witch and her crow have something to do with it." Sirena stopped in front of the mirror to gaze upon her reflection once more.

"These witches," she said with disgust. "They have been a plague on our family for centuries. But this one we might be able to use to our advantage. If she has the power to cross the veil between worlds, she can be very, very useful indeed. "She turned her head slightly to look at her sister. "Go, summon Willow. We need to get our hands on that crow. It can be the key."

"Yes, sister," Jasmine said as she bowed her head at her sister's command.

Sirena reached to touch the glass of the dark mirror. As she did, the mirror moved and rippled like water, turning foggy, like swirls of smoke, until an image appeared.

"Not all is lost. We have her friend, another witch. Pity, this one didn't even know she was of the blood," Sirena said as a shape of a woman began to appear in the swirling black reflection, "and when we have her crow as well, she will have no choice but to come to us."

"What about the police?" Jasmine asked her sister, her voice a low whisper. "Don't bore us!" Sirena scoffed, "We know the detective is suspicious of us. He might even know that the women all had the blood of the old world. He is probably aware they were all here, in our house. Still, we are not worried about him. "Sirena's lips curled up into a snarl. "We might have some use for him, and when this witch's body turns up, he will have even more of a reason to come seek us out."

"Maybe taking her wasn't a good idea," Jasmine said as she slowly lifted her shimmering eyes to glance quickly at Sirena.

"The police have never concerned us before. Why would they now? Don't worry, sister. He's not important; all that matters is the girl. She is the one we need. Once we have her, it's all the power we will ever need. We will no longer have to live on borrowed time," Sirena said, her expression changing to a warm smile as she approached her sister and touched her arm lovingly.

"Will she have to die like the others? All this death, we don't know how much more of this we can take," Jasmine said as a tear ran down her face.

"Oh, Jasmine always blubbering," Willow said as she walked briskly into the room. "Why should we care about those witches anyway? We know what they did to our family, yet here we are crying over them." Willow pushed her sister as she brushed by her and walked in front of the black mirror.

"We understand, but it's getting dangerous now. We are afraid; that is all," Jasmine replied as she regained her balance after Willow almost knocked her off her feet.

"Afraid? Why would we be afraid of them? Look at the power we possess. They should be the ones who need to fear us." Willow said as her large silver blue eyes fell back onto Jasmine. "It's as if we doubt our sister's power." Her mouth turned up into a mischievous grin. "We would never doubt our sister. We wouldn't be here if it weren't for her sacrifice," Jasmine said as she wiped the tear off her cheek.

Willow closed the gap between her and Jasmine. She gently kissed Jasmine's cheek and wiped away her tears. She then turned back to the mirror as she stepped close to Sirena. Together they gazed upon the image swirling in the smoky reflection.

"She was a fun one," she whispered in Sirena's ear, "put up a fight, but nothing we couldn't handle. We loved hearing her cries and pleas for her life. So pathetic. So, we took a little longer to drain her completely," Willow sneered.

Sirena snapped her head to look into Willow's eyes. "Cruelty does not impress us, sister," she said sternly. "We despise these witches as well, but what we do is out of necessity. It's the deal we made. The deal we made to save all of us."

Willow stared at her sister, anger flickering in her blue silver eyes. "Really, sister? The deal made for us or the deal we made to cover our sins."

Sirena slapped Willow's face hard, leaving a red handprint across her cheek and splitting her lip. Willow, surprised by the strike from her sister, kept her head down, her long hair covering her face. She slowly turned her head to look at Sirena, her eyes glowing, as the bruise on her face and lip disappeared like they had never existed.

"We don't have time for this." Sirena's attention turned to Jasmine. "We will go deal with the detective since even that simple task seems to be too difficult. "She focused her pearl-like eyes back on Willow. "Sister, go find us that crow. We will not ask again. Do you hear us?" Sirena's voice echoed throughout the room, like a roar, shaking the walls of the house.

Jasmine covered her ears and closed her eyes, as Willow stared at her sister in defiance. She finally nodded her head reluctantly as Sirena brushed by them both, her long robe trailing behind her, out of the room.

"Why provoke us, Willow? We owe everything we have to

Sirena," Jasmine said, as she carefully approached her sister, lightly placing her hand on Willow's shoulder.

"Yes, of course, we owe," Willow said as she pushed Jasmine's hand off her shoulder, "but we are sick of being ordered around. We have all this power, but can never enjoy it." With that, she walked out of the room, bumping into Jasmine as she passed. "We are going to go play."

Jasmine stood alone in the room. She walked closer to the large mirror, as the floating outline of a body could still be seen in the black swirling smoke. She watched the image for a long time, until a noise at the window caught her attention. She quickly ran to the window just in time to see a crow with a broken beak jump off the windowsill and fly off. She recognized the crow. It was the same one that she had seen that night in the garden with Ember. She stood quietly at the window and watched the bird fly away into the rain. If that crow was Ember's seer, then Jasmine was certain it saw and heard everything that had just been said in the room. She thought about alerting Willow, even warning Sirena that the bird might have been watching them, but she didn't. Instead, she just watched as the crow flew away from the house into the storm.

CHAPTER 22

SALEM, MASSACHUSETTS 1914

Water dripped from the gaping hole in the roof, down through the beams and rafters of the burned-out mansion. The wallpaper, once bright with intricate patterns, now peeled off the walls and smelled of mold. The floorboards, lifting and expanding with the moisture of the leaking rain, creaked and cracked as the house crumbled around itself. Birds and mice nested in every dry corner they could find.

It was dark, damp, and cold, but Sirena preferred the abandoned house to the hospital. After she had healed enough to leave the burn unit, she was moved to the psychiatric wing, where she would be locked in a room alone for days on end. She lost all sense of time and space. With the daily doses of heavy medications, she had no idea how much time had passed or how long she had been locked away. The only human contact she had was the occasional lawyer who would come with papers for her to sign, always avoiding eye contact with her horribly scarred face and body, or the endless parade of doctors and nurses.

She hadn't spoken a word since arriving at the psych

ward, only living in her own memories. She repeated the events of that terrible night every day. The faces of her fiancé and her family imprinted deep in her mind. Her guilt gnawed at her, rotting her from the inside out, until one day she decided she couldn't take it anymore.

She waited for the right moment when the late shift nurses were distracted and made a run for the stairwell that led to the kitchen. She hid behind some crates of food and waited for the midnight deliveries and then slipped out unnoticed, running for the tall gates that surrounded the hospital.

She used the little strength she had to pull herself over the fence and to the ground. She ran through the dark woods, branches scratching her face, her bare feet bleeding from the sharp stones and tree roots. She ran until she reached the burned-out shell of what used to be the majestic Hale mansion. The porch bowed under her weight as she walked through the unlocked door of the house. Sirena stood in the dirty, wet foyer and looked up at the mahogany staircase, once polished to a mirror shine, now charred and broken. Black soot stained the ceiling, walls, and paintings, making them unrecognizable. She walked through the house, the smell of smoke still in the air, and tried to picture the way it had been before the terrible flames.

She wandered aimlessly throughout the empty house, for how long, she wasn't sure. Days melted into months, then years, as she aimlessly stared out the cracked windows at the world going on around her. She finally built up enough courage to go up to the attic. She trembled as she approached the door and carefully walked up the dark, narrow stairs to the floor above. Hardly anything remained on the top level. The star-filled sky was completely visible; the entire roof was gone, and only parts of it remained intact.

Sirena looked up at the sky and felt the cool night air on

her skin. She didn't remember the last time she had stood outside under the moonlight. She felt as hollow and lonely as the old house. She was all alone in the world, scarred and hideous, and all by her own hand. The sadness and guilt of what she had done hung over her like a shroud. She had asked herself why only she was spared, but now she understood. This was to be her punishment. To spend life in this purgatory, a ghost walking through the burned memories of what once was, and what almost came to be. She did not feel sorry for herself nor prayed for absolution; she accepted her fate.

As she turned to leave, something caught her eye. A small reflection of light peeking through the darkness. She followed the light to a far corner of the attic. She could see a hint of gold scrollwork partially covered by a dirty sheet. She pulled it off to reveal a large gold-framed mirror. It had been untouched by the flames and appeared to be almost brand new. Sirena could not recall ever seeing the mirror anywhere in the house in the past. But there it was, leaning against the charred wall.

She looked at her reflection in the mirror for the first time since the fire. The hospital staff had kept her away from reflective surfaces during her stay for fear that her appearance would be too much for her to handle. Sirena forced herself to look upon what she had become, what her jealousy and anger had turned her into. She reached up to touch her once beautiful face as tears fell from her remaining eye.

"You have always been a monster; now you look like one," she said to her own reflection in the mirror.

As she turned from her reflection, a strange voice floated through the air. At first, Sirena thought it was just the wind blowing through the holes in the house. She turned to look in the direction the voice had come, but only saw herself in the mirror, so she began to walk away and heard the voice again. This time louder and clearer, only then did she realize it was coming from the mirror itself. She looked closely to see if it was just her mind playing tricks on her, and at that moment, the crystal-clear silver mirror began to move, distorting her face and body even more.

Sirena slowly began to walk backwards as the mirror swirled, like a whirlpool of dark water. Streaks of black began to appear in the circling image until the entire mirror was a slick oil-stained color.

"My child, you have finally found us," the voice from the mirror said. "We have been sleeping for so long, waiting for you."

"What do you mean you have been waiting for me?" Sirena said out loud to the mirror, her own voice sounding foreign in her ears. "What do you want?"

"We are your birthright child, kept away, hidden for so long, trapped in an endless dream," the voice said, sounding like a chorus of people speaking at once.

"My birthright? What do you mean?"

"We are bound to you and your blood, we have been for centuries," the voice continued. "If thou set us free, you can have all that you desire, as those who came before you did."

"Those that came before me? "Sirena asked as she leaned closer to the mirror.

"Yes," the voice hissed. "We have served your blood since they crossed our sea; they called to us, and we answered, giving them everything they desired in this new world, as we can give you all you desire."

The mirror swirled and cleared to show Sirena's scarred and disfigured reflection. Sirena covered her eyes at the sight of her own face. "Please, stop. I don't want to look at myself. I'm hideous!"

"Look again, child," the voice said softly.

Sirena slowly lowered her hands and gazed upon her

reflection. She gasped, this time seeing a beautiful woman. The burn scars on her face and body had disappeared. Her dark almond-shaped eyes glowed back at her, now a shimmering silver color. A bundle of long, full hair flowed with perfect corkscrew curls. Her body was lean and muscular, with full breasts, round thighs, and long legs. Her skin was smooth and glowing as if it were made of bronze. Sirena couldn't believe what she was seeing. She reached out to touch the mirror, and immediately the beautiful image disappeared and returned to the way it was before.

"No!" Sirena screamed, not wanting to see her true self. "Please, bring it back. I want to be beautiful, even if it's not real."

"But it can be real; you can have beauty, wealth, fame. Sickness or the passing of time will never touch you again. Thou wilt be a part of us, share our power. Just set us free and it will be so…forever."

"How…. how do I set you free?"

"Thou must go to the sea, make a sacrifice of blood, your blood, and the pact will be sealed," the voice said to Sirena.

"If I do that, I will be beautiful forever?" Sirena asked, "I can have whatever I want?"

"Yes, anything thou ask," the voice replied.

"I want my sisters back," Sirena said as the mirror hissed and swirled faster.

"Bringing the dead back to this world is a great task," the voice answered. "What comes back from the underworld is not always the same."

"I thought you said you could give me all I desired if I set you free. I will, but in return I want my sisters, and I want us all to be beautiful, forever."

The voice was silent for a moment. "Agreed, but be warned, child, the price for the dead to walk the earth is a costly one. Thou wilt be bound to them, bound to death, so death is what thou must give back."

'I don't care what the price is. I'll pay it. Anything is better than this," Sirena said as she looked at the rubble around her.

"Wait until the clock strikes three. Your sisters will come to thee; then go, go to the sea, spill your blood, set us free, and forever a beauty you will be," the voice said loudly as the dark water turned and swirled faster before it disappeared.

Sirena ran downstairs to the ground floor of the house and into the library. She saw the old grandfather clock at the far end of the room. It was stuck at the time the fire had reached it. As she got closer, the hands on the clock began to move around the face, faster and faster, until it stopped at one in the morning. It chimed once and began to tick like it had been wound up by some invisible force.

She sat on the dirty carpet in front of the clock and rocked back and forth. She had to wait until three, but she didn't know what exactly was going to come through that door. She laid her head down and tried to fight the sleep that had come over her, but she gave in.

The chimes of the old clock startled Sirena awake. She sat up and looked to see what time it was.

"Three," she said aloud as she looked around the room, her heart pounding. The house was silent, the ticking of the clock the only sound. Suddenly, the clock stopped, and Sirena heard the hinges on the front door creak as it opened.

She was too scared to turn around and look as she heard footsteps approaching behind her. Sirena could smell the odor of decay filling the room as mud dropped to the floor around her. She slowly rose from the floor but did not have the courage to turn around and see what had walked through the door.

"Sister," she heard a raspy voice say over her shoulder.

Sirena turned slowly to see her two sisters standing in the

library with her. They were hardly recognizable; most of the flesh had rotted away, exposing skull and bone. The skin that remained was black like coal. Their eyes were glazed over with a white film, their clothes shredded and covered in dirt and mud. Sirena recoiled at the sight of them.

"Sister, what has happened? I don't remember anything, just the dark. It was so dark and cold," a voice said coming from the creature that resembled her sister Jasmine.

"I remember," Willow said, her head bent to one side in an unnatural position. "I was stuck in an endless nightmare because of you."

Willow began to walk toward Sirena, her leg dragging behind her, backing her up against the wall.

"Please, Willow, I'm sorry. I brought you back to make it right. I can make things the way they were. Better even," Sirena pleaded.

Willow stopped inches from her sister's face, as her mouth turned up in a hideous grin, exposing even more of her jawbone and teeth. "I see you got what you deserved," she said as she looked at Sirena's disfigured face and body. "How are you going to make any of this right?"

"I found a mirror upstairs. A voice came from it, and it said we can have everything we want! The voice brought you back. I asked it to, and it did," Sirena said, her tears rising up in her voice.

"It brought us back, to live like this?"

"No, the voice said it can make us like we were, better, and we will never get sick or grow old," Sirena said, trying to convince her sister of what she had heard. "It said we need to go to the sea, and everything will be as it was! Please, you must believe me!"

"Willow, listen to her. She brought us back," Jasmine said as she moved slowly closer to her sister. "She can heal us, and we can all be together again."

Willow backed away from Sirena and peered at her with milky white eyes. "Fine, sister. Take us to the ocean. Let's see if you can keep your promise."

Sirena shook her head and began to pull dusty sheets from the furniture. She threw them over her sisters to cover them as best she could.

"Hurry, we have to go now before the sun comes up," Sirena said as she covered herself with a sheet and moved towards the front door, her sisters behind her.

They walked down to the harbor as quickly as they could, staying in the shadows so they wouldn't be seen. They all walked down to the water's edge and stood on the rocky beach. Sirena threw the sheet off her and picked up a sharp piece of sea glass that was by her feet. She held it as she stepped into the cold water, her sisters following behind her.

Sirena took the piece of sea glass in one hand and dragged it across the flesh of her arm. Crimson blood poured into the dark water.

"Here we are. I spilled my blood, like you wanted. Now you are free! Show yourself!" Sirena yelled, her voice carrying over the sounds of the waves hitting the rocks.

The air was still and the water motionless. Suddenly, a vibration came from the darkest recesses of the ocean. Sirena looked as far ahead as she could to see something swimming towards them, cutting through the water, picking up speed as it got closer. Right before it reached them, it seemed to have disappeared once more under the surface.

Sirena looked around but saw nothing; the water was still. Suddenly, she felt something rub against her legs. Scarp scales entangled between and around them, rippling through the water. She could see long, scaled bodies, silver and green, the color of a sturgeon fish, rolling and flipping, breaking the water's surface. Then in front of Sirena, a face came slowly out of the water. She could see, even in the darkness, that it was the face of a woman, but only her eyes were visible; the rest of her face remained hidden under the dark, murky water of the harbor.

The eyes that stared back at Sirena were silver, shining like coins. Behind the mysterious face, Sirena could make out the scaly, horned, sturgeon-like tails rising and falling out of the water.

"You came to us, my child," Sirena heard the voice say, without the face moving from under the water.

"Yes, and I gave you my blood. I have set you free," Sirena said back to the strange aquatic creature in front of her.

"Yes, thou hast released us from our dream," the voice said, the face disappearing under the water and appearing again closer to Sirena. She could feel the sharp scales cut through the skin on her legs as the creature wrapped itself around her.

"I did what you asked. I brought you my sisters. You said you would heal us, make us beautiful," Sirena said to the silver eyes staring back at her.

"Yes, thou did, and the pact has been made, sealed with thine blood. We will give thou everything thou heart desire, child, but before we do, know the price of what thou hast received."

"I gave you my blood," Sirena replied as the one scaled tail began to turn into many. She could now see other sets of shining silver eyes appearing from under the water, peering all around her.

"Life must be paid with life, and only beauty can sustain beauty," the voices said, now coming from all directions.

"Thou must bring us the souls of the ones who carry the blood of the old Gods. The ones they call witches, the ones who walk between worlds. Only that blood can give thou what thou seek."

"Wait! You didn't tell me that, you never said anything

about bringing you people," Sirena screamed as the tails undulated around her.

"It's the bargain thou hast struck! Thou hast bound by blood to us and to each other. Bring us souls or suffer our wrath," the voice hissed loudly as the scaled tails undulated quicker all around her.

Sirena turned to look at the decayed shells that were once her sisters. She had brought them back; she had promised them beauty and life. She could not go back on her promise. She turned to the face with silver eyes.

"Yes," she said softly.

With that, the tails came up out of the water and wrapped around all three of the sisters, dragging them down to the cold depths of the ocean until nothing but small bubbles remained on the surface.

* * *

THE MORNING SUN kissed the harbor with the first streams of golden light, reflecting like glittering gold on the ocean waves. Small bubbles broke the water's surface, growing bigger and coming faster.

Beautiful voices, singing in unison, floated from under the surface as three gorgeous women, with silver eyes, appeared from under the water, singing the hypnotizing melody, their hair slicked back away from their faces, showing off their stunning features. They walked slowly out of the sea, their long lean limbs moving gracefully with the rhythm of the tide, the sunlight shining on their smooth naked bodies. Water beaded off their perfect skin as they walked out of the sea to the beach, leaving nothing behind except echoes of their magical voices.

CHAPTER 23

The hot water from Thomas's shower washed all the dirt and mud from Ember's hair and body. She lathered the soap over her skin and remembered how Thomas's hands had felt when he touched her. The previous night in the cemetery had been the most passionate experience she had ever had in her life. She couldn't believe she had let herself doubt Thomas was not being truthful with her, that he was out to hurt her. She had a deep connection with him that was undeniable, but she could not ignore her instincts. After they made love, Thomas wrapped her in his jacket and brought her to his loft. She didn't want to be alone; her worry for Chloe still hung over her.

Thomas walked into the bathroom and stepped into the shower with her. He embraced her from behind and kissed her neck. Ember smiled to herself, feeling so safe in the hot water with Thomas' body close to her. He reached for a shampoo and squeezed some out in his hands. He lathered Ember's dark hair gently.

"I don't think I've ever let anyone brush my hair, let alone wash it," Ember said as the water rinsed the soap out of her hair.

"It's the least I can do," Thomas whispered in her ear.

Ember turned to face him. "Thomas, I'm still really worried about Chloe. I tried calling her again before I got in the shower, and her voicemail is full. It's not like her."

"Ok, I'll see what I can do to find out where she is. I'm sure she's fine. Maybe she decided to go away for a few days."

Ember bit her lip and debated whether she should tell Thomas the truth about how she saw Chloe with the Hale sisters. The truth about who she was and what she could do. She stepped out of the shower and put on one of Thomas's fluffy warm robes. She walked out of the bathroom and lay on his bed. Thomas joined her a few moments after.

"Thomas, I have to tell you something. Promise me you will keep an open mind."

"Of course I will," Thomas said as he wrapped a towel around his waist and sat down on the bed next to her.

"I am a witch; I was born a witch. Magic has always run in my family. I never understood the power that I have until I got here and met Lydia. She has not only taught me so much but helped me connect with the Goddess and to my true power," Ember explained as she stood up and walked towards the window. "She took me to her coven, and I had an experience, one that changed me forever. I was able to travel to another plane, in between, the world that parallels our own. There I connected with the Goddess, and she told me of my purpose and my power. She told me danger was coming, and that I would be put to the test, that only I could stop these terrible things that were going to happen. I didn't understand what danger she was talking about, but now I think I know."

Ember turned to look at Thomas, who was sitting at the edge of the bed, listing. "Tell me, what dangers?" he asked.

"The murders, I think I know who's been killing those girls. I think they were hunted because of who they were, witches, like me. Maybe some of them didn't know that they had the gift of the craft, but I am certain that they all were. "

Thomas stood up from the bed and moved closer to Ember. "You are right, I had made that connection to all the victims, that's the one thing they had in common, that and they all went to parties at the Hale mansion."

"What, they all went there?" Ember asked, surprise in her voice, "You are sure?'

"Yes, I have evidence to prove it. That's why I went there, to talk to the eldest Hale sister, but I was given the brush off. Then Jasmine shows up in my office, wearing almost nothing."

"But Chloe isn't a witch," Ember said to herself as she chewed on her thumbnail.

"Why do you say that? Why do you think Chloe is involved with the Hale sisters?"

"I saw her with them, at a restaurant. Well, I didn't see them. Shadow did," Ember said as she looked into Thomas's eyes.

"Shadow saw them?" he asked, his curiosity piqued.

"Shadow is more than my protector; he's my connection to the other world, to the Goddess. I can see through his eyes, hear what he hears. We can communicate with each other."

"So, you can control your crow?"

"In a way, yes, what he sees, I see, and the last time he saw Chloe, she was with the Hale sisters. I feel something terrible has happened to her, and I believe the sisters have something to do with it. I know this might all sound crazy, but you must believe me."

Thomas ran his fingers through his thick blonde hair. "I believe you, Ember, and it does sound crazy, but like I told you last night, I've seen some strange things myself lately."

"What have you seen?"

"For lack of a better explanation, ghosts. I've seen the ghosts of two of the murdered girls, maybe three, fuck I don't know. The first time I thought was in the cemetery the day we met, then it happened here, in my loft. I thought I was losing my mind, or the booze had finally taken its toll on me, but it happened again, last night in my office. Jasmine saw it too, and she recognized who it was. She ran off, scared. So, yeah, I believe that those sisters are involved somehow."

"Then we have to go there now. Chloe might still be in the house," Ember said as she looked around for something to wear since her dress was ripped and dirty.

"Ember, we can't just go barging in there without cause. We still don't know where Chloe is or if she's even missing. I can't just walk in there and start throwing accusations, especially ones based on visions and ghosts. The Hale sisters have friends in high places. We have to tread lightly."

Ember shook her head in agreement, remembering Sirena's veiled threats of ruining her reputation and implied accusations that Thomas had something to do with the murders. Both their thoughts were interrupted by Thomas's cell phone vibrating on his dresser. He picked it up and looked at the screen. "It's the office. I have to take this."

Ember watched as Thomas answered his phone and stepped away from her. She could hear someone's voice on the other end, but couldn't make out what was being said. She studied his face closely, looking for any expression that would clue her into what he was hearing. But he remained stone-faced, his eyes icy as he looked back at her. Then all the blood ran from his face, and his jaw clenched tightly. He hung up the call and looked at Ember with a strange blank look in his eyes.

"What, what's wrong?" Ember asked, walking closer to him, the strange look on his face worrying her.

"A jogger found a body of a woman, washed up on the beach near Winter Island," he said in a monotone voice, his eyes dropping back to his phone.

"It's Chloe, isn't it! I know it is," Ember yelled, her eyes filling up with tears.

"The woman was found with her identification in her purse. It's not Chloe," Thomas said as he reached out to hold Ember in his arms. "It's Lydia."

* * *

THOMAS SHUT the engine off as he pulled his SUV up to the yellow crime scene tape. He sighed and took Ember's hand in his. "I am so sorry, Ember; I know how much she meant to you. "

Tears fell from Ember's eyes onto the white dress shirt she had borrowed from Thomas.

"I can drop you off at home. This might be too much for you," Thomas said, concern in his voice.

"No, I'm ok. I owe it to her to be here," Ember said as she tried to wipe the tears from her face.

"Ok, but stay here. I don't want you to see this."

Thomas got out of the car and walked over to the gathering of police cars and ambulances. He ducked under the crime scene tape as he approached the group of officers and emergency medical personnel who had assembled near the beach. He could see his boss, Captain Torres, on the beach kneeling by a yellow blanket.

"Hey, Captain, I came as soon as I got the call."

"Cole, where the fuck have you been?" Torres asked as he

stood and pulled Thomas aside, away from the scene. "What have you been doing? This case has gotten completely out of control. Now I have another victim on the beach, and you haven't given me shit."

Thomas rubbed his forehead. "Cap, I have been working on this case; that's what I've been doing. It's all I've been working on."

"Really?" Torres asked as he looked up to see Ember standing on the other side of the crime scene tape wearing Thomas's shirt.

Thomas turned to see what Torres was looking at. "She's been helping me with this case; she has provided some good information."

"I'm sure she has," Torres said with disdain. "God dam it, Cole, all I need now is you thinking with your dick. You have fucked this case to the point of gross incompetence. I have given you all the resources available to us. Not to mention space to be run this investigation on your terms, but you have run it into the ground."

"I have suspects, Cap, I have some good information that the Hale sisters are involved," Thomas began to explain.

"Stop, Cole! The Hale sisters? Are you kidding me? I've entertained this bullshit before, but I can't anymore. This has gone too far. I am taking you off this case and bringing in the feds to take over. You have given me no choice."

"Fuck, Cap, don't do that. I'm so close. You have to trust me."

Captain Torres sighed and looked at Thomas. "You have forty-eight hours, Cole. That's all I can give you. Get me some results, or I'm pulling you off this case."

Thomas nodded in agreement. "Forty-eight hours, ok."

"Not only is my ass on the line, but yours is too. Forty-eight hours, Cole, or I'll have your badge and gun," Torres said as he turned and walked off the scene.

Thomas ran his fingers through his hair and sighed deeply. He glanced over at Ember and walked back over to the body under the yellow blanket.

Crime scene technicians collected bits and pieces of evidence and placed them in brown paper bags, sealing them with red evidence tape, as Thomas kneeled and lifted the blanket. Lydia was lying on her stomach with her head turned to the side. Her lips and fingertips were a deep shade of blue, her eyes slightly opened with a cloudy white film, water dripping from her nose and mouth.

"How long do you think she's been in the water?" He asked one of the technicians.

"Hard to say right now, probably less than twelve hours."

Thomas put on some latex gloves and lifted the collar of Lydia's shirt. Long red scratches marred her neck and back; her shirt was torn and shredded like an animal had clawed at it.

"Good news, though," the technician said, interrupting Thomas's concentration. "We found a hair on the body, blonde, definitely doesn't belong to the victim."

"Take that all to the lab, put a rush on it," Thomas replied curtly.

The technician nodded his head as he walked away, and Thomas's attention drifted to Ember, who was suddenly standing right next to him.

"Whoa, Ember, I told you to stay in the car. You don't want to see this," he said as he stood up, pushing her back gently to block her view.

"Please, I need to see," Ember said, as she broke through Thomas's arms and bent to get closer to Lydia's body. Thomas kneeled beside her. "Ok, tell me what you see."

Ember reached out her hand and placed it over Lydia's, closing her eyes. In an instant, her normally yellow eyes opened and had changed to pure black as she stared off into the distance.

The visions came to Ember quickly. Lydia had been in the shop when she was surprised by someone who had approached her. She had argued with that person and then lifted her arms up to defend herself from the savage attack that came without warning. The vision turned black for a few seconds, but when it came back into focus, Lydia was being dragged by her feet. She left finger marks in the sand as she tried to find something to hold on to.

Ember tried to focus on who or what had Lydia, but it was blurry, like it was being shielded somehow. Lydia chanted a protection spell, but whatever was attacking didn't seem affected by her words. The attack became more violent, long fingers and nails reaching up to Lydia's throat, as she desperately tried to say something.

'The book, look in the book,'-Lydia struggled, 'look with the Goddesses' light, and you will see.' As the words left her mouth, Ember saw Lydia being taken to the seashore. As the water splashed around her, Ember got one look at the creature. It was a dark creature; the only features Ember could make out before they disappeared under the dark water were two large glowing silver-blue eyes.

In seconds, Ember was taken from her vision. She blinked as her eyes turned back to their usual warm gold.

"I saw, I saw what happened to her," she said, looking at Thomas, her hands trembling.

"What did you see? Tell me."

"She was in the shop; someone came in and they started arguing. Lydia was trying to cast a protection spell, but whatever it was broke right through it." Ember said her voice struggling to keep back the tears, "It tore her apart, and then she was taken here, to the water; it pulled her under."

"What did? What pulled her under?" Thomas asked as he looked at Ember.

"I'm not sure, but it wasn't human," Ember said as she looked straight into Thomas's eyes. "There's something else. Lydia tried to send me a message. I'm sure of it. She said to look in the book, so that I'll be able to see with the Goddess's light."

"Do you know what book she was talking about? What does that mean?" Thomas asked.

"No, I don't, but I know she trusted me to find out."

"Ok, I need you to go back to the store before I send cops and forensics there to process it. Go see what you can find," Thomas said as he stood up and took Ember's hand.

"I'll go, but where are you going?"

"I'm going to have a talk with the Hale sisters," Thomas said as he helped Ember to her feet.

"Thomas, be careful. They are dangerous, more than I think we realize. I will have Shadow go with you; he can watch your back."

"Your crow? Ok, I'll take all the help I can get," he said with a small smile.

"What about Chloe?" Ember asked as they both made their way back to the car.

"Don't worry, Ember. I'll find Chloe," Thomas said as he walked over to the driver's side of the car.

"If it's not too late," he said under his breath.

CHAPTER 24

*E*mber watched as Thomas's car drove away from her down the cobblestone. She stood in front of the shop, closed her eyes, and called for Shadow. Within minutes, his wings were flapping above her head.

"Hello Shadow," she said as he took his place on her shoulder.

He rubbed his head against her dark hair as if to comfort her. Ember slowly opened the door to the store. She wasn't surprised that the front door had been left unlocked. As she stepped inside, she saw tables overturned and items thrown around the room. She knew Lydia had fought for her life with everything she had. But whoever or whatever had attacked her was too strong for her to fight off.

"Lydia was protected. Whoever did this to her was powerful," Ember said to Shadow as he jumped off her shoulder onto the front desk. He squawked loudly as if to get her attention. "What do you know, boy? Show me."

Ember looked deep into his dark, round eyes and took a deep breath. She was taken back to the stormy night as Shadow flew through the rain over the Hale mansion. She could see through the window into Sirena's room as she stood in front of a swirling black mirror.

Shadow answered with their short squawks.

Ember immediately understood what her friend was telling her. "That's right, Lydia did say something about a book; it must be here."

Ember moved the wheeled ladder and climbed to the top of the shelf. She quickly ran her hands over each dusty book, looking for the old, worn black leather book Lydia had read from when she had asked about the Hale sisters.

Shadow squawked as Ember's hand touched a black book with stitching on the spine.

Ember pulled the book and climbed down. "This has to be the one she wanted me to find." She sat on the floor and opened the book in her lap. Ember thumbed through the worn tea-colored pages of the handwritten book. It was full of names, dates, and stories on several families in Salem, going back before the trials. She read about the land disputes between the Putnam family and the Eastys, Towne, and even her own family, the Wildes. She read about Cotton Mather and his father, Increase Mather, and how they had been heavily involved in the witch hysteria, as well as Samuel Parris, whose daughter, Elizabeth, first cried witch against their indentured servant, Tituba.

She turned the pages faster to find the chapter on Reverend John Hale and his family. She read that he had been a well-respected man who had studied at Harvard. How, as a young boy, he had witnessed the hanging of Margaret Jones and other women in Boston for the crimes of witchcraft. Hale seemed to be an enthusiastic participant in the trials up until his wife Sarah was accused; then he seemed to have a sudden change of heart, somehow keeping her out of jail and off the gallows.

As Ember lifted the book to get a better look at some small

writing, two folded pieces of paper fell out of the pages into her lap. She unfolded the first paper. It seemed to be a page torn out of a journal. It described a journey by ship from England to the Massachusetts colonies. The writer described how passengers on the ship began to disappear mysteriously and how strange voices could be heard from *the* water at night. It continued to say that creatures were seen emerging from the waves.

The ship finally made port, but with less than half of its crew and passengers. The ones who did survive the journey seemed affected somehow, like under a spell. A list of names was written on the border of the page, and one caught her attention: Robert Hale. John Hale's father. So, the Hale family had been on that voyage. The ship's name, The Arbella, 1630.

Her attention turned towards the second folded piece of paper, a worn newspaper clipping from the late 1800s. It was a short story announcing the Hale family's adoption of an infant. It went on to read that the Hales had not been blessed with a child, so they traveled to an orphanage to find a baby girl.

"They have another sister?" Ember asked aloud.

But where was she? Who was she? No one had ever mentioned a fourth sister. Ember didn't know what to make of this hidden secret, but she was certain she should keep this to herself, for now.

She placed both pieces of paper in her pocket and flipped through the rest of the book, stopping at a drawing of a sea creature that strongly resembled a mermaid. Written under the picture was an old story about mysterious sea creatures, known as sirens, who would lure people to their deaths with their song. The story went on to say that the sirens would choose some, those they considered worthy to make a blood pact, granting them powers, and even eternal life.

She looked down at the bottom of the page to see a warning, written in red ink. It read, 'Beware the call of the sirens, for it brings death to all who hear it.'

Ember closed the book with a sigh. She looked up at Shadow. "I don't think this is the book Lydia was talking about. I didn't see anything that can help us here," she said as she stood and looked around the shop in frustration.

"How am I supposed to find what book she was trying to point me to?' Ember paced the floor. "She said something about the Goddess' light, what could she have meant by that…"

Shadow answered with a low grumble. Suddenly, she heard voices at the front door. She ducked under one of the counters and looked over at the door. She saw a group of what appeared to be police officers gathering on the sidewalk. She remembered that she hadn't locked the door when coming in.

She motioned for Shadow to follow her out the back door. She exited in the alley unseen and quickly made her way down to the street, Shadow on her shoulder. When she reached her apartment, she realized the front door to her unit was slightly open. Her heartbeat quickened as she approached the open door and heard someone inside.

She slowly walked through the door and stepped as quietly as she could into her living room. There was an intruder moving around in the kitchen. Ember held her breath as she hid behind the wall and waited for whoever had broken in to come around the corner. She looked around for something to protect herself with, but there was nothing close. She breathed a sigh of relief when she saw Shadow, perched high on the molding, feathers ruffled up, his chest puffed out, ready to attack with his sharp beak and talons. She looked at him and gave him a slight nod, letting him know to be ready. Just then, a tall familiar figure walked out of the kitchen.

"Tristan!"

"Jesus, Ember! You scared the stuffing out of me," Tristan said with a startled jump.

Ember flung her arms around his neck and hugged him tight. "What are you doing here?"

"Well, since you haven't answered any of my calls or messages in weeks, I took it upon myself to check on you. I got here and I wasn't surprised that your front door was unlocked," he said as he looked at Ember in Thomas's over-sized shirt.

"What's going on here, Miss?"

"Oh, I um, got my dress dirty," Ember said as she brushed a strand of hair behind her ear.

Tristan gave her a small grin and sat on the couch. "Dirty, eh?"

Ember sat next to Tristan and put her head on his shoulder as Shadow flew over and jumped on the arm of the couch as if to introduce himself.

"And who might this be?" Tristan asked as he reached his hand out.

"This is Shadow. He's my friend."

"He's so cute, "Tristan said as he looked back at Ember. "Ok, so what's going on? Why haven't you called me back? Why are you sneaking around corners in your own house? In a guy's shirt no less."

Ember rubbed her tired eyes. "I don't even know where to start, so much as happened."

"Well, you better start talking because I've been worried sick about you," Tristan said as he got up and walked over to the kitchen. "I'll make the tea, you talk."

He opened and closed cabinets until he found the kettle. As he filled it with water, Ember walked to his side and leaned on the counter. "I'm sorry for not getting back to you. But so much has been going on."

"Apology accepted, just start from the beginning, or from who wears the tall slim fit," Tristan said as he looked around the kitchen for tea. "What kind of tea do you have, girl?" He looked over Ember's shoulder to see her grandmother's book on the table behind her. I bet there's some good tea recipes in there. I should look in that book, and only that book."

Tristan's words struck her like a bolt of lightning. "What did you say?"

"No, I'm just saying everything you ever need to know is probably in your grandmother's book. I'm sure there are some good recipes in there."

"Oh, my Goddess! I didn't even realize, Tristan, you are a genius," Ember said as she gave him a kiss on the cheek.

"I am? I mean, of course, but wait, I'm confused. What are you talking about?"

Ember grabbed her grandmother's book and opened it. She didn't know what she was looking for, but she was sure that whatever Lydia wanted her to find had to be written on those pages. She scanned each page closely, reading Carmen's cursive handwriting.

"Lydia, she told me to look in a book. I thought she meant one of her books. I didn't even think she could have been talking about grandma's book."

"Who is Lydia? Em, you need to back up," Tristan said as he sat next to Ember at the kitchen table.

Ember looked up from the book. "You are right. I'm sorry. I have left you out of my life. That's not fair to you. You are one of my dearest friends."

Tristan listened intently as Ember filled him in on everything that had happened since she moved to Salem: meeting Lydia, the coven gathering, and the vision she had. She told him of Shadow, how he had come to her, and the connection she had with him. Everything from the murders of the women in town and how they all had a connection to witchcraft. Lydia is dying, and her friend Chloe is going missing, and of course, Thomas.

Tristan lifted an eyebrow as she told him about the rainy night they shared in the cemetery. She felt her cheeks turn red as she told him how she ended up wearing one of his shirts. She changed the subject before he could ask any questions and told him all about the Hale sisters.

"I know all of this might be hard to believe, but there's something wrong with those sisters. I don't think they are entirely human, and I believe they are responsible for the murders. Tristan, I know they killed Lydia. I saw it in my visions. Whatever attacked her was definitely not human, not even a witch as powerful as her could fight it off."

"I believe you, Em, of course I do," Tristan said as he put his hand over hers, "but why are you looking in your grandmother's book? Do you think that there might be something in there that can help?"

"Lydia said something before she died; I think it was a message to me. She said to look in the book, that I would see it under the Goddess' light," Ember said as she looked back at the book in front of her.

"See what exactly? What are you looking for? A way to stop these sisters?"

"I honestly don't know, but I am certain it's in these pages," Ember said as she continued to flip through the pages.

"I know my grandmother made some sort of sacrifice for me, and I know she left me her necklace for a reason, to protect me. So there has to be something in her book, and I think Lydia knew it."

"Ok, well let's keep looking until we find something," Tristan said as he slid his chair closer.

Together they went through every page of the book, reading every spell, herbal remedy, and incantation written by Carmen, but nothing seemed to fit. Ember let out a sigh as she closed the book.

"Look, you are tired, and you can't think when you're tired. Why don't you go and take a hot bath and get some sleep? When you wake up, we will look again with fresh eyes," Tristan said as he stood up and put the book back on the counter.

"Will you stay? I really don't want to be alone," Ember asked as she walked into her bedroom. Shadow squawked as if to remind her that he was there, and Tristan laughed. "We will both stay with you, don't worry."

She gave him a small smile as she motioned to Shadow to come to her. Shadow took his place on her arm. "No, not you. I have a job for you."

Ember walked to the kitchen and opened the window to let Shadow hop onto the sill. "Go, my Shadow, fly to the Hale mansion. Be my eyes, and my ears, find Chloe, and protect Thomas, but be careful, they are hunting us, all of us."

Shadow opened his large wings and flew off into the twilight.

CHAPTER 25

The Hale mansion looked dark and ominous against the setting sun. Thomas slowly parked his car a couple of houses above so as not to alert anyone to his presence. He wanted to catch the sisters off guard.

He checked his 45 Glock sidearm and made sure he had extra clips, just in case. As he put his gun back in his shoulder holster, he heard a scratching noise on the roof of his car. He opened the window to see Shadow hop down and land on his side mirror.

"Hey there, Shadow. I see you have been put on watch duty," Thomas said as the bird nodded his head in agreement. "Ok, well, best thing if you take the high ground, get a good look around the house, and let me know if someone is trying to sneak out, or in." The large crow made a short, low sound and flew off in the direction of the mansion. "I can't believe I just gave orders to a bird….and he understood me," Thomas said to himself as he shrugged his shoulders. "Not the strangest thing I've seen lately."

Thomas stepped out of his SUV and gently closed the door. He walked on the sidewalk to the mansion's large front entrance, looking around to make sure no one surprised him. He looked up and could see Shadow circling overhead.

Thomas banged the brass knocker on the thick wood door and waited. He could hear footsteps approaching and then stopping on the other side of the door. He knocked again. This time, the door opened slowly. Thomas expected to see the tall older man who worked for the sisters as a butler. But instead, he was surprised to see a statuesque, beautiful woman in a long silk dress and robe with fur on the neckline and cuffs.

"Detective Cole, we presume," the woman said as her glossy red lips parted in a seductive smile.

"Miss Hale, it's a pleasure to finally make your acquaintance," Thomas assumed that he was looking at the eldest sister.

"Please, call us Sirena. Won't you come in?" she said as she stepped aside to let Thomas walk through the open door. "We were informed that you had called on us the other day. We apologize that we haven't been able to get back to you. Some important personal matters to attend to, you understand."

"Yes, of course, your sister Jasmine did come to my office in your stead," Thomas replied as he followed Sirena into the parlor.

As Sirena stood in front of the large fireplace, the glow of the fire outlining her curves through the white silk, she let out a small chuckle. "Can never be certain what our youngest sister is up to."

Thomas sat down on one of the Victorian-style couches as he tried not to be distracted by Sirena's barely there dress. He was sure that her attire or lack thereof was for his benefit.

"So, tell us, Thomas, may we call you Thomas. What can we do for you?" Sirena sat on the loveseat across from him, her hair spread out over the gold trim of the small couchette and her long tan legs peeking out from the high slit in her robe.

"I prefer Detective Cole, just to keep it professional, if you don't mind. I'm here to ask you about the young woman who has been murdered."

Sirena glared at him with her glowing eyes. "We see. It's such an incredibly sad situation. Those poor women."

"Yes, indeed. Did you know any of the women?" Thomas pulled out a printout of all the victims' pictures from his jacket pocket.

Sirena leaned in closer and took a quick look before looking away. "Hard to say, Detective. We know many people. Well, they know us in any case. It's possible we might have crossed paths at one of our many events."

"Well, I'm asking if you knew them personally, hosted any of them at any point in a more personal setting?" Thomas asked, watching her closely. Sirena stood up from the loveseat and walked over to a small table. She poured a bright green liquid into two glasses out of a glass decanter. She placed one of the glasses in front of Thomas. "No, thank you, Miss Hale. I am on duty."

"Oh, come now, Detective. We know you must be parched. How many days has it been since you had a drink? Your shaking hands tell me it's been a few." Sirena placed small metal spoons on top of the glasses and topped them off with a cube of sugar.

Thomas watched as she poured ice water out of another decanter, as he tried to hide his trembling hands. He hadn't noticed it had been a while since he'd had a drink. Being with Ember had consumed him so much he hadn't felt the awful feeling of withdrawal, but now, being in the dark warm room, hearing the drip of the water through the sugar into the green beverage, the thirst in his throat was almost intolerable.

Sirena stirred the sugar in the glass with the small spoon and handed the glass to Thomas. "Absinthe, they say, is the drink of the divine. We would have to agree."

Thomas hesitated but gave in to thirst at the back of his throat and drank the strong anise-flavored spirit. It burned going down, but instantly Thomas felt more relaxed. Sirena poured him another drink, which he accepted enthusiastically, not waiting for the sugar water mixture. He leaned back on the couch and placed the empty glasses on the table.

"Now, we can have an honest conversation," Sirena said as she poured more Absinthe in his glass. You are here because that dirty witch girl has convinced you we have something to do with those murders. We must admit, we did underestimate her ability to seduce you so quickly, but you men are all the same, so weak-minded."

Thomas drank the third glass of Absinthe quickly as he listened to Sirena's voice. He tried to respond to what she was saying but felt like he couldn't speak, a strange feeling coming over him. Sirena laughed seeing him struggle. "Weak-minded, but you are so beautiful, Thomas. We can see why she is so taken by you."

Thomas tried to get up but found his legs were weak and unsteady and his arms numb. He tried to focus on Sirena, but his eyesight became blurry, as if he was looking through a dirty window. He tried to focus on the room he was in. The soft glow of the fireplace cast long shadows on the wall. He watched as the shadows stretched long and tall. They danced across the wall and to the ceiling. The shadows formed into bodies of women twirling all around the room. He closed his eyes, trying to refocus on the ghostly figures as they grew on the walls. He blinked his eyes and turned his head to the wooden carvings of mermaids around the fireplace mantle.

The room appeared to grow larger as the fireplace was suddenly further away from him. Through his blurry vision, he could see the carved wooden pillars begin to move and take shape, the mermaids coming alive as their arms reached out to him, beckoning him to them. Thomas closed his eyes. "This isn't real," he said, his words slurring.

"It's not only the wormwood, love, but also a bit of nightshade," Sirena said as she walked over to Thomas and sat on his lap, straddling her tan legs on either side of him. "What a shame, to waste a face and body like this." Sirena unbuttoned Thomas's shirt and ran her cold hands over his chest. "We once loved a man like you, so handsome, so full of promise, but he was a disappointment, as everyone always has been."

Thomas could barely move or speak. His eyes grew heavy as he fought to keep them open, the potion of Absinthe and nightshade making the room spin, as the figures moved and danced around him. He was completely helpless as Sirena kissed his lips and whispered softly in his ear.

"Oh, Thomas, it's too bad that you didn't listen to your boss when he told you to tread lightly. If only you had listened." Sirena licked Thomas's ear as she said. "We must confess to you, since we are so much closer now…. We did kill them," Sirena hissed, her crimson lips turning up in a snarl.

She placed her hands behind Thomas' neck to steady his head. "Of course, we all did our part. We sisters work together. We gave them life; it's because of us that we have all of this," she said as she took off her robe and slowly pushed the thin straps of her dress down over her shoulders, exposing her bare breasts.

"Now, don't think us evil, Thomas. We are doing a great service by ridding it of the plague of witches. They bring nothing but pain and destruction to the world, even your beloved crow girl." Sirena dug her long nail across Thomas's cheek, leaving a deep cut, blood dripping down to his collar. "We are truly sorry it had to end this way. You had such potential, but this is the way it must be. Imagine the shock and horror when they find you dead, by your own hand, in your home, full of evidence that you, in fact, were the murderer all along. Killing those witches then hiding the evidence so you wouldn't be discovered."

Sirena ran her fingers across Thomas's neck until she felt his pulse. Thomas struggled to move, to reach for his gun, but he was paralyzed.

"You should have told your dirty witch that we will always win," she said as she began to push the tip of her fingernail into his throat. Thomas felt her sharp nail begin to break his skin. He closed his eyes and accepted his fate. His thoughts went to Ember. The night they had shared in the cemetery, how beautiful she had looked in the rain, how her heart had beaten with his. Thomas could feel death begin to swallow him, and he gave in to the darkness.

Suddenly, the front door burst open with a huge gust of hurricane-force wind, so hard it ripped the hinges off the frame.

Snowflakes tickled Ember's eyelashes, as her eyes fluttered open. She could feel the cold snow falling on her face and underneath her. Shadow's familiar call rang out in the distance. She sat up and looked around at the beautiful frozen snow-covered valley, the tall, majestic pine trees swaying with the wind in the distance. Cold water ran over the rocks in the dark stream behind her. It took her only a moment to realize she was back in that world, the world in between. She stood and brushed the snow off her dress. Ember looked up in the gray, clouded sky to see if she could spot Shadow circling above her, but he was nowhere to be seen. She was about to call to him when she heard a very familiar voice over her shoulder.

"My little one, I have missed you so." Ember slowly turned to look towards the voice that had brought her so much comfort as a child. She threw her arms around the woman standing next to her.

"Grandma!" Tears ran from her eyes and onto Carmen's red knitted sweater. Ember inhaled deeply, her grandmother's perfume, lily of the valley, making her heart ache with how much she had missed her.

"I have missed you so much. I have been so lost without you," Ember said through her tears, now coming too fast for her to hold back.

"There, there, Ember. You are not a lost child. You are exactly where you are meant to be," Carmen said as she pulled Ember away. "Now let me look at you." She ran her hands over Ember's messy hair." I see the hairbrush still eludes you." Ember laughed through her tears at her grandmother's joke. "You have changed so much, but still the girl I remember," Carmen said as she stroked Ember's cheek lovingly, wiping away the tears.

"Is this real, or am I dreaming?" Ember asked, looking at her grandmother, who stood before her.

"You are dreaming, child, but this is very real. You know this place, and it knows you, yes?" Carmen hooked her arm to Ember's. "Walk with me, Ember."

They both walked in silence for a while, hearing only their footsteps crunch in the snow. Ember broke the quiet first. "I'm sorry, Grandma. I'm sorry for not being there when you passed. I should have been. I just couldn't bear the thought of seeing you suffer. I didn't want to see you in pain or sick. I wanted to remember you like you are now, like I knew you. I know it was selfish, and I have never forgiven myself."   Ember choked on the sadness and regret that had suddenly come over her. She turned her face to her grandmother. "I should have been there. I don't know what happened, but maybe I could have done something," she said as her voice trailed off.

"Ember, you mustn't do that. What I did, I did for you, and I wouldn't change anything for the world. There is nothing for you to be sorry for."

"What did happen?"

Carmen continued walking, holding Ember closer to her. "We have never hidden who we are. Even though it caused fear in some, we understand those who live with fear are consumed by it. Sadly, it was a lesson I failed to teach your mother, and I lost her. She died of heartbreak and regret, but I would not fail you. So, I surrendered myself to the illness that had overtaken my body, knowing when I did pass on to the next world, my power would pour into you," she said as she looked at Ember.

"Living out in the open is freeing, powerful, but it can also attract those who mean to take that power. They feed off it. They think it can grant them all they desire, but they soon find that taking power they are not worthy of can only lead to ruin. Sadly, this makes many of us hide our true selves, but hiding only makes us weak."

Ember looked down at her feet. "Why didn't you tell me?"

"I had seen what you were going to face, that the curse that had been dormant for so long was going to be awakened once more. It is a sickness of the heart and mind; it infects those who live in fear and feeds off their weakness. It lies and turns neighbor against neighbor, family against family. The more lives it takes, the stronger it becomes. This is something you had understood on your own."

"Salem, that's what happened in Salem, to Sarah?"

"Yes, Ember. I looked into those silver eyes, and felt evil itself," said a voice from the trees. Ember looked in the direction of the voice and saw a woman wearing a plain brown dress. Strands of dark hair blew across her face as the rest was neatly tucked under a white bonnet.

"Sarah, you are Sarah Wildes?"

The woman walked closer to them, taking small steps, her hands folded in front of her. "It came to me one dark night, on a cold wind. A voice so beautiful I thought it must be from heaven. I followed the voice to the harbor. That was when I saw evil coming from murky depths. It did not speak, but I could hear its words in my mind. It promised me riches, beauty, even life eternal."

Sarah paused to move closer to Ember. "I tried not to listen. I prayed to God to help me, to give me the strength to fight the foul creature. It said that if I did not give myself to it, that if I did not set it free, a curse would seep into the land from the water. A darkness would spread to all of us. That is when I heard them."

"Who did you hear?" Ember asked as she turned closer to Sarah.

"The crows. I saw they gathered around me, as if they were one. They protected me and scared off the creature. I ran back home under the cover of their wings. I knew I was safe, but not for long. If anyone had seen me that night, I knew the cries of witchcraft would lead me to the noose, so I said nothing. That following winter was the worst we had ever experienced, and with it came the darkness. I knew it was the same evil I had encountered in the water. But I was too late to stop it. It must have gotten to others, and it spread like a sickness."

Ember glanced at her grandmother for reassurance as Sarah continued. "Many of us were accused and lost our lives to this curse. It kept us in darkness, like a prison of dark water where it would feed off our souls... off our power. It needs ones like us, ones who carry the old blood in our veins. Some were able to escape, but not until they sent that evil back to the depths it had come from. But now it's been released, and by those of the same line that unleashed it onto this world."

"The Hale sisters, they made a pact with this creature, as many have done before. That's why they kill women, like us. They need a worthy sacrifice for the creature to maintain their beauty, to sustain their life. The blood of witches. But what Sirena has done is so much worse. She has made the darkest of deals, one with the dead. By having that creature bring her sisters from the land of the dead, she has put not only her life in danger, but this world as well. She has given that creature the ability to punch a hole in the veil that separates the world of the living and of the dead. That evil cannot have power over both realms, and it can never have power over this one."

Shadow made his appearance as he flew down from the treetops and landed on Ember's shoulder with a flutter of black feathers. Hello, Shadow," Ember said as she snuggled her friend.

Sarah and Carmen bowed their heads as Shadow spread and ruffled his wings proudly, both knowing that the crow was made of the Goddess.

"Grandma, Sarah. The Hale sisters took my friend Chloe and killed my mentor Lydia, and all those other witches… Why? What are they?" Ember asked as she looked at each of them in turn.

Sarah's eyes locked with Ember's. "They are of the sea, ancient creatures of myth and legend. They have been swimming through the oceans of the world for eons."

"Mermaids?" Ember asked as she intently listened to Sarah.

"No, Ember. What the Hale sisters have become is something far worse. They are sirens, and they possess the most evil of powers. They can control the minds of others, bend them to their will, confuse and cloud memories with their voices, drawing humans to them. They can shape shift into all forms of creatures, even birds, "Sarah said as she looked at Shadow with concerned eyes. "And there is one prize that they covet above all others. The blood of witches."

Ember blinked as she took in all that Sarah was saying. It

all made sense now. The Hale sisters' strange glowing eyes, the way they moved, the marble-like appearance of their skin.

"How do I stop them? How do I defeat these creatures?"

"The Goddess walks with you, child. She has sent her messenger to be your guide," Carmen said as she took Ember's hands in hers. "Look deep in his eyes and see what lies inside."

"For under the Goddess's light you will see, you will see how you will defeat the three," Sarah continued as she now held Ember's other hand. A circle of light began to form in the center of the three women. As it grew brighter, Carmen's book appeared. Ember could feel the burning heat building in her hands as purple flames ignited between the women, lighting up the pages in the book as quickly flipped, finally stopping on a page revealing a spell that had not been visible before. Now the words, previously hidden, glowed in a bright purple.

"Goddess night, on the crow's flight,
Come to your daughter and help her fight.
With sword and shield, be at her side, and bind the
Sirens where there is no light."

All three women chanted the spell from the book as the purple flames grew brighter. Ember closed her eyes, the burning feeling spreading all over her body. When she opened them, they had turned a deep, dark black and glowed with the reflection of purple flames. Power took over her and was like nothing she had ever felt. It coursed through her body and out of her fingertips. Now, she could see through the flames, beyond them, to the material world where she saw Thomas at the Hale house, trapped by Sirena. Her legs straddling him, hands at his throat.

"No! She has Thomas!" Ember yelled out. She knew she only had seconds before Sirena took his life, trapping his soul in that dark, empty place.

"Go now, my child, go through the flames. It will take you to him. Do not fear. You have the power of our blood, and you have the power of the Goddess and all those She commands. Go save him and our sisters, set them free, and banish those bitches back to the darkness where they belong," Carmen yelled, her voice loud and intense. Ember let go of the woman's hands and stepped close to the bright purple flames.

"What if the darkness takes me, Grandmother? What if I get lost? What if the fear that took Victoria takes me?"

"You must fight it, girl. Trust in yourself. Trust the ones who have touched your heart, especially him…The necromancer. He holds great power. He believes in you, as I have always believed in you." Ember quickly turned back to her grandmother. "Who is the Necromancer?"

"Trust your feelings, child. Believe, and you will save us all."

Ember stepped into the purple flames as they consumed her completely. Before she was on the other side, she yelled out to Carmen, "I will, I promise. I love you, Grandma!"

With that, Ember fell fast, down into the flames. She could hear Shadow's cries in her ears as the real world rushed up to meet her. With a jolt, she was back, Shadow on her shoulder. As she looked around at her surroundings, she realized she wasn't in her bed, where she had fallen asleep. She and Shadow were standing in front of the Hale mansion. She blinked as Shadow's vision merged with hers. She could see everything, every detail, every movement around her through her all-black eyes. The bright purple flames illuminated her skin as they ignited all around her. The pages of Carmen's book, now in her hands, glowed with the same purple light. It burned her fingers, as the heat built up inside her, a fury she could not contain.

With laser focus, her eyes fixated on the heavy wooden front door of the house. She knew Thomas was inside, his life in that siren's hands. Without a moment of hesitation, Ember ran for the door. Her legs were moving so fast that her body was a bright streak of purple fire as she burst through the door, blowing it off its hinges and through the foyer like an explosion of wind and flames. Ember stopped her momentum abruptly as she entered the house. She slowly turned her head to see Sirena on the floor in front of Thomas, a look of terror on her face.

Ember stepped into the parlor, her eyes scanning everything in the room. She looked at Thomas; he had barely moved, even after the loud explosion that shattered the door and shook the entire house to its foundation. Ember inched closer to Sirena, as she scrambled to her feet and lunged at Thomas, her claws reaching back for his throat.

"Get your hands off of him, bitch!" Ember yelled.

Shadow jumped off her shoulder and flew directly at Sirena. She screamed as she raised her hands, trying to shield her face from his sharp beak and talons. She ran to the other side of the room, crashing against the wall, desperately doing her best to flee from his attack. Ember slowly walked to Sirena, her black eyes watching as Shadow pecked and scratched without mercy. With a wave of her hand, Ember withdrew Shadow's attack. He flew and landed next to Thomas with a loud caw.

"No more pretending, Sirena. I know who you are and what you have done," Ember said as she looked at Sirena curled up against the wall.

Sirena unfolded her arms from her face and looked past Ember, a flash of relief in her glowing eyes. Before Ember could turn to see what was behind her, she felt a sharp pain in her chest, a stabbing pain, as if someone had driven a knife into her heart. She doubled over in pain and screamed as her grandmother's book fell from her hands onto the floor. She turned her head to see Willow standing behind her, smiling, her claws wrapped around Shadow's neck.

CHAPTER 27

"We have your pretty little birdie, witch," Willow said as Shadow pecked at her hand, struggling to free himself from her grasp.

Ember struggled to get to her feet, the pain in her heart taking the wind out of her as Willow tightened the grip on Shadow's fragile neck.

"Let him go, Willow," Ember said, trying to catch her breath and fight through the pain in her chest.

"Back away from our sister and we will!" Willow snarled, her blue-silver eyes glowing brighter than ever.

"Willow! Stop this," Jasmine yelled as she burst into the parlor, seeing what her sister was doing.

Ember turned towards Willow, trying to focus her vision, which had become wild and erratic as Shadow fought against his captor. She rubbed her hands together, intensifying the flames, making them burn brighter and hotter, the magic in her hands flowing out of her body, surrounding her.

"If you hit us with whatever shit magic you think you have, we will snap his neck,' Willow responded, seeing Ember's plan for attack.

"Sister, please. We can handle her without hurting her seer," Jasmine pleaded with her sister.

Willow whipped her head around to look at Jasmine. "Shut up, Jasmine! Defending this disgusting witch and her bird? Why? Are you not our sister?"

"Willow, wait. We might be able to strike a deal with the witch," Sirena said as she stood up and turned to look at Ember. She wiped some blood away from her lips with her hand, smearing red lipstick across her face. "Impressive, Ember. We knew you had power; we just didn't know how much. So, we decided to give you just a little push."

Ember's black eyes looked quickly around the room, her head tilting from side to side as she focused back on Willow. "If you hurt Shadow, you will bring down a wrath I will not be able to control."

"Ember. We meant what we told you at our first meeting. We are your friends. We don't want to hurt you, or your Shadow. We want you to join us, to be one of us, as our fourth sister," Sirena said, her voice sickly sweet.

"Sister, that can never be! A witch in this house," Willow protested as she kept her grip on Shadow.

"Don't listen to Willow, always jealous of those who hold more power," Sirena said as she turned her back on her sisters. "We know you think what we have done is cruel, but you are so young. You do not understand that at times of great need, sacrifices must be made for the greater good."

"Murdering innocent witches, that is the greater good?" Ember asked as she took a few steps closer to Willow, never taking her eyes off her. "Also, don't you already have a fourth sister?"

Anger flashed across Sirena's face, Ember's question catching her off guard as Ember moved in closer. "How do you know…." Sirena began to say.

"Stop, don't get any closer," Willow interrupted, drawing Sirena's attention back to Shadow squawking in pain.

Sirena's expression changed to a toothy grin. 'We know you think they were innocent, but if you give us a chance, you will understand. You will have everything you have ever wanted. To be accepted, loved, and admired. You will never have to look down when you pass people in the street. You will have beauty and power beyond your wildest dreams," Sirena said as she looked over at Thomas, "and you will have the man you love. All you have to do is join us, share your power with us, and we will need to take lives no more."

Ember's mind raced; she knew she couldn't trust Sirena, but as she looked at Shadow and then over at Thomas, now waking up from the absinthe and nightshade haze, she knew she had to do something. She knew Sirena was clever, but not as clever as she thought she was.

"Fine, let Shadow and Thomas go, and I'm sure we can come to some agreement," Ember said as she lowered her hands, the flames dimming slightly.

"Ember, no, don't listen to her," Thomas said from behind Willow as he struggled to get to his feet.

"Of course, anything you want, just agree to join us, and no harm will come to your loves," Sirena said over her shoulder to her sister. "Willow, give the crow to me."

Willow looked at her sister, her eyes glowing with rage. "Sure, she can have her bird back," Willow said as she held Shadow out in front of her. "And she can bury him next to her friends." She snapped Shadow's neck with a loud crack and threw his lifeless body at Ember's feet.

Ember screamed, the pain in her chest excruciating, as if her heart had exploded. She fell to her knees next to Shadow's lifeless body, tears of anger falling on his feathers. Jasmine stood motionless with her hand over her mouth, not believing what her sister had just done. Sirena whipped around and screamed at Willow, "Stupid girl, what have we done?"

Willow stepped in close to Sirena, snarling, "We are sick of listening to you. We are the powerful ones. We should be doing what we want. We don't need your permission, just like we didn't need your permission to kill her mentor or her best friend."

Hearing Willow's words enraged Ember. Hot tears burned as they came down her face. The purple flames lit up bright, burning and spreading until she was completely illuminated by them, making her hair float like ribbons of purple fire. At the sight of the raging fire before them, the three sisters began to back away from Ember's terrifying image, as her feet levitated off the floor and she began floating in their direction.

"Ember, we can fix this. We can bring your Shadow back. We have done it before. If you become one of us, you will have him back," Sirena said as she walked in Ember's direction, her hair coming to life and moving like snakes all around her head. "I don't want to hurt you, but I will," she said, her lips curling into a snarl.

Ember knew what she must do. She could hear the voice of the Goddess speaking to her.

'Call them Ember, use their power.'

She closed her eyes as an eerie hush fell over the house. Suddenly, a whirling sound could be heard all around the outside of the mansion. Low at first, then slowly building in intensity. Scratching and pecking at the large windows, all around them. A strong gust of wind came from behind Ember and swooped up from the chimney, blowing out the fireplace, plunging the entire room into darkness, the only light coming from the purple flames that surrounded Ember. The sisters' eyes glowed silver as they looked around the room, desperately trying to see what was circling the house, trying to make an entry, coming for them.

"Ember! What is happening? What are you doing?" Thomas asked as he finally made it to his feet and got as close as he could to her.

Ember turned her attention to him, her black eyes burning, "Thomas, either help me fight them or get out of my way."

With those words, all the windows exploded, spreading shards of glass everywhere, as hundreds of crows flew in, filling up the entire room. They came from all directions, coming together to form a circle around Ember. The sisters all ran out back, out the broken glass doors that led into the gardens, running from the swarm of black wings. Ember stood and watched the sisters retreat, trying to find safety from the hundreds of sharp beaks and razor-like talons. She lifted her left hand above her head and pointed in the direction the sister had run off to. In an instant, the crows stopped circling Ember and flew into a long formation moving in the direction Ember commanded, following the sisters outside.

Ember's eyes could see everything the crows saw; they were all connected as one sharing the same sight, the same strength. She slowly levitated through the broken glass, out to the garden. She could see, through the eyes of the crows, that the sisters had run off in different directions. But Ember knew exactly which sister she was coming for first.

The large black mass of crows flew fast to catch up to Willow as she ran through the maze of bushes, filling the air with their battle cries. Willow looked back to see the crows getting closer. She screamed as she tripped over a tree root and fell in the dirt. The crows encircled Willow as she tried to fight them away with her hands, frantically hitting and punching them, but they quickly overpowered her.

Ember's feet touched the earth in front of Willow. With a

slight movement of her hand, the formation of crows parted and took their positions in the bushes and trees around them.

"You thought that by murdering my Shadow, you were going to lessen my power. But you didn't. You unleashed it," Ember said as she stepped closer to Willow, the crows watching, waiting for their next command.

"I know you murdered Lydia for no reason other than to feed your own cruelty. You were a mean, dark, jealous, soulless person in life, and you remain the same in death."

Willow cackled at Ember's words. "You are so right. We killed your friends because we could. We enjoyed it. There's nothing that you or your birds can do about it. You can't hurt me, so bring it, witch."

Ember breathed in deep. She tilted her head up towards the night sky and closed her eyes. It happened in a flash. A blur of black hair and feathers as Ember spun around quickly, her body disappearing and transforming into hundreds of black wings as she became one with the hundreds of crows as they flew straight at Willow. They engulfed her, lifting her body off the ground. The crows' sharp beaks pecked and scratched at Willow, violently, leaving gaping, bleeding holes all over her face and body. She screamed as they picked at her flesh. Blood sprayed over their feathers as they tore and ripped, their sharp beaks stabbing and pulling at her eyes, until they plucked them out of the sockets and threw them in the dirt beneath them.

Thomas stumbled out of the house and into the garden. He could hear screams of pain in the distance. He followed the cries until he reached the violent scene. He leaned on a tree and watched as the crows ripped Willow apart. Blood and chunks of flesh splashed everywhere. The assault continued until Willow's mangled body dropped to the ground in a puddle of blood. In a whirl of wind and wings, the crows transformed back into Ember's form right in front of his eyes.

"Ember, is that you?" Thomas asked as his eyes and his brain could not comprehend what he had just seen.

Ember looked over at Thomas, her black eyes showing no emotion. Thomas searched her eyes for the beautiful, shy woman he had fallen in love with. "Ember?'

She said nothing to Thomas and turned to look down at Willow, her once-blonde hair now soaked red with blood. She kneeled next to the battered body and looked at the empty sockets where her eyes used to be.

"I can hurt you, and I will hurt you," Ember whispered to Willow as she struggled to breathe. She scratched blindly at the ground, trying desperately to get away from Ember.

"Ember, enough!" Thomas yelled, "Lydia wouldn't want you to do this. Chloe wouldn't either. You are better than this!"

"Am I?" Ember asked, looking back at him, his reflection visible in her black eyes.

"Yes, Ember, you are. This isn't you. You are not a killer. You would never murder anyone."

"This isn't murder, this is justice. "

Ember stood, and she raised her arms above her head. The crows that had been waiting and watching from the trees jumped and took flight, circling all around her. She smiled as their feathers brushed against her skin.

"Go bring me the other two," Ember commanded as the crows broke off and split in a different direction, searching for Sirena and Jasmine. Ember turned her attention back to Willow as she clawed at her own face.

"Why are we not healing?" Willow gasped, "Sirena! Help us!"

"Sirena can't help you, Willow. No one can," Ember said as the purple flames from her hands cast a glow over the blood on the ground. "You won't heal; you and your sisters are bound by my magic now. Your powers mean nothing to me," Ember said, taking Willow's face in her hands, the flames burning the flesh that remained.

"Ember," Thomas said as he walked behind her, "I know they deserve this, all the pain they have caused. They will suffer, but it doesn't have to be by your hand."

"It's not by my hand, Thomas. My sisters, my ancestors, and the Goddess, it is by their hand. I am simply their sword," Ember said as she threw Willow's head in the dirt. "Now, I will ask you one last time, will you fight with me?"

Thomas looked at Ember's black eyes. "Yes, I will. I will stand by you, now and forever."

Ember kissed his lips hard. Thomas could feel the heat from her mouth on his as the flames grew and spread between them. The fire hurt his skin at first, but Thomas held her closer and kissed her harder. He surrendered to her kiss, to her flames.

"Good," Ember said as she parted her lips from his, the purple glow now surrounding them both. She turned back to Willow, still whimpering and crawling in the dirt, looking for her plucked eyes. Ember walked to where one of the eyeballs lay. She pressed the eye into the ground with her bare foot, feeling the blood between her toes. "Let's go. This isn't finished..."

CHAPTER 28

The mass of crows flew back to Ember and Thomas. They hovered over their heads like a dense dark cloud, dropping Sirena and Jasmine in front of their dying sister, Willow. They pecked and tore at the two Hale sisters before taking their places high in the trees.

"Sirena," Willow whimpered as she reached for her sister, mustering up the last bit of strength she had.

"Willow," Sirena said with horror in her silver eyes as she looked at her sister's bloody, mangled body. She turned and glared at Ember. "What have you done to us?"

"You have done this, Sirena. You have brought this on your sister and on yourself," Ember replied. "By your own vanity and hubris. You only have yourself to blame." Ember said as she stood over Sirena. "I might decide to take pity on your sisters, if you let mine go."

Sirena laughed. "Let them go? Even if we wanted to, that's impossible. They belong to us, to the sea. They are bound forever."

"To the sea? Really," Ember asked as her piercing black eyes stared back at Sirena, "Then to the sea we shall go." With that, Ember turned around quickly, her long black hair swirling around her, growing longer and darker until it morphed, and her entire body disappeared into hundreds of crows. The others who waited in the trees instantly took flight from the branches and joined with those who flew around them. As a mass, they swirled around all of them like a tornado of feathers. It created a gust of wind that began to lift them all off the ground. Thomas could feel his feet being lifted by the wings all around and underneath him. He closed his eyes and let himself be carried into the sky. It carried all of them away, like a storm cloud through the night sky.

The great cloud of crows dropped the group on the sandy banks of Salem Harbor. It took Thomas a moment to realize where they all were. The crows, still overhead, moved silently like ghosts, flying in a circle until they transformed back into Ember's long wild hair. The entirety of her figure unveiled behind it like a black curtain. He watched as Ember walked over the rocks and sand to where Sirena lay face down. Ember picked Sirena up by the neck and held her out in front of her with one hand. Sirena struggled to free herself from Ember's grasp, fighting Ember's newly acquired strength with her own. She dug her long claws into Ember's skin, as her long curls came alive and entangled Ember's arm all the way up to her face.

"You can't break the spell, witch. What's done is done. You might be able to control those birds, but that means nothing to what dwells beneath the water," Sirena said as she desperately tried to free herself, her eyes glowing bright in the darkness, "and only we command them."

Sirena threw her head back and screamed, the same high-pitched banshee scream that Jasmie had unleashed on Thomas in his office. It was so loud and powerful that it blew Ember down onto the sand. Ember covered her ears to try to shield herself from the horrible noise. Thomas dropped to his knees and covered his head. The vibrations of her voice shook the crow's flight, and they began to drop from the sky into the water. Ember was still able to see through the eyes of the crows that remained in flight. She could see over the still dark harbor water as something began to stir off in the distance. Something was swimming fast towards them, cutting the water with its sharp fins. Sirena, seeing the waves in the water and the sand shake under their feet, ended her siren call. She approached Ember, a look of triumph on her face. She flipped Ember on her back violently and straddled her, pinning her down in the sand. Sirena hissed as her dark tendrils of curls wrapped around Ember's body.

Ember looked into Sirena's eyes. "You were right. You were right about me. About wanting to be loved and accepted. That is all true," she said as the weight of Sirena's body kept her from moving. "But I realized what kept me back. Made me live in doubt, stopped me from seeing the true nature of things. But now, my eyes are open, Sirena, and I see everything." Ember looked up at the sky, past Sirena's shoulder, at the crows flying above them. "And you don't command me."

The crows, hearing Ember's call, swooped down and attacked Sirena. She waved her arms frantically above her head as she lost grip on Ember and ran to the water's edge. Ember knew she only had seconds before she used the voice or disappeared under the water. She closed her black eyes and brought her hands together with a loud clap, dispersing the crows away from Sirena and back to her. They flocked around her as Ember's skin began to once again glow bright with purple flames. The crows dipped and flew into the flames from Ember's body, creating a stormy purple orb all around her. From the growing light of the orb, Carmen's book appeared and dropped on the sand by Ember's feet.

"I didn't understand Lydia's last words to me, but I do now. Everything I need to fight can be seen under the Goddess's light," Ember said as the book opened and the pages flipped quickly, stopping right in the middle. The wind off the ocean came in swiftly, parting the clouds in the sky, letting the moonlight shine down on the book's pages, revealing the hidden spell, the words glowing a bright purple color.

"Under the Goddess's light…. Moonlight," Ember said as she began to read.

Sirena, seeing the book, began to back away from the shore, deeper into the water. Her glowing eyes turned to the sea, looking for the creature to come and protect her. "Come to me now, save me," she screamed, her voice carrying far across the water. The waves began to part, and the water began to vibrate as the creature arose from the depths.

"You have betrayed the Goddess. You have betrayed She who is three, and with the power of the moon, I banish thee," Ember read from the book. She looked up to see a monstrous creature break the water's surface and rise in front of Sirena. Long green armor-like scaled tails slithered out of the water. Using its strong tail to hold its body out of the water, the sea monster swam around Sirena, its face emerging from the surface.

The creature's sliver eyes glowed like flames that reflected bright off the water. Its mouth, full of jagged, sharp teeth, opened into a hideous, wide grin as it spoke. "Who are thou to command us?" It hissed at Sirena as one of its horned, sharp-scaled tails whipped out of the water, striking Sirena in the face and throwing her body back to the water's edge.

It slithered on top of the glassy water towards Ember, close enough to where she could smell the putrid stench of dead fish coming from its black mouth. "Ah, you are the one.

The witch we have been waiting for. Our sirens have finally brought you to us. And now we will have you."

"You won't have me, or any other witch. You are going back to where you came from," Ember said as she looked back at the book. In a heartbeat, one of the creature's tails came out from the water and knocked the book out of Ember's hands and up the sandy embankment.

Thomas, watching the entire scene, saw the book fly through the air and land on the sand. Out of the corner of his eye, he could see Jasmine standing not far from him, her eyes glowing as she watched him. In a split second, they both ran towards the book, Thomas reaching it first as Jasmine fell at his feet. He reached for his gun and pointed it at Jasmine. "Don't move or I will shoot."

"Please, we don't want to stop you! We want to help you," Jasmine said, desperation in her voice.

"Help me? Why would you want to help me?" He stepped back away from the siren, keeping the barrel of his gun on her.

"We speak the truth. We do want to help you. Please, there's no time. You must read the incantation and banish us back to the sea," Jasmine said as she stood and moved her body closer to Thomas.

"Me? I'm not a witch, I can't do magic," Thomas answered as he focused on the words, still shining in the moonlight. Jasmine looked at him, her silver eyes glittering like pearls. "You have the power to control the dead, of reaching through the veil to the other world. That's why Lila and the others appeared to you, and only you. The creature has no power in that world, but you do."

"I can control the dead, how?" Thomas looked up into Jasmine's beautiful face with doubt. What was she saying? How could he be sure that she wasn't trying to trick him somehow? Seeing the conflict in Thomas, Jasmine moved towards him, the end of his gun pressed against her chest. "There is no time to explain. You must read from the book. You must open the veil and free the souls that have been trapped. Once you have summoned the witches, it will make Ember stronger, and the creature will be vulnerable. But you must be quick; the veil cannot stay open for long," Jasmine said, pleading with Thomas to hurry.

Thomas turned his head slightly and studied Jasmine. "Why are you helping us?"

Tears ran from her eyes. "We love our sisters, but it was wrong what Sirena did. We don't belong here. We are dead, and we should have stayed dead." Thomas heard her words and looked deep into her silver watery eyes and knew she was telling the truth.

He slowly holstered his gun and reached out to take Jasmine's hand. "Thank you," he said warmly.

Jasmine wiped the tears from her face. "Go! You must hurry, read. We will distract the beast."

Thomas took a deep breath and began to read. A strong gust of wind blew down, creating a sandstorm all around them, making it difficult to see.

"Keep going, it's the creature trying to stop you," Jasmine screamed over the wind.

As Thomas brought the book closer to his face, he suddenly felt a sharp pain in the back of his head, and everything went black. Jasmine watched wide-eyed as Thomas fell to the ground after Willow struck him with a large piece of driftwood.

Jasmine screamed as she saw Willow's hollow eye sockets, her blonde hair, red with blood. "We don't need to see; we can hear. Maybe stop yapping like always, sister," Willow said as she raised the wood over her head to strike a final blow to Thomas.

"No," Jasmine cried as she jumped and tackled her

injured sister to the ground. She grabbed the driftwood before Willow could reach it and struck her in the left temple as hard as she could. Blood sprayed over the sand and rocks. Jasmine threw the wood down and crawled over to Thomas. She shook him violently." Wake up! Please!" she yelled.

Jasmine felt the earth-shaking underneath them. She looked to the ocean, where Sirena was face down in the water, not moving.

The creature's shiny tail wrapped around Ember's neck and torso, pulling her into the water. The crows swooped down trying to defend her, clawing and biting, but the scales of the creature were too hard and thick for them to penetrate.

They circled and regrouped overhead, cawing loudly, desperately trying to find a way to stop the creature from dragging Ember down into the deep ocean.

Thomas slowly regained consciousness as he rubbed the back of his head, feeling a large lump and warm blood. He tried to shake off the blurry double vision and looked for the book. He dug through the sand until he found it. He stood, still feeling woozy from his head injury. He flipped the pages until he found the spell and began to read loudly.

"I call upon you, Her who is many, and many who is Her. Dark Goddess, queen of Battle, ride on the dark wings of your crows. Raise your sword and open the veil between worlds."

The creature snapped its head to look at Thomas as he read. It hissed as a forked tongue rolled out of its monstrous mouth. Its scaled tails undulated through the water faster in Thomas's direction, still keeping a tight grip on Ember. Thomas's attention was interrupted by the creature splashing through the water, moving closer to him.

"Keep reading!" Ember yelled, the purple flames from her

hands growing brighter as she fought the creature's crushing armored tentacles

"Hear me now, dark Mother, hear my call. Give me the power of the river of death, of the land soaked in blood, give me the power to command all that dwell in darkness."

The creature snarled and growled. It twitched and recoiled its tails away from Ember. Its glowing large eyes focused on Thomas as it slithered through the water's edge.

"Who is this that calls upon Her? Thou hast no power here," the sea creature growled as bile dripped out of its mouth.

"By the maiden, mother, and crone. I command you release the souls of the ones who are of the old Gods," Thomas chanted as a grey mist formed over the water.

The mist moved and swirled up to the sky like a waterspout, growing larger as it approached the beach. Thomas looked out over the sand to see a blue light slowly growing inside the missile of the vortex as it moved. The light was glowing brighter as it floated above the water tornado. The blue light split and divided, forming floating transparent apparitions of women, silently hovering over the dark water. The creature howled and shrieked as the apparitions circled around it, pushing it back into the dark water.

Thomas rushed beside Ember as she raised her hands to command the crows to fly and join the ghostly forms. The creature clawed and whipped its tails in the water, fighting the souls of the witches that had been summoned by the spell. They reached out with ghostly hands and choked the creature, all the while the crows picked at its scaled tails, as green and black blood dripped down over its body.

Jasmine ran up to Ember and Thomas. "Only one thing can destroy it now, our blood, "she said as she stepped into the water, dragging Willow's unconscious body behind her. She pushed her way through the water, letting go of Willow as she approached Sirena, still floating motionless. She cradled Sirena in her arms; tears fell from her cheeks as she gently kissed Sirena's lips. "We are so sorry, sister, but this is the way it must be."

Sirena began to wake from her blow to the head and looked at Jasmine. "Sister, what are we doing? No! Please." She desperately tried to break away from her sister's embrace, her eyes wild with fear. She looked over to the shore where Ember and Thomas were standing. "Stop this! You can still stop this. Please, I beg of you, spare my sisters!"

"No," Ember said, her black eyes like mirrors. "The Goddess demands justice, and justice she will have." Ember clapped her hands together, bringing all the crows down on the creature at once, like a fist of wings and feathers.

Sirena's tear-filled eyes fell on Willow's body as the creature thrashed in the seawater. She let out a scream as she saw her sister face down in the waves. Jasmine smiled through the flood of tears and sobs, as she placed a hand on Sirena's head.

Sirena turned to look into Jasmine's eyes, seeing what her intentions were, but powerless to stop it. Sirena knew that it was time. It was all over. She watched Jasmine slowly lift a long claw-like nail to her own neck. She let out a shriek of pain as Jasmine sliced deep across her throat. Dark blood poured from the gaping wound, down over Jasmine's chest and mixed with the salty sea water.

"In the name of the dark Goddess, I banish you from this world, with your blood and the blood of all who came before, to the black sea where you came. May the same blood that gave you power, bind you forever to the depths. May the mother of the sea hold you in her arms, forever," Ember said loudly, her voice carrying over the dark water.

The creature, weak and shredded, green and black blood oozing from gaping holes in its tails, slithered over the surface to Jasmine's and Willow's lifeless bodies. Its sharp scaled tails coiled around them, tearing at their flesh as it pulled and squeezed. It slowly began to retreat into the murky depths, dragging the two Hale sisters down with it.

Sirena stood helplessly in waist-deep water and watched her sisters being taken to their deaths by the same creature that had given them life.

She stumbled out of the water and collapsed on the beach, her head buried in the sand. As she lifted her face slowly upwards, Ember could see that the magical silver in her eyes had disappeared. Her skin, once so beautiful, had been torn to shreds by the creature's scales and claws; her beautiful features were now a bloody mess of lacerations and bruises.

Ember stood over Sirena, the crows still flying above her head. "I know you think I'm going to kill you. I want to, and you deserve it, but you will suffer a fate worse than death. You will live, in this body, alone, with only your guilt and pain to keep you company. You will live the rest of your very long life trapped in a nightmare; in the prison you built for others. Just you, and the blackness of your heart."

The purple flames that had surrounded Ember now dimmed, until they disappeared under her skin. Her eyes returned to their bright yellow color. She reached for Thomas's hand as they both looked at the ghostly apparitions that still floated gracefully over the water. Ember could see the figures of Lydia and Chloe, smiling down at her.

Thomas held her close, his hands in her thick hair, as he gently turned her face to his. "I told you I would never let you fall," Thomas replied as he gave her a long, deep kiss. They both stood there as the crows flew around the souls of the witches and gently carried them off into the moonlight.

"They are free," Ember said, her face nuzzled against Thomas's chest, "thanks to you."

Thomas placed a kiss on the top of her head. "Yeah, you are going to have to explain all that to me later, but for now I just want to hold you. I love you, Ember." Thomas held her close as she looked up at him. "I love you, with all my heart."

"I love you more," Ember replied with a cheeky smile.

"The sun is coming up in a couple of hours. We need to get back to the mansion," Thomas said as he looked down at Sirena, curled up on the sand.

"Back there? Why?" Ember asked as she bent to pick up her grandmother's book.

"Because this bitch is going to jail for murder," Thomas said as he looked at Sirena. "We can't have them come here. I mean, how do we explain this?" He picked Sirena up by one arm. "Let's go, sweetheart. You are about to give a full confession."

Thomas began walking off the beach toward the street, dragging Sirena by the arm. He looked back at Ember. "Are you coming?"

"Yes, I just, I can't go back there. But can you find Shadow? Bring him back to me?" She asked as one tear fell from her eye. "He was more than my friend; he was my connection to that other world. Without him, I might have lost that magical place forever."

"Ember, Shadow is a part of you, and you of him. He will always be with you; you haven't lost anything. I'm sure you will see him again."

Ember looked up at the star-filled sky. "You're right. I know I will."

CHAPTER 29

$\mathcal{Y}$ellow crime scene tape circled the Hale mansion as neighbors stood on the street with curious stares, wondering what had happened in the house the night before. They watched as Sirena was taken away, handcuffed to a stretcher, screaming and kicking madly, the shredded and scarred skin on her face and body red and raw. She hollered incoherent words as she was placed in the back of an ambulance. Thomas stood on the front porch of the mansion and watched the ambulance rumble down the street.

"I should have never doubted you, Cole," Captain Torres said as he walked out of the house behind Thomas, "but who would have thought that one woman could be capable of all this?"

Thomas rubbed his hair and glanced over at his boss. "I knew it, I just had to prove it."

"Well, we have plenty of evidence in the house. She kept trophies. It shouldn't be that hard to tie it all to each victim. I just can't believe she would kill her sisters as well. You think they were going to turn on her? That's why she killed them?"

"It's possible, but we aren't going to get any answers from her. She's completely insane," Thomas said as he turned to walk back into the house.

"Still can't figure out how she pulled this off for so long. And the way she murdered those girls was brutal, and for what? What was her motive?" Torres asked as he shook his head.

Both walked into what was once the main parlor. Plates of broken glass covered the floor along with black soot from the fireplace. "Do you think she blew up the place? Gas maybe?" Torres asked. "Trying to burn the house down, cover her tracks."

"Hard to tell. Fire Marshall is looking into it. Regardless, I don't think we will ever find the bodies of her sisters. At least not all of them. They did find some parts out back. We will have to wait for the DNA, but I'm certain it's one of the sisters, " Thomas said as he watched the forensic team sift through the piles of debris.

"She leaves the bodies of the other victims in the water but disposes of her sisters in a way we will never find them. Doesn't really match her pattern. You are sure she wasn't working with anyone?"

Thomas looked at Torres. "Sirena Hale is the only suspect. She's been doing this under our noses for months, hiding in plain sight. My guess is the sisters saw something they weren't supposed to or maybe tried to bribe her. I don't know, but whatever it was, it signed their death warrants."

"Well, go home, get some sleep. I'll make sure the boys finish up here. I'm going to want a full report tomorrow."

Thomas turned to look at his captain with a side eye.

"Ok, Cole. No later than the end of the week, and make sure there are no loose ends. I want this case airtight," Torres said as he looked out one of the broken windows. 'I see the vultures have circled."

. . .

THOMAS TURNED to see several media and news vans pull up in front of the house.

"You want me to handle it?" Torres asked as he put his hand on Thomas's shoulder.

"Yeah, boss," Thomas said softly.

"You got it," Torres said as he made his way towards the door. "Hey, I'm proud of you, Tommy."

Thomas shook his head and gave his captain a smile. He watched as Torres walked outside and up to a reporter with a microphone in her hand.

He glanced around the room, trying to remember everything that happened the night before. But a lot of his memory was clouded. He walked carefully through the broken glass and turned over the furnishings. He could see a small bit of black feathers under a pillow. He carefully lifted it to see Shadow's lifeless body. He gently picked him up and wrapped him in his jacket. He had made a promise to Ember, and he was intent on keeping it.

"Do you want us to bag and tag that?" One of the forensic technicians said from across the room as he watched Thomas pick up the crow.

"No, it's just a dead bird. Must have flown in and got hurt by the glass."

The technician shrugged and went back to what he was working on. Thomas walked out of the room through the back, avoiding the mass of media that had gathered out front. He walked out through the back garden, keeping his head down as he passed more technicians collecting evidence. He cut through the neighbor's yard and back onto Chestnut Street where he had parked his car.

Thomas turned the heater on to the highest setting and closed his eyes as the warm air hit his frozen hands and face.

He lay back on the headrest and took a deep breath, trying to process everything that happened the night before. He was thankful the case had come to an end and there would be no more dead women washing up on the shores of Salem, but he couldn't help but feel a sense of uncertainty, of uneasiness. Not that he doubted his actions, he knew the sisters were guilty and deserved what happened. He was confident there was more than enough evidence to secure a conviction, even if there might be some unanswered questions. He was sure the people of the city wanted this terror to be over and were not going to ask many questions. Especially questions that might lead to the supernatural. It would be way too unbelievable, even for this town.

Thomas's sense of uneasiness came from Jasmine's words to him on the beach. He remembered what she had said to him, of him having power over the dead. How he was able to read from the book and somehow free the trapped souls of those women. He had never had anything like that happen to him before this case, so why now? He never had any magical beliefs, and he certainly never considered that he would have abilities.

He rubbed his stubbled face and tried to put those thoughts in the back of his mind. Too much had happened to make sense of it right now.

He reached into his jacket and carefully unwrapped Shadow, placing him on the seat next to him. For a brief second, he thought it might be best if he buried Shadow so Ember wouldn't see him like this. The last thing he wanted was to put her through any more pain. But he had given her his word. He pushed the ignition button and listened to the engine warm up. After a few seconds, he put the car into gear and drove down the street towards Ember's apartment.

* * *

Ember tiptoed softly into her apartment, not wanting to wake Tristan, who still slept on the couch. He hadn't even noticed that she was gone. She knew it would be difficult to explain how she had disappeared from her own bed, so she wanted to avoid it.

She softly closed her bedroom door behind her. She looked over at her unmade bed and saw Shadow's favorite pillow, and her heart ached. She looked up to the ceiling, trying to stop the tears that were building up in her eyes. An overwhelming feeling of loss washed over her all at once. She couldn't hold back the tears anymore. She threw herself on the bed and cried not just for Shadow, Lydia, or Chloe, but also for Sirena. A part of Ember felt incredible sadness for her, for everything she had done, and for the punishment she would have to face.

She got up from her bed after a few hours and looked at herself in the mirror. She was a mess; her long hair was tangled and full of sand. Her face and dress were dirty and tears-stained. She looked down at her hands and realized it wasn't dirt, but blood.

She ran to the bathroom sink and scrubbed her hands with scalding water and soap as she sobbed. She collapsed on the bathroom floor, the pain in her heart too much to bear. She knew what she did had to be done, but she had never seen that side of herself. She didn't even know it existed, the dark rage that had taken over her. She lay her head back and wondered if that was who she truly was. Had she been denying herself all these years?

After another hour, Ember pulled herself up from the tile floor and looked at her reflection once more. She studied her face and tried to find a small glimpse of the girl in the simple dress that looked at herself in the large mirror on that last day at her childhood home. She wondered if she was still there as she looked back at her blood-stained hands. She turned the bathtub faucet all the way on and watched the hot water fill the old tub as she slipped out of her dirty dress. Ember slowly lay back and let the steamy water wash over her.

A loud knock at the front door startled Tristan awake. He looked around the apartment and saw Ember's bedroom door was closed, and assumed she must still be sleeping. He got up from the couch and looked through the peephole in the door to see a tall, handsome, blonde man on the other side. He smiled as he opened the door. "You must be tall and slim fit?'

Thomas looked confused, not understanding why there was another man answering Ember's door. Then he remembered Ember telling him about her friend in Connecticut.

"And you must be Tristan. Ember told me all about you. I'm Thomas."

"Yes, I know, the detective. Pleasure, come in," Tristan said as he stepped to one side, giving room for Thomas to enter the apartment. "Ember is still sleeping. She must have been exhausted because I haven't heard a sound from her."

Thomas stood awkwardly in the living room. "Sorry, she didn't tell me you were in town."

"Oh, it was last minute. I was worried. I hadn't heard from her in a while. But you know how she is," Tristan said as he walked into the kitchen. "Can I get you anything? Coffee or tea? You look like you were rode hard and put away wet."

Thomas hadn't noticed how messy his appearance was. "No, thank you. I'm fine," he said as he quickly noticed that Tristan had no clue about the events of the previous night. "I'm just going to check on Ember. There are a few things that I need to tell her."

Tristan smiled and nodded as Thomas opened Ember's bedroom door. The room was empty, but he could hear the water running in the bathroom. He knocked softly on the door before opening it. "Ember."

She looked up to see Thomas standing in her doorway. "Hey," she said softly as she pulled her knees close. Thomas sat on the edge of the bathtub. "How you holding up?"

"I'll be ok. Is it done?"

"Yes, it's done. I took care of everything. It's over," he said as he stroked her head.

"And Shadow? Did you find him?"

Thomas reached into his jacket and pulled out a small bundle. He had wrapped Shadow's body in a scarf. Ember reached out her hands and held the bundle close to her heart. "Thank you, Thomas."

"Of course. I will make sure he is taken care of," he said to Ember as he took the bundle back from her and walked out to place him on his pillow in the bedroom. Thomas walked back into the bathroom and leaned against the door. "I kept your name out of the investigation, so you won't have to go through any questioning."

Ember nodded as she hugged her knees even closer. "Have they found Chloe's body?"

"No. Not yet, but they are looking. I know they will bring her home. I met your friend Tristan. He doesn't seem to know anything about last night," Thomas said as he sat back down on the edge of the tub.

"No, I told him only what he needed to know yesterday," Ember replied as she looked up at Thomas. "I owe you so much."

"You don't owe me anything, Ember," Thomas said as he leaned in close. "I told you there is nothing I wouldn't do for you."

Ember raised her head, and her lips found his. She kissed him softly as he held her cheek tenderly.

"I need to feel you," he said as their lips parted for just a moment. Ember kissed him deeply as she pressed her naked body against his, pulling him into the tub with her. Water overflowed and splashed onto the floor as Thomas fell on top of her in the hot water. Ember laughed, seeing his clothes soaked as he struggled to take them off.

"Wait, I have a perfectly soft bed in the other room," she said as she stood. Thomas, not being able to take his eyes off her breasts, kissed them as he held her closer to him.

Ember stepped out of the tub and wrapped herself in a towel, waiting for Thomas as he quickly peeled off his wet clothes.

In the bedroom, he ripped the towel off of Ember's body and pushed her onto the bed. He stood naked in front of her as his eyes roamed over every inch. She reached to pull him to her, but he grabbed both her hands and pushed them down on the bed above her head. He held her as his mouth explored her body.   Ember gave in to his powerful hold on her and closed her eyes.

CHAPTER 30

The flames of the bonfire blew in the cold wind. Ember stood by the fire holding Tristan's hand as Thomas walked up to her holding Shadow's body. Ember took Shadow from Thomas and walked over to the fire. She raised her head up to look at the moon; she didn't feel sadness. She was happy she was able to send her friend back to the Goddess, back to his mother. She gently placed the small bundle in the flames and watched as the fire burned through the scarf, showing his once beautiful onyx feathers.

"Goodnight, my Shadow. May your crossing through the veil be a peaceful one."

Thomas walked up behind Ember and put his hands on her shoulders. They all stood watching as the smoke rose up to the sky, as if carrying his spirit away from his body. Ember smiled as she watched the smoke travel towards the moon.

She turned to embrace Thomas, as he bent down and buried his face in her hair.

"I'm so sorry, Em," Tristan said, sadness filling his voice.

Ember and Thomas had spent the day explaining everything they could to Tristan about what had happened. He listened and didn't ask many questions. It looked to Thomas that he was just relieved that his friend was safe and unharmed.

"I'm going inside," Ember said as she broke her embrace with Thomas and walked back into the apartment.

Tristan walked up next to him. "Thank you for protecting her. I feel better knowing she has someone looking out for her."

"I love her."

"I know you do," Tristan said with a smile. "I'm going to take off. My husband is probably getting ready to send out a search party."

Thomas laughed. "You aren't going to say goodbye to Ember?'

"She knows I hate goodbyes." Tristan said as he began to walk away. "Oh, there's one more thing. Ember gave this to me before she left, but I think this was for you all along."

Tristan pulled out the silver chain and locket from his pocket and handed it to Thomas. He looked at the initials engraved on the locket - TRC.

"My name is Tristan Richard Cadwell," Tristan said as he looked at Thomas.

"Mine is Thomas Robert Cole," Thomas said with a surprised look on his face.

"I've never told Ember my middle name." He smiled." Like I said, this was meant for you. I was just keeping it safe."

Thomas stood looking at the locket and smiled. For the first time in his life, he couldn't explain something and didn't really care. He put the chain around his neck and walked inside to find Ember standing by the large window in the living room. "I used to stand here and see Shadow on the fence across the street. Chloe would walk past him, and he would squawk at her so loudly, scaring her out of her skin. She would just laugh." Thomas held her by her waist. "I miss them and Lydia."

"I know you do," Thomas whispered in her ear.

"Tristan left without saying goodbye?"

"Yeah, he said you would understand," Thomas replied.

Ember turned around to face Thomas and saw the locket around his neck. "He gave you this?" Ember asked as she touched it.

"He did," Thomas answered. "He told me this was meant for me. Even though you might not have known it. Did you know his middle name is Richard?"

Ember shook her head. "No, I suppose I didn't."

"My middle name is Robert," Thomas said with a smile.

Ember backed away from Thomas and stared into his eyes, a look of surprise on her face.

"What? Is something wrong?"

Ember paced the room as she looked at Thomas. "Something my grandmother said to me, when I saw her and Sarah in the in-between. They said to trust the necromancer."

"Ok, what does that mean?" Thomas asked as he followed Ember around the room.

"What was it that Jasmine told you on the beach? That you have the power to control the dead, to walk between worlds, right?"

"Ah, yeah, something like that. I don't know what she meant. She wouldn't tell me."

"It means my love, that necklace was for you. It means you got this tattoo for a reason." Ember said as she lifted his sleeve to show the crow tattoo on his forearm. "It means you, we, were always destined to be together, and like Shadow, you are not only my protector, but my key to the in-between."

Thomas looked at Ember intensely. "How? Tell me."

Ember stood close to Thomas, as she reached up and held his face. "Stay with me. No matter what."

Thomas nodded as he breathed in deep.

She looked deep in his blue eyes. "In your eyes like ice I see, the door to the world beyond that you will open for me."

In an instant, the world around them turned upside down and quickly fell away. Thomas felt like he was falling down a black hole, faster and faster until his body came to an abrupt stop. He slowly looked around at his surroundings to see snow falling from the sky and rubbed his eyes. He was in a beautiful snow-covered valley surrounded by a thick forest. Pine trees swayed in the wind, while snowcapped mountains stood silently in the distance. He stood and tried to regain his bearings as he looked around. He walked toward the babbling creek running through the snow. He closed his eyes and listened to the quietness, only hearing the water splashing off the ice-covered rocks. He took in the silence of the winter world.

"I was right," a voice said from behind as a bonfire magically ignited next to him.

Thomas turned to see Ember, snowflakes shining like crystals against her black hair. He ran to her, picked her off her feet, and swung her around.

"This is incredible! Where are we?" he asked as he placed her back down on the snow.

"This is the in-between. It's not our world, but also not quite the other world," Ember said, her cheeks pink from the cold.

"It's amazing! How did we get here?"

"You," Ember said. "You have the ability to walk between the veil, maybe even cross it all together."

"I never knew I could do any of this," Thomas said as he took Ember's hand, "Now I can because of you."

Ember smiled. "There are some people who want to meet you."

Ember motioned Thomas to look over to the tree line. Through the snow, Thomas could make out figures walking towards him. It wasn't until they got close to the fire's light that he recognized them. There they all stood. All the women the Hale sisters had killed. They stood in the snow as Thomas looked at each of their faces.

He looked at the woman standing closest. "Annabel," Thomas said as the young woman smiled at him. "Molly, Lila, Jennifer, Elise, and Claire," Thomas said as he looked at all of them in amazement.

"We all came to thank you, Thomas," another voice came from behind. Thomas turned to see Lydia and Chloe standing next to Ember.

"Lydia," Thomas said as he hugged her tightly. He turned to Chloe, the bright yellow bow in her hair standing out against the dark grey sky. He embraced Chloe. "I am so sorry. I failed you," Thomas said to her. "I failed all of you," he said as he stepped back to look at all the women standing before him.

"No, Thomas," Claire said, "you set us free."

"We are all here, free from that dark place thanks to you," Chloe said as she looked at him warmly.

Ember walked up to Thomas. "You did this, Thomas. You saved them, in the only way they could be saved."

Thomas held back tears as he looked at all the women, all of them looking as they did in life.

"Finally, you have found each other," another voice said from the trees.

Thomas and Ember looked up to see Carmen and Sarah walking towards them. Carmen embraced Thomas. "Let me look at you, my boy," she said as she admired his face.

"You are far more handsome in person than you were in my dreams."

"Thomas, this is my grandmother, Carmen, and my ancestor Sarah," Ember said as she took Carmen's hand in hers.

"We have all come to thank you both," Carmen said warmly as she squeezed Ember's hand, "all of us."

Ember looked out to the tree line. All around her stood women, dressed in the clothes of different time periods. "Who are they?" she asked her grandmother.

"They are your family, your army. We are the keepers of traditions, of the old ways. We have protected the sisterhood for centuries, and now it is your turn."

Ember looked at all the faces of her sisters standing around her, and her heart filled with pride. Suddenly, a bit of sadness came over her. "And Victoria?" she asked as she turned to look at her grandmother. "Is she here?"

Carmen smiled at her granddaughter. "No, but she isn't far. You will see her, child. When the time is right."

Ember smiled back at Carmen, understanding the meaning behind her words. She would see her mother again, but not today.

In the distance, a dark figure emerged against the white backdrop of the in-between. All the women bowed their heads and went down to one knee as they saw the woman in a black cloak walking towards them beside a large pure black stallion.

The woman approached Ember, the long mane of her horse the same color as her hair. Ember bowed as she realized it was the Goddess.

"My Lady," Ember said as she looked at Thomas, who still stood. She pulled him down to his knee.

The Goddess approached Ember and tilted her head with

a gloved hand. "Rise, my child." Ember slowly rose to look into the Goddess's purple flame eyes.

"I never doubted you for a second," she said. "I always knew how strong you were, even though you never saw it in yourself." "Your grandmother always knew; she and all of my daughters have always watched over you. You have done so well."

"Thank you, dark mother," Ember said, "I know the power I have, and I owe it all to you."

The Goddess smiled and looked over at Thomas, still on one knee. "I see you enlisted the help of the Fae." She said as she walked to stand in front of Thomas. "Let me look at you. It's been a millennium since I've gazed into the eyes of those who are born of twilight."

Thomas rose slowly to his feet, a look of confusion in his eyes. "I'm sorry, ma'am. I don't know what you mean."

Ember looked at her grandmother. "Fae, I thought you said he was a necromancer," she asked.

"I thought he was, my Lady," Carmen said to the raven-haired woman who stood before them all.

"An easy mistake to make. For the Fae folk are nearly extinct, only half-bloods remain, like your friend," the Goddess said as she looked back at Thomas. "You have always felt it, have you not? The ability to see things humans cannot. To hear whispers on the wind. The power to see, not just the ones who have crossed the veil, but to see what is to come. The inner light that you possess can not only give you the power to see into the darkness, but command it. "

"I'm sorry, I don't understand," Thomas said as he searched the Goddess' face for answers.

"You will, in time. You will learn how to use all your gifts. For now, please accept my deepest gratitude for helping us," she said as she bowed her head slightly to Thomas. She turned back to Ember, "I know you have lost so much, your sisters, and your Shadow."

Ember looked at Lydia and Chloe and smiled, but the thought of Shadow brought tears to her eyes.

"Do not cry, child. All is not lost. Shadow is much a part of me as he is of you," the Goddess said as she wiped away her tears. "You don't think that I would ever take him from you?" Just then, Shadow appeared over the Goddess' head, his majestic wings spread out as he flew and landed on Ember's shoulder, squawking happily.

"My Shadow," Ember said as she hugged her feathered friend. The Goddess turned to Thomas. "I can return Shadow to this world, but only you can help him cross the veil."

Thomas nodded as he watched Ember smile and kiss Shadow's head. "Anything for her."

The Goddess walked towards the woman, still on one knee. "Rise, my children, for the darkness has passed, but it's not gone. It will lie in wait, under the waves, waiting for its chance to yet again spread its evil to all worlds. Now that we have joined forces with the most ancient ones, the Fae, we will only be stronger. Together, we shall be those who protect against it and protect we shall."

The Goddess walked over to her large horse, put her foot in the stirrup, and flung her other leg over the black leather saddle. She looked one last time at Ember. "Remember child, do not forget who you are, and who walks with you." With a nudge to her horse's flank, she rode off until she disappeared through the trees and over the snowy mountains.

Carmen put her hand on Ember's shoulder. "It's time to return to your world, darling girl."

Ember hugged her grandmother tightly. "Will I see you again?"

"Of course, we will all always be here," Carmen said as she looked over at Thomas. "Protect my girl."

"Yes, Ma'am," Thomas said with a smile as he took Ember's hand. The wind picked up, swirling the snow around them.

"I love you; I love all of you," Ember called out over the howling wind. In a flash, she was lost in a sea of white so bright that it blinded her.

CHAPTER 31

The sound of the swirling, roaring wind filled Ember's ears. The white light in front of her eyes was so bright it blinded her.   She could still feel Thomas's hand in hers, sense his presence close to her. She slowly blinked as her eyelids opened.

"Ember. It's ok. Look at me," Thomas whispered in her ear. She opened her eyes fully and let them adjust to the bright sunlight. They were both standing in a sunny green field, tall grass with bright purple flowers all around them. A large, twisted moss-covered tree shaded them from the bright sun in a cloudless blue sky. Wildflowers of all different bright colors swayed in the warm breeze in the distance, as pollen floated all around them.

"What is this place?" Ember asked as she walked over to a moss-covered log. She looked as rabbits peeked their small heads out of holes in the dry logs to look at her curiously.

"This is my in-between," Thomas said as he looked over at Ember. "I don't know how we got here, but I have seen this place before, in my dreams. I just didn't think it was real."

Ember outstretched her arms and spun around in the field of flowers. "It's so beautiful!"

She stopped as small firefly creatures buzzed around her; they glowed a bright blue as they whipped around her hair. Thomas took her hand and pulled her close to him, his arm around her waist, and kissed her softly. Shadow squawked loudly from his perch in the tree, his dark features blending beautifully against the purple flowers. Ember laughed. "Can we stay here forever?"

"I'm afraid not, but we can come here whenever we want," Thomas said, as he picked a piece of pollen out of Ember's tousled dark hair.

"That is good enough for me," she said as she kissed him under the purple flowers.

"You know your powers will work here too, I'm sure of it," Thomas said as he pulled his lips from hers.

Ember looked up at him, with a mischievous grin. Then up to her feathered friend in the tree. "Shadow, let's fly!"

With that, Shadow jumped off the tree branch and glided down to Ember. As he spread his wings, Ember's hair spread out all around her and instantly changed into dozens of crows. With Shadow in the lead, the crows spiraled high in the sky then spread out like a black wave over the green field.

Thomas smiled as he watched the crows dance. It all felt like a dream, and he didn't understand how or why, but he didn't care. His heart filled with joy, feeling the sun on his face and watching his love fly as high and fast as she could.

The crows came fast, a blur of wings, whipping around the tree, shaking purple flowers free from the branches. They swooped down, and in a flash of onyx hair, Ember appeared. She ran to Thomas and threw her arms around his neck, making him lose his balance as they both fell on top of the soft grass. Ember giggled as violet petals landed all around them.

Thomas touched her face. "You could fly to the moon and back, but I will always keep my feet on the ground for you."

Ember kissed his lips, the sun shining off his silver locket, and reflecting a rainbow prism on his skin. Ember had never felt so free and happy. She knew in her heart this moment wouldn't last forever, but she knew she and Thomas could make their forever anywhere. The world was open to them, and she knew together anything was possible.

"So now what?" Ember asked as she sat up and ran her fingers through her hair.

Thomas propped himself up on one elbow and looked at her lovingly; he thought she never looked more beautiful than she did at that very moment. "What do you mean?"

"What happens now, with everything?" Ember asked as she twirled a strand of hair around her finger.

"Well, first I want to sleep for like a week," Thomas laughed, "and then I have to work. I need to make sure that everything is done right to close out this case. Not to mention, I haven't forgotten about Chloe. I have to bring her home."

Ember looked down at the grass. "I haven't forgotten about her either," she said as she stretched out next to Thomas. "We will find her together," she said as Shadow landed in the grass next to them.

Thomas scratched his head, ruffling his feathers.

"I think it's time to go home," Thomas said as he leaned over and kissed her lips lightly.

"Yes, let's go home."

The Summerland they were in began to turn fuzzy, like a picture out of focus, and then in an instant, they were back in Ember's apartment, lying on the floor, the soft midday sunlight creating patterns on the floor around them. Shadow squawked happily to be back on his favorite spot on the couch as he nestled in for a long-needed rest.

Ember touched her forehead to Thomas's, so grateful they both could put all the darkness behind them. They spent the next day in her warm bed, enjoying being close to each other. Ember loved the smell of his skin and the touch of his hands. She smelled his pillow after he got up to shower, rolled over, and looked out the window at the morning light. As happy as she was, the future seemed insecure as thoughts of Chloe and Lydia ran through her mind.

She knew they needed to find her friend. She couldn't bear the thought of her body being somewhere cold and alone. Then she thought of Lydia. The shop had been so important to her, and it was one of her most cherished possessions. Ember couldn't allow the store to close, now that Lydia was gone. She sat up in bed and wrapped the sheet around her; she knew exactly who to go to for help.

She quickly got dressed and could hear the water running, so Thomas was still in the shower. She quietly walked into the kitchen, as Shadow squawked loudly. "Shh, boy. Come on, we have somewhere to go."

Ember wrote a note for Thomas, saying she was going for a walk, and she would meet him later at his loft. She threw on her coat and headed out the door, Shadow flying overhead.

It was a cold, bright morning; Ember pulled up the collar on her black coat and walked quickly down the street. She turned down the small alley and stopped at the red door. Shadow flew down and took his place on her shoulder as she knocked three times. After a few minutes, the door opened.

"I knew you would come," Mya said as she stood in the doorway, dressed in an elegant black pencil skirt dress, her silver hair pulled back in an elegant French twist, and her makeup, usually applied perfectly, a bit smeared around her eyes, as if she had been crying.

Ember followed her through the door and down the stairs to the dark room with the pentacle painted on the floor. The smell of incense smoke filled the air. On the altar at the front of the room, many candles burned, their flames flickering and casting shadows on the dark walls. In the center of the table, surrounded by candles, was a picture of Lydia, and right next to it was a green leather book. Mya stood in front of the altar for a moment before she turned to face Ember.

"Lydia crossing the veil was a great loss to us. She was a most honored sister, and her presence here will be missed. But it was just like Lydia to not stay gone for long."

Ember looked at Mya with a confused look. "She came to you?"

"Oh yes, in a dream, when you released her from that dark prison where she and our sisters were being held. She told me what you and Thomas did. How you defeated the Three. We will be forever in your debt."

"You don't owe me anything, Mya. What I did, what we did, was what was right. It was my fate." Ember said as she walked closer to Mya.

"Yes, indeed," she smiled. "Lydia loved you like a daughter, and she wanted me to give you this." Mya turned around and picked up the green book from the table. "It is tradition that when a witch dies, her Grimoire is either burned or buried with them. But, in some special cases, the book is passed on to a descendant. Lydia did not have family of her own to speak of, so she wanted you to have her book.' She held the book in both hands as she passed it to Ember. "It is a great honor to have a witch's most loved and protected possessions. Keep it close to you; keep it safe, for it holds the mysteries of our order."

Ember took the book and held it close to her. "I absolutely will cherish it and guard it with my life.'

Mya smiled at her. "I know you will, dear."

"Mya, the reason I'm here is to ask you a favor. I didn't know where else to go."

"Anything, darling," Mya said as she sat in a large leather chair and motioned for Ember to take a seat next to her as Shadow jumped off her shoulder to perch high in the rafters.

"It's about the shop. Lydia loved it so much, she dedicated her life to it, and it meant the world to her. I can't stand the thought of it closing. I want it to continue, to flourish, in Lydia's honor. I know she was a member of the coven, and I know you two were so close. I can only trust you to keep the store up and running. I know that's what Lydia would have wanted."

Mya reached out for Ember's hand." Oh, my sweet girl, that is so touching, and I agree. The shop should continue, expand even."

Ember breathed a sigh of relief and smiled. "Oh, wonderful. I am so happy you are willing to take it over."

"You misunderstand, Ember. The store isn't for me, but for you. Lydia passed on her estate, including the store, to you. There's a sealed envelope in the book; you will find all her last wishes and instructions for you there."

Ember sat back in surprise and shook her head from side to side. "No, this is too much, I can't accept this," she said as tears welled in her eyes.

Mya squeezed her hand. "It is done, love; I am certain you will do right by her wishes and make the shop more successful than ever."

Ember nodded as she rose from her seat, Shadow flying down to her shoulder. "Thank you so much, Mya."

"Wait, my love, one more thing. Now that Lydia is no

longer with us, there is a spot open in the coven. We would be so honored if you took Lydia's place."

Ember paused for a moment and turned to look at Mya. "That is a great honor. Thank you so much for offering. I know I still have so much to learn, and I want to do that on my own. Just me and my Shadow. But thank you."

Mya folded her hands in front of her. "Of course, I completely understand. If you change your mind, our door is always open."

Ember smiled at Mya as she walked back up the stairs to the sun-drenched street. She held the book close to her as she made her way through the maze of busy people, just living their lives, not knowing how close their world came to being swallowed up by darkness. Some gave her glances as she passed them on the sidewalk, Shadow on her shoulder. But for the first time in her life, she didn't mind. She walked with her head held high, smiling at their curious expressions. To her surprise, they smiled back.

CHAPTER 32

It had been a month since that night on the beach when the Hale sisters were sent back to their underwater prison, and Sirena had been put on trial for the murders. They rushed the proceedings after the police found Chloe's body floating in the water close to Marblehead.

Ember sat at the back of the courtroom and watched as the once-striking, beautiful, and statuesque Sirena slouched in a chair, her head down, looking at the floor. She didn't even look up as she pleaded guilty to the deaths of the women. Her musical voice was now reduced to a whisper.

The condition of her plea was that she would spend the rest of her days confined to a state hospital. As the bailiff led Sirena out of the courtroom, everyone tried to get a glance at her horribly disfigured face, but she looked back and met Ember's eyes just for a second. That's all the time Ember needed to see the pain in Sirena's expression. Ember couldn't help but feel some pity for her, but she knew this was what she deserved. She had done this to herself.

It had started snowing as Ember walked down the steps of the courthouse. She strolled towards the old Burying

Point Cemetery. As she entered through the iron gates, she saw Thomas standing in front of the old oak tree, snowflakes in his hair and on his navy peacoat. She walked behind him without making a sound.

"Is that my wildflower?" Thomas asked, without turning around, sensing her presence.

Ember embraced him as he turned to face her. "It's getting quite difficult to surprise you now since you have been learning how to use your Fae skills."

Thomas laughed as he kissed her cheek. "So how did it go?"

Ember sighed as she hugged him tighter. "Sad actually."

"Well, she's going where she needs to be," Thomas replied as he tucked Ember's head under his chin.

"I know," she said as the snow began to fall faster, covering the ground with a fresh coat of white. "It's over now, and I will never think of her again."

"Do you think she can say the same?" Thomas asked.

Ember didn't respond to Thomas's question; for she already knew the answer, they both did.

They stood in the silence of the snow falling around them, holding each other. Shadow broke the winter quiet with three loud squawks as he glided down from the grey sky. He circled them, flying gracefully, more beautiful than ever, his black feathers standing out against the falling snow. Ember watched her friend fly, so carefree, and her heart soared. Shadow swooped down, close to Ember, something shiny in his broken beak.

"What you got there, boy?" Ember asked as Shadow dropped the sparking object before flying back to the oak tree.

Ember caught the object right before it hit the ground. She opened her hand to see a large sparkling ruby and diamond ring. She looked up into Thomas's blue eyes. "Thomas?"

"It took a lot to convince Shadow to let me propose. Took even more to get him to surprise you. I think I'm growing on him," Thomas said as he kneeled in front of Ember and took her hand in his.

"Ember, from the first minute I saw you, standing right under this tree, I knew I loved you, and I've loved you more each day after. I want to spend the rest of my life falling in love with you." Thomas slid the ring on Ember's finger. "Will you be my wildflower, forever?"

Ember bent and threw her arms around Thomas's neck. "Yes, yes, I will be your wife," she said as tears ran down her face.

The snow fell harder, turning the world around them into a white wonderland. Above them, Shadow flew through the snowflakes, circling above the tree line and into the grey clouds. His wings spread wide as he squawked loudly, and slowly other crows flew out of their hiding spots, joining Shadow on his flight through the winter storm, all of them moving together, as one, into the endless sky.

EPILOGUE

The thick metal door slammed hard, echoing through the cement hallways of the hospital. Sirena had gotten used to the noise and the stale smell of her cold, damp cell. It was empty other than a bed with a thin mattress, a dirty pillow, and a metal toilet in the corner.

When she was first brought to the hospital, after her arrest, she wouldn't allow anyone to come close to her. She would scream violently and throw furniture at anyone who came near her. It took four male nurses to hold her down long enough to sedate her. Then, they threw her in isolation, a small windowless dark room.

She was in that room for so long she lost all sense of time.

She sometimes didn't know if she was asleep or awake. When they finally let her out, they locked her in a cell with bare floors and only one small window, and there she stayed, day after day. Doctors and therapists came in and tried to evaluate her, but Sirena said nothing. She would just stare at the walls, not saying a single word.

The doctors declared her unfit to stand trial, but the prosecutor wouldn't accept her not having her day in court.

So, her public defender convinced her to plead guilty to a life sentence at the hospital. Sirena just shook her head; she knew what it was like being in a hospital, but this was more like a prison.

Day after day, she sat locked in her barren cell. The only comfort was looking out the small, barred window and seeing the blue sky. When the sun set, and the room became dark, it was the worst time for her. Sirena would awaken in the darkness, screaming from horrible nightmares. She would dream of her sisters, rotting away on the bottom of the ocean, fish and sea creatures eating their flesh, picking them apart. She would wake up, but she could still see their faces. She was alone, her screams her only companion.

* * *

A TALL, elegant woman with long, flowing red hair walked through the doors of the state hospital, the sound of her red-bottom stiletto pumps clicking through the halls. She stopped at the front desk and adjusted the large sunglasses on her face.

"Excuse me," she said to the nurse," I'm here to see Sirena Hale."

"Are you family?" the nurse asked.

"No, I am an old friend of the family," she said, her red lips turning up in a smile.

"I'm sorry, but that patient isn't allowed visitors unless it's family, and it needs to be approved."

"I'm sure we can skip all those formalities," the woman said, cutting off the nurse. She lowered her sunglasses and peered at the nurse with glowing silver pupils.

"Yes, of course. Right this way," the nurse said as she led the woman down the corridor to a large white door. She pulled a mass of keys out of her uniform pocket and unlocked the metal door that led to a small hallway with rooms lining both sides. They stopped at the door marked with a number three.

The redhead smirked when she saw the number on the door. "Unlock it and leave me your keys."

"Yes, ma'am," the nurse said as she unlocked the cell door with a loud clanking.

"Now leave, and you never saw me."

The nurse turned and walked back to her station. The woman closed the door behind her. Sirena stood by the window, her back to her.

"I must admit, seeing you like this almost makes me feel bad," the woman said as she walked closer to Sirena. "Almost."

Sirena slowly turned to look at the woman who was standing in her room. It took her only a moment to recognize her, "Willow?"

"Hello, sister. Did you miss me?"

The End

ACKNOWLEDGMENTS

This book is not just a story; it's my story. A story of how I allowed others to take my power and my sense of self and how, against all odds, I fought my way back.

I have always wanted to be part of something larger than myself. To belong. To have a moment in the spotlight...

Growing up, I was the awkward, clumsy, shy, chubby girl with messy hair that everyone made fun of, bullied, or ignored. I didn't have many friends. So, I lived in the fantasy worlds I created. It was my escape from reality; there I could be anything I dreamed of.

In the woods, I was a beautiful fairy queen. Underwater, in my backyard pool, I was a graceful mermaid. In my basement playhouse, I was a powerful witch making bubbling potions. Locked in my bedroom, I was a singer and dancer, as I twirled around in long skirts listening to Stevie Nicks from my record player.

So, imagine having the opportunity to live your childhood fantasies. To be glamorous and beautiful dancing on a stage. To swim underwater in a mermaid tail and hear the cheers and applause through the thick glass of porthole windows. To be a star. Those thirty minutes underwater meant everything to me. It was my greatest love. Then I watched as my greatest love became my undoing....

This book was my way of healing, not just the woman that I am today, but the little chubby girl with the messy hair that I was. It's my love letter to her. To let her know that she will be ok. That she will move on. That she doesn't have to retreat into her fantasy worlds anymore. She can be who she wants to be in the real world.

I couldn't have come this far without those that I love around me. My friends, my supporters, who have always had my back. You all inspire me every day. No matter what crazy situation I found myself in, your words of encouragement kept me going. You all were my guiding light in the darkness.

To my brave husband Jeff. The love of my life, the only man strong enough to walk with me. Who has never faltered, never given up, never let me fall. You fell on the sword for me so many times. And you did so with honor and integrity. You taught me to never look down, to always hold my head up, and remember who I am. You have given me more than a beautiful life; you gave me the power to believe and love myself. For that, I will be forever grateful.

This book is for you.

To my beautiful daughter Kassandra. Your talent and determination will always inspire me. I see the universe in your eyes, endless and full of possibilities. I am so incredibly proud of the woman you have become. I am honored to be your mother. You will forever be my tiny dancer.

This book is for you.

To my stepsons, Matthew and Andrew. I wish I had known you sooner. But I am blessed to have you in my life. Watching you grow into the strong, confident man you are has made me so happy. Having you both in my life has made it complete.

This book is for you.

To my Tata. My beloved Grandmother. You were taken too soon from this life. I cherish every single moment I have had with you. It is burned into my heart and my memory. I know you still walk with me; I hear your voice in the wind; I feel your hand on my head as I sleep. I feel your presence always. Thank you for giving me strength.

This book is for you.

To those who meant harm to me. Thank you for being my muses. By pushing me off your small stage, I was forced onto a larger one. The heartbreak that I suffered from your actions and words reminded me to fight for how powerful I am. No matter what obstacles were put in my way, I could overcome them. To not stay hidden behind the curtains that you put up for me and take my place in front of the spotlight and tell my story. To not be afraid.

This book is for you.

And lastly, to all the awkward, chubby, shy, clumsy girls with messy hair. All of those who feel less than, left out, unseen, marginalized, or forgotten in the shadows.

Believe in yourself, you are stronger than you know. There is power in being different. Embrace that power. It will be your sword and shield. Now, no matter how many times you fall, get up and keep fighting. Don't let fear ever hold you back from telling your story. Tell it, write it down, scream it from the rooftops.

You are seen, you are heard, you are loved.

This book is for you.

ABOUT THE AUTHOR

Born in San Juan, Puerto Rico, to a military family, Mia spent her childhood in New England before moving to South Florida. She travels frequently to the northeast, falling in love with its picturesque landscapes and changing seasons. Mia has been a practicing witch and pagan for over 30 years and devotes her time to educating others on the craft and what it means to be a modern-day witch. She has had a long career serving her community as a firefighter paramedic, along with being a wife, mother, model, performer, writer, makeup artist, and digital creator. She lives in Fort Lauderdale with her husband and beloved Husky Sansa.

www.ingramcontent.com/pod-product-compliance
Lightning Source LLC
Chambersburg PA
CBHW061639190726
48289CB00006B/1664